Praise for Christina Freeburn's Mysteries

"A snappy, clever mystery that hooked me on page one and didn't let go until the perfectly crafted and very satisfying end. Faith Hunter is a delightful amateur sleuth and the quirky characters that inhabit the town of Eden are the perfect complement to her overly inquisitive ways. A terrific read!"

— Jenn McKinlay,
New York Times Bestselling Author of *Copy Cap Murder*

"Christina's characters shine, her knowledge of scrapbooking is spot on, and she weaves a mystery that simply cries out to be read in one delicious sitting!"

— Pam Hanson,
Author of *Faith, Fireworks, and Fir*

"A fast-paced crafting cozy that will keep you turning pages as you try to figure out which one of the attendees is an identity thief and which one is a murderer."

— Lois Winston,
Author of the Anastasia Pollack Crafting Mystery Series

"A little town, a little romance, a little intrigue and a little murder. Join heroine Faith and find out exactly who is doing the embellishing—the kind that doesn't involve scrapbooking."

— Leann Sweeney,
Author of the Bestselling Cats in Trouble Mysteries

"Battling scrapbook divas, secrets, jealousy, murder, and lots of glitter make *Designed to Death* a charming and heartfelt mystery."

—Ellen Byerrum,
Author of the Crime of Fashion Mysteries

D0108942

"Freeburn's second installment in her scrapbooking mystery series is full of small-town intrigue, twists and turns, and plenty of heart."

– Mollie Cox Bryan,
Agatha Award Finalist, *Scrapbook of Secrets*

"A great read that had me reading non-stop from the moment I turned the first page...kept me in suspense with plenty of twists and turns and every time I thought I had it figured out, the author changed the direction in which the story was headed...and I liked the cast of characters in this charming whodunit!"

– *Dru's Book Musings*

"Witty, entertaining and fun with a side of murder...When murder hits Eden, WV, Faith Hunter will stop at nothing to clear the name of her employee who has been accused of murder. Will she find the killer before it is too late? Read this sensational read to find out!"

– *Shelley's Book Case*

"Has mystery and intrigue aplenty, with poor Faith being stuck in the middle of it all...When we finally come to the end of the book (too soon), it knits together seamlessly and comes as quite a surprise, which is always a good thing. A true pleasure to read."

– *Open Book Society*

"A cozy mystery that exceeds expectations...Freeburn has crafted a mystery that does not feel clichéd...it's her sense of humor that shows up in the book, helping the story flow, making the characters real and keeping the reader interested."

– *Scrapbooking is Heart Work*

NOT A
CREATURE
WAS
STIRRING

NOT A CREATURE WAS STIRRING

A Merry & Bright

HANDCRAFTED MYSTERY

Christina FREEBURN

HENERY PRESS

Copyright

NOT A CREATURE WAS STIRRING
A Merry & Bright Handcrafted Mystery
Part of the Henery Press Mystery Collection

First Edition | January 2019

Henery Press
www.henerypress.com

Trade Paperback ISBN-13: 978-1-63511-434-8
Digital epub ISBN-13: 978-1-63511-435-5
Kindle ISBN-13: 978-1-63511-436-2
Hardcover ISBN-13: 978-1-63511-437-9

Printed in the United States of America

To my three amazing (adult) children who have enriched my world and life so very much. While I miss your "younger" days, I'm looking forward to watching you spread your wings, achieve your dreams, and go out there in the world and adult. I'm so proud of all of you.

ACKNOWLEDGMENTS

A huge thank you to my editor Maria and all the other wonderful members at Henery Press for helping me make this book awesome. It's been a while since I was in the head of a new character and I'm thrilled that Henery Press was willing to give Merry a chance.

For all the women who have taken their love of crafting and turned it into businesses that support their family—keep crafting, ignore the naysayers.

Also want to give a shout out to one of my new favorite shows *Making It*. It's so awesome to see crafting/hand crafts getting some respect.

ONE

A rancid smell washed over me. I flicked an admonishing glare toward my companion. "Are you kidding me?"

Talking was a mistake. The smell penetrated me. I gagged. Removing a hand from the steering wheel of my new-to-me RV, I quickly opened the window. I was managing to drive the mammoth beast, but not with so much confidence I wanted to do it one-handed. The fresh air, with a slight twinge of exhaust, smelled better than my furry companion.

"I'm Dreaming of a White Christmas" flowed from the radio. The cold air complemented the Christmas music. I loved Christmas. All of it. Music. Movies. Decorating. Wrapping presents. Baking. Crafting. There was never too much Christmas for me. Thanksgiving was Thursday and my mind had bypassed it to focus on Christmas. For me, the Christmas season started in August and lasted until the first week of January.

My livelihood was built around the season: Merry and Bright Handcrafted Christmas, an Etsy store I started with my best friend Brighton Lane. Today, I was traveling to Morgantown, West Virginia for a huge holiday craft bazaar at the Armory. The living quarter space and the underneath storage compartments of the Class A RV were packed with handcrafted Christmas decorations and gift options. The first couple of craft shows of the season netted me a nice profit, and if the one at the Armory made as much as last year, I was halfway to my dream of no longer preparing taxes and working in the pro shop at the local golf course, allowing me to focus on crafting.

The smell wafted toward me again. "You smell like the dead."

Was he? I glanced at the cage belted in the passenger seat. The guinea pig looked like a melted multi-colored furry blob with feet. I had aimed the air vents on Ebenezer. Was the sun shining through the window too much for the critter?

"Ebenezer?"

"I Want a Hippopotamus for Christmas" played. I had intended to take it off my playlist, but Ebenezer loved it. The first time Ebenezer heard it, he moved around in a circle until it ended. He remained a blob. My heart beat faster. If only I could safely rattle his cage while I drove.

Tears pricked my eyes. I kept two children alive and relatively happy, for twenty-one and twenty-three years respectfully, and yet I couldn't keep a guinea pig alive for more than a week. My first pet and I killed him. My traveling companion. Since my children moved out and I was now divorced—again—Ebenezer was the most significant other in my life.

He rolled over and gazed at me.

So, it wasn't death causing the stench. It was his natural odor. I had thought the adoption people were cruel, placing him far away from the cats and dogs. Now I knew they just hadn't wanted to chase off any potential adopters with his smell. "It's a good thing you're cute, Ebenezer."

I had named my new pet after the main character in *The Christmas Carol*, who later in his life "...knew how to keep Christmas well, if any man alive possessed the knowledge." I, like Ebenezer Scrooge, found joy and a purpose in keeping Christmas well.

Christmas changed everything for Scrooge, as it had for my parents forty-five years ago when they found me on Christmas Eve—a sickly infant placed in a large stocking on the church steps. They adopted me and named me Merry because "We knew we'd have a Merry Christmas because of you."

A mix of love and pain crowded my heart. My parents were in their early forties when they adopted me, and aging wasn't kind to them. My father suffered from arthritis before cancer took him eight years ago. My mom now resided in an assisted living facility. Some days she remembered me and her grandchildren, other days she didn't.

A car zoomed past, bringing my full attention back to the road. I reached the crest of the hill. This was the part of the drive I dreaded. Gripping the steering wheel tighter, I leaned back as if the movement would help slow the momentum. "As the saying goes, what goes up must come down."

Ebenezer whistled. I wasn't sure if the sound was giddiness or fear. Or neither, because he was a guinea pig and had no feelings whatsoever on this predicament.

The impulsive buy of the RV might very well be the death of me. Maybe that was why my former stepdaughter brought the motorhome to my house and offered it at a rock-bottom price. She hoped I'd crash. Two weeks ago, I divorced her father, and Cassie was having a hard time with my decision, and with her dad's quick remarriage to Bonnie, the person Cassie blamed for our divorce.

My glasses slipped down my nose and I locked my arms to stop the instinct to push them up. I had hoped the Christmas music would calm me, but my go-to cure for anxiousness wasn't helping. On the way home, I might have to go with one of the Christmas CDs I stored in the glove compartment as the play list on my phone lacked the calming effect.

I reached my favorite part of the drive: crossing the bridge over Cheat Lake. Ripples of waves bounced across the water. The sun gleamed off the surface casting a pinkish hue as it set. It was a spectacular and tranquil sight, and I envisioned one day being able to move there—near the beauty and peace of that view—and closer to my children who now lived in Morgantown.

If they stayed, I reminded myself. So far, neither my son or daughter had committed to living in West Virginia or moving from the state that I had planned to become our home. I knew one day I'd need to help take care of my parents and living in the low-cost area they had chosen for their golden years allowed me to fulfill all my financial needs: children, parents, me. Plus, with my love of Christmas, how could I not move to a place called Season's Greetings, West Virginia?

The music lowered, and a ping came through the speakers. A text. I kept my eyes on the road and hoped it wasn't from my neighbor. A neighbor promised to notify me if my garage door opened. It was a little off the tracks, making it hard to secure. I should've made time to fix it rather than adding it to the after-the-craft-show to-do list.

I merged off the interstate and made my way to the Armory. A large banner directing people to the fifteenth annual Christmas Holiday Bazaar waved in the distance. Excitement jingled through me. This year, I was at the craft fair in my RV, my mobile craft studio and home away from home. I was ready to take on the weekend—and my new life.

I turned down the road leading to the Armory. The building loomed before me and workers had already placed signs directing people to the show. The gravel lot for shoppers was empty, waiting for tomorrow when people would rush for spaces or settle for a parking space near the overnight parking area which was quite a distance from the door.

The overnight/RV parking lot was starting to look like a small town with campers, trailers, and other Class A vehicles filling up the space. I spotted my friend Grace Turner's trailer toward the front of the lot. Her son Abraham was outside hooking up the utilities. I waved. His eyes widened, and he waved back before hurrying into the camper. I maneuvered the RV to my borrowed spot in the far end corner of the overnight RV lot. My other part-time job that kept my financial teeter-totter from slamming down to the ground was at the local golf course, and a golfer, who had a standing reservation weekend from August until the beginning of December at this lot, loaned me the spot in exchange for personalized t-shirts and wooden signs for his wife's scrapbook room. He was thrilled to finish Christmas shopping without venturing from the golf course.

After parking, I scooped Ebenezer out of his cage and grabbed my cell phone. "Let's show you, and our new home, off to Auntie Bright." It wasn't unusual for me and Bright to go a week or two without contacting each other during our busy season except for noting in our project list on Google Docs which order was ours to complete.

Right around the time my father died, Brighton and I "met" on a Facebook group devoted to using electronic die cutting machines. Chatting through Messenger, Bright and I discovered we had similar tastes in crafting, TV shows, and a love of all things Christmas. Our friendship was built on Facebook messaging, emailing, and picture attachments. If anyone asked who knew me best, the answer was Bright, even though we've never met in person.

The phone pinged, a reminder I hadn't read a text, and vibrated in my hand. Cassie. *So, can I come get it?*

She had left something in the RV. I shifted Ebenezer, making sure he was cradled securely then texted back. *Can't today. I'm in Morgantown. The craft show.*

I can come to you. It's important.

I'll be back home Sunday night.

Ebenezer pawed at the small kitchen countertop, wanting down. I inched away from it.

I need it sooner.

The girl wasn't the best driver and I didn't want her zipping to Morgantown at night. *The RV is packed. No way to find anything in here tonight. I'll look tomorrow when I unload. What do you need?*

Ticket. I'll come tomorrow.

The RV had become the spot Cassie hid whatever she hadn't wanted her father to find. Samuel was a good dad, it was his one redeeming quality, but he never saw a flaw in Cassie's behavior, and she tried to stay on that pedestal. After she sold me the RV, she dug out two parking tickets, a racy note from her boyfriend, which I regret having set my eyes on, and a letter that she immediately tore up.

I'll look for it. I typed. *When do you need to pay it?*

Not that kind of ticket. It's for an event.

Where you going?

Not your business. There was a pause before another text popped up. *You're not my mother.*

Ouch. She was right. I wasn't her mom. It wasn't my business where she went or with whom. *If I find it, I'll let you know. I'll be back on Sunday. You can get it then.*

I'll find it. Don't trouble yourself.

Don't trouble yourself. Cassie's way of ending a conversation. I weaved through the abundance of Christmas products I handcrafted and opened the door to allow some extra light into the space. I took multiple pictures of the inside: kitchen area, dining area, and living room. I wanted proof of how it looked when I went to an event, better to determine what alterations I wanted to make to the RV to suit my needs.

I planned on converting some of the kitchen cabinets into supply storage and turning the dining area into a studio space that would hold two electronic cutting machines and my laptop. Right now, the upholstery and counters were dark blue and gray, not quite my liking. At the after-Christmas sales, I planned on buying upholstery fabric in creams to redo the benches and couches. I envisioned pillows with silver trim and gold accents. Silver and gold was my favorite color combination with a little bit of poinsettia red mixed in.

Positioning myself sideways, right shoulder facing toward the door leading into the living space rather than facing the camera head on, I pressed Ebenezer to my cheek. His fur tickled my chin. I tapped the camera icon on my cell and flipped the view. I held out my arm, squinting at the screen to make sure me, my companion, and part of the soon-to-be mobile craft studio was in the frame. *Click.* I examined the picture. Perfect.

Our new craft studio, I typed and hit send. I scurried back to the passenger seat and placed Ebenezer back inside his cage while I was out hooking up the electric and sewage systems. I wanted the task completed before dark.

What is that? Bright messaged back.

I typed back: *Ebenezer. My traveling buddy. Isn't he cute?*

Not the ball of fur. The studio space. Did you buy a shed? Trailer? I thought new toy meant you upgraded your die cutter to the Cricut Maker.

I had coveted the ultimate edition of Cricut and planned to buy it this weekend, but it wasn't in my budget since I bought the RV. A large portion of my savings, and the money I had painstakingly saved for my son's college tuition, went to the purchase. My children's father had offered to pay the full amount, but I wanted—needed—to help with their tuition. Scotland's job with the Morgantown police department offered tuition reimbursement, so he was going that route to finish his degree. I hoped Cassie spent the money responsibly. Not my worries. It was on her dad. Samuel was careful with "his" money yet had a habit of frittering away others' money on marketing schemes, business ventures, and whatever else he thought would make his life better. One of the reasons for our divorce.

I bought a recreational vehicle. I responded.

Did you win the lottery? Heard someone in West Virginia won a nice wad of cash. Show me the outside. Following the words was a row of happy face emoticons.

While I was out there, I'd hook everything up before the light completely vanished. In the few minutes I had spent messaging Bright, the sun slipped further behind the mountain. I had stopped at Ace Hardware and picked up duct tape, rope, gloves, garbage bags, and an array of tools to have on hand in case I needed to make any repairs. The RV appeared in perfect condition, but I was sure there was another reason—beside Cassie's new stepmother Bonnie wanting the teen to move into it—that had made her sell it to me. Cheap.

The air had a bite of cold. The unseasonal warmth was leaving, and true winter weather was on its way. I dared say even some snow. I just hoped it didn't fall until I returned home. There was no way I wanted to drive the beast in the snow. I messaged Bright a few pictures of the vehicle then started hooking up the electrical, water, and sewer hose. Before leaving home, I had watched a lot of videos on YouTube on how to accomplish the task.

My phone pinged. It pinged again. And again. Bright had a lot to say about my RV. I went inside into the warmth, took a bottle of water from the refrigerator, and curled up in the leather recliner that faced the thirty-two-inch flat screen TV. This was the traveling life. All the comforts of home. Crafts. Christmas movies. Snacks.

Ebenezer squealed. A long, drawn out pitiful noise. Poor guy. He was used to roaming around. He had never chewed on any product before, but I had also never had my pieces out in the open where he could nibble on them. I had four-foot wooden trees made from pallets, boxes of hand-painted wooden and ceramic ornaments, stacks of decals, and garland cut from weatherproof material, stored in the living quarters.

My phone pinged again. I forgot about Bright. Tilting my hip up, I pulled my cell phone from my pocket, eager to see what she had to say about the on-the-go Merry and Bright studio. Unexpected tears pricked my eyes as the words pelleted my heart.

What were you thinking? Bright messaged in all capital letters, followed by what seemed like hundreds of question marks. *I can't believe you bought that.*

The sadness ebbed away as anger built. I was a grown woman. I could purchase whatever I wanted. It was my money. My parents' investments and my father's life insurance paid for most of my mom's care. I met our monthly expenses every month with a few sacrifices here and there. I was always waiting "until" before I embraced what I wanted to do, and today decided to go for it.

I love it. I banged the virtual letters of the small keyboard. *The mobile craft studio will help our business grow. I can go to more craft shows. No more hotel costs and minimal for food.*

I think getting an RV is a great idea, Bright responded. *I'll even chip in. The mobile studio benefits me too.*

I felt heat licking my cheeks. Was that why she was upset? Because I had made a huge business purchase without consulting her? *I had no intention of splitting the RV purchase. Sorry for not running it by you first.*

Get over the money thing. My issue is the who you bought the RV from. That RV looks like the one Samuel "bought you" as a present for your mom to move into.

My cheeks flamed. I was caught. Samuel hadn't liked the amount of money I was contributing to my mom's care, so his great idea was moving her into the trailer, "She'll love living close to you. You're great at taking care of people." The plan had nothing to do with what was best for my mom, the purpose was to free up funds for Samuel's business ventures. It was the start of the end of our new marriage.

Cassie's new stepmom felt it was time for the high school senior to "adult" and part of the plan was for Cassie to live in the trailer. After being gifted the RV, Cassie figured if there was no motorhome to live in, the woman couldn't kick her out of her house, so she drove it over to my house and offered to sell it to me.

It was a steal, I typed.

That's what you should worry about. I can't believe you trusted Samuel.

I didn't, I responded back quickly. *Cassie owned it. I bought it from her.*

You know what they say about the apple and the tree.

Protectiveness zapped through me and a familiar anger burned in my gut. My hands clenched. Mama Bear was roaring to life. There was one thing that made me furious, bordering on murderous, anyone going after my cubs. And in my heart, Cassie would always be one.

And you know what they say about assumptions. I messaged back.

I know you care about her, goodness knows someone should. I stalked her Facebook page. She posted horrible things about her father and later apologized to him. Then she wrote you were heartless and wanted karma to strike you down. She knew the divorce was his fault but thought you should've stayed for her.

And I had. For a month longer than I should have. I hadn't wanted to be another woman who up and left Cassie. Samuel had lived in Morgantown when Cassie was a baby but moved back to Season's Greetings after Cassie's mother left them, leaving a note stating she wasn't the mother type. Since then, I believed Samuel had searched for a mother for his daughter and kept failing. There was a stepmother before me. And a fiancé before her. Now, her current stepmom was trying to force her out of her home.

I had fallen for Samuel when I was at my neediest. For the last twenty-three years, the focus of my life had been my children. The jobs I took were based on what was best for them and their schedule rather than for me. When my youngest, Scotland, got a job at the police department in Morgantown and moved, I went into a tailspin. I questioned every decision I had made and wondered about my purpose since I was no longer primarily a mom. The one thing I feared more than anything in the world, besides harm coming to my children, was being forgotten.

My children had warned me about Samuel. Neither Raleigh nor Scotland had liked the man. I believed it was because I hadn't dated anyone since their father and I divorced, and my children always wanted me back with their dad, even disregarding the fact their father was remarried. I should've heeded my children's advice about Samuel.

Ebenezer whistled and pressed his body against the cage. Did I want to risk him stinking up everything? I could put the Christmas trees and totes in the outside storage crawl space. Since I wasn't driving anywhere, my concern of the trees hitting each other and scratching off the green paint was no longer valid.

Ebenezer needs out. I'll send you pics of the booth tomorrow.

It's a guinea pig. You don't have to walk it.

But he does need to be aired out. He stinks to high heaven. I didn't want to fight with Bright. She was my best friend. It was best to end the conversation now.

"You need a bath." I reached into the cage and paused. Earlier, I had held Ebenezer under my nose. I hadn't smelled him.

Ugh! Cassie must've hidden rotting food in the RV. No wonder she sold it to me for half the going rate. I walked right into her master plan for revenge. Would my creations—my work—absorb the stench? Once again, my heart got in my way. I left Ebenezer in the cage. Until I found what Cassie hid in my RV, I didn't want Ebenezer roaming around. He might eat it and get sick. Maybe whatever was causing the smell wasn't Cassie's fault. Our town was being overrun with feral cats and one might have gotten trapped somewhere. I wasn't aware of a way a cat could wiggle itself into the main living space, but cats were resourceful creatures and capable of anything.

First thing: emptying out the living quarters. I laid a couple of plastic garbage bags on the ground near the hookups, then wrangled out a wooden tree and placed it on the bags to protect it from dirt and any rocks that might scratch the paint. The security lights in the trailer section of the parking switched on. At least I didn't have to carry the flashlight with me. It was hard enough lugging out the trees without supplying my own light source.

"Merry Christmas, Mama said you need help." The deep rumble came from behind me.

Smiling, I turned and greeted Abraham. "I could use it. I have a lot of trees to bring outside."

At six foot two and a solid wall of muscle, Abraham was an opposing figure. His expression was always serious, lending itself to the menacing nature of his appearance. It was deceiving. Abraham was a sweet soul in a fear-inducing body. He had a cognitive disability, which made him miss social cues and caused his mother a lot of angst as people took his ignoring personal space as a threat. It brought joy to my heart knowing she felt safe to send him over to help without following him.

"I'll get them for you, Merry Christmas."

For years, I've explained to Abraham that my name was just Merry, but he had latched onto the way I explained my name and the two are forever linked.

"Thanks. I could use the help."

Abraham stepped into the living area. "It smells horrible in here."

"I know." I followed Abraham into the RV. "I think someone left some food in here before they sold it to me, or a cat got stuck somewhere and died."

Abraham spun around, a horrified expression twisted his features. "A cat died? I love cats. Cats are nice to me." His pitch amplified with every word.

I grimaced, regretting voicing my cat theory. Abraham loved animals. Most times more than people. What if it was a dead cat? I didn't want that image stuck in Abraham's head. My gaze fell on Ebenezer. Perfect.

As Abraham carried out the last tree, I picked up Ebenezer's cage and grabbed a blanket off the bed. The temperature had dropped, and I wanted Ebenezer to stay warm. Technically, he wore a fur coat, but I wasn't sure how long it would take to find the source of the smell and didn't want Ebenezer to lose a lot of body heat.

Abraham placed the tree on top of the pile then tucked the garbage bags around them. "Keeps them nice and dry. I love Christmas trees. You did a good job on these, Merry Christmas."

"As a thank you for helping, you can pick one to take home."

Abraham shook his head. "Helping doesn't require a present. I help because it is the right thing to do." He tilted his head and smiled. "Who's your friend?"

"This is Ebenezer. I was hoping you could keep an eye on him while I tidied up the RV. Ebenezer hasn't had any fresh air today. I brought a blanket out for him since it's cold."

"I can do that for you." Gently, Abraham took the cage from me. "That's an awfully big blanket. It won't fit inside his cage."

"It's to cover it."

Abraham frowned. "Then Ebenezer won't be able to see the stars. I'll let him use one of my gloves as a blanket. We'll sit by your trees and protect them until we can move them inside."

My heart sparkled. Abraham was such a sweet soul. "Your hands will get cold. Ebenezer will be okay not looking at the stars."

Abraham pulled out a pair of wool gloves from his coat pocket. "I carry extra in case someone needs them."

If more people were like Abraham, the world would have less strife. I walked back up the stairs and flipped the switch for the slide-outs to open. The stench blossomed. I gagged and covered my nose with my hand. I ran back to my bedroom and dug out a pair of knee length socks embroidered with reindeer. I unrolled them and tied one of the socks around my nose the other around my mouth. Thankfully, I had the foresight to pick up gloves and trash bags. I was going to need them.

I opened every window. The smell was strongest around the kitchen and dinette, the best place to start the search. I ran my hand over the dark gray granite counter top that doubled as a sink. Tears dotted my vision. I swiped them away. This was a minor annoyance. Before long, this would be an aggravating memory that one day I'd laugh and roll my eyes about. I stuck my finger in the hole of the granite cutting board that hid the kitchen sink and lifted it. Nope, not in there. Too easy. Cassie would make me work for the solution.

Retrieving a step stool from the pantry, I thoroughly checked the upper cabinets. Right now, the cabinets over the fridge stored supplies I might need for personalizing some of my products. The 12x24 mats fit up there perfectly along with paint and brushes for any necessary touch-up to the wooden trees.

I crawled under the dinette. The smell felt thick here. The dinette seats were also storage. I remembered that from when Samuel and I originally toured the RV at the dealership. Cassie had given me the spiel of all the storage space I'd have for my crafts: underneath storage compartment, the bed that was over the driver's area, under bed storage in the bedroom. She listed them all except for the dinette. There were small half-moon smudges of dirt on the edge of the upholstery. Yep. This was the place.

"I should've searched this—" I yanked the seat up.

The smell smacked me in the face. Breath clogged in my throat. Samuel, neck tilted at an awkward angle, stared up at me. His body was squished into the five-foot-long space. One hand near his ear, the other palm up on his chest. Brown eyes opened and vacant. I swayed. The room darkened.

Screaming, I slammed the lid down and collapsed onto the dinette. I flung myself off, clipping my cheek and arm against the dinette table. Pushing myself backward on my hands and derrière, I put distance between me and the awful truth. My back pressed against the wall.

Gasping sobs escaped from me. I brought my knees to my chest and wrapped my arms around my legs, rocking myself back and forth to try and settle my heart and mind.

Samuel was dead. Murdered. In the RV I had just bought from his daughter.

Oh God, what had Cassie done?

TWO

"Merry Christmas! Merry Christmas!"

Abraham screamed my name. Shook my arm. I couldn't move. React. Talk. I felt so cold. My gaze wandered over to the dinette bench.

Whatever expression was on my face caused Abraham to rush over and reach for the seat. "I'll get it out."

He thought there was a dead animal in the storage compartment. I couldn't let him see Samuel. I sprung to my feet and grabbed his arm. "Don't open it!"

Too late. Abraham stumbled backward, a look of horror on his face. He stared at me with wide eyes. "That man. He's dead."

I nodded. What else could I do? The police. Call the police. With a shaking hand, I pulled out my cell. How would I explain it? How could I? I didn't know what was going on. Why was Samuel in my RV? Dead.

I grabbed Abraham's arm. "We have to leave."

"That man. Did he hurt you?" Abraham glared at Samuel's body.

"I didn't know he was in there. He scared me when I saw him." I tugged Abraham toward the door.

"How did he die?"

"I don't know. We have to get out of here." Cassie's name flittered into my head. No. Not possible. The voice of suspicion was persistent. *Why was she so insistent on selling you the RV today?*

Abraham refused to budge. "Maybe he needs our help."

"No, he doesn't." My voice took on a high-pitch, nearly

hysterical quality. "Let's go."

"Merry? Abraham? What's going on?" Grace, Abraham's mother, stood on the threshold of the RV.

Relief flooded through me. I pulled her aside and whispered furiously what I discovered in the seat storage area as I kept an eye on Abraham. He was still standing in front of the dinette with his hands tucked into his back pockets. The tilt of his head suggested he was struggling with my "don't touch" order.

"Abraham, where's Ebenezer?" I threw out the only idea that might get him away from the bench.

"He's outside near the trees. You screamed. If someone screams that means they're in trouble. I came to help."

Grace took her son's hand and pulled him away from the dinette area, avoiding looking at Samuel's body. "I am so proud of you for protecting Merry. I thought something was wrong, so I called the police. Can you wait near our trailer and point out Merry's to them?"

Abraham nodded. "I'll bring Ebenezer with me so he doesn't have to stay out in the cold."

"Thank you," I said. "That's a wonderful idea."

"We should wait outside." With a steadying grip on my elbow, Grace led me out.

I shivered. She unwrapped one end of her shawl from her shoulders and draped it over me, pulling me to her side. We stood there, side-by-side, staring at my dream that had now become my nightmare. The stars twinkled overhead. I gazed up, wishing with all my might this was a horrible dream. The cold penetrating through the shawl, and into my body, told me this was reality. A horrible reality I'd have to explain to the police. But how?

Why was Samuel—a dead Samuel—in my RV? The RV that his daughter had sold me. Was that why she was desperate to sell? My stomach clenched. I placed a hand on my stomach and drew in small puffs of air.

"What happened?" Grace tightened the shawl around us.

"The RV smelled horrendous. I was looking for what was

rotting. I didn't know it would be my ex-husband." My body quaked. Bile rose in my throat. I sucked in breaths through my nose, hoping to settle the sick feeling.

This was supposed to be a fantastic weekend. The beginning of my dreams coming true. I could expand Merry and Bright Handcrafted Christmas and make it my only full-time job. No more seasonal jobs. Focus on Christmas crafting year-round. There was travel in my future. The RV allowed me to visit the places in the United States I had read and dreamt about.

Sirens filled the air. Red lights swirled near the entrance of the recreational vehicle parking. I shivered harder.

Grace slipped out from the shawl and wrapped the other end around me. "Do you want me to call Scot—"

"No!" I didn't know much right now, but I knew I didn't want my son here. Scotland hadn't been on the police force long and I didn't want him running down here to help me out of this legal kerfuffle. Being a police officer was his dream and I didn't want this complicating his life. This was my problem.

"I can't believe this is happening." I moaned and planted my face into my hands.

"It'll be okay." Grace squeezed my shoulder. "You did nothing wrong."

My breath tightened in my lungs. Would the police think I did something wrong?

A car door slammed near us. The wail of the siren stopped, but the red light continued to swirl around. A uniformed officer walked toward Grace's trailer. Abraham stepped out, holding Ebenezer like a football, and pointed toward us. The officer pivoted and headed in our direction.

"Do you think I'll be blamed because he's my ex-husband?"

"It's strange that he was in your trailer..."

"I just bought it." Something in me screamed not to tell her about buying the RV from Cassie.

"That's even odder."

My lips quivered.

Grace's eyes widened. "I'm not blaming you. I know you'd never kill someone. And if you did, you sure wouldn't bring him with you to a Christmas craft show. This..." she spread out her arms, "is your happy place."

That it was. And Samuel ruined it. Think sympathetic thoughts. It wasn't like the man murdered himself.

An ambulance pulled to a stop a few feet from us. A paramedic hopped out and walked over to us as another pulled a gurney from the back of the ambulance.

"A young man said the victim was over here."

I nodded and pointed at my RV. Victim. Samuel was a victim. His body was in the RV that was once his and now mine. I shuddered. Body. Samuel was no longer here.

"The dead man is in that RV." Grace wrapped an arm around my shoulders and tucked me into her side. Her comfort wrapped around me. My trembling slowed.

"Is anyone else inside?"

I shook my head.

"No," Grace said, becoming my voice.

The paramedics went up the steps of the RV. "Wait out here."

I had no intention of stepping one foot in there with Samuel stuffed in the bench.

A female officer walked over to us. She looked like she had just reached the age to legally buy alcohol. Scotland's age. "It was reported that a man died in a recreational vehicle. Do either of you know the victim?"

I tried to speak but no sound came out. Instead, I nodded.

"Samuel Waters, her ex-husband, was in her RV." Grace gave me a one-armed hugged. "She's shaken up. She didn't expect to see him."

"He startled her, there was an altercation, and she—" The officer created a scenario.

"No!" I found my voice. "He was just in there."

"Does that mean he forced himself into your RV?" The officer asked.

"Not exactly." I'd have to try harder to explain the situation coherently. I drew in a deep breath and slowly released it, hoping it settled my heart rate and the anxiety racing through my body. Speak slow. Focus on one word at a time. "He was in the dinette bench. It can be used for storage."

The officer settled a look on me that was halfway between pity and suspicion.

I cringed. That sounded bad, like I decided to take my dead ex-husband on a road trip.

"She didn't know he was in there." Grace rubbed my arm in a soothing manner.

"How long ago were you divorced?" The officer asked.

"Two weeks ago. The divorce proceedings lasted longer than our marriage," I said.

"It was a contentious divorce?"

"Yes, he fought everything. I only wanted what I brought into the marriage. I wanted nothing from him."

"Was your husband trying to get alimony from you?"

I shook my head. "He just didn't want the divorce hearing to end. He liked forcing me to see him. The judge granting the divorce scheduled us to come in at different times to sign so I didn't have to see Samuel again. He just—" A sob strangled the rest of the words.

Grace squeezed me to her side. "I'd like to take my friend to my RV. She's had a rough evening. She'd been looking forward to this weekend for months. There is a Christmas craft fair, and Christmas is her thing."

The officer tapped a pen on her notebook.

"I'd like to get this over with." The sooner I answered the questions, the sooner it was over, and the better chance Scotland wouldn't get wrapped up in this in any way. I didn't want word floating around the station that *his mother* was coming in for questioning regarding her ex-husband's death.

"Did your ex-husband know this event was important to you?" Something sparked in the officer's eyes that I couldn't decipher.

"I mentioned it when we were married," I said. "He kept

texting and messaging me that he needed to talk. It was extremely important. I told him I meant it when I said I never wanted to see him again. I blocked him from my Facebook page, so I doubt he remembered it was this weekend."

"Did you keep those messages?" The officer asked.

"A few."

"Can I see them?"

Nodding, I pulled up my text messages and handed my cell to the officer. She scanned through them and handed it back to me.

"Samuel tried to rent a booth a few days ago," Grace said.

"What?" My eyes widened. "You didn't tell me."

Samuel wasn't a crafter. He hadn't been interested in my business except for how much I made and telling me to "dump that partner of yours."

"I didn't want you being anxious about coming," Grace said. "He was told there wasn't a space left."

The officer scribbled furiously in her notepad. "How did you find out?"

"I'm on the committee that organizes the event," Grace said. "Another member mentioned it because he was demanding. She wanted us to know in case he showed up to sell."

"Has that happened before?" the officer asked.

"You can't even imagine," Grace said. "Last year, someone tried to claim they were another vendor to take their spot. Fortunately, we caught them before we had a huge problem on our hands. The committee member had written down Samuel's name and was going to alert the registrars in case he tried it."

A paramedic stepped out. "The guy is dead. We need a coroner."

The officer nodded and pressed a button on the radio attached to her vest as she entered the RV.

Poor Cassie. Tears stung my eyes. She was now an orphan. Her mother had abandoned her sixteen years ago.

Cassie had to be told. Would the police do that? Would I have to? Should I call Scotland? He had training in how to deal with a notification. I cringed. Notification. Raleigh was getting her master's degree in adolescent psychology. Maybe she was the better person to break this horrible news to Cassie?

Cassie might already know. The evil thoughts trickled in. One after the other. *She sold you the trailer. For cheap. It's her dad shoved in your dinette. Dead. What better revenge than to end both of your lives? Samuel's literally. Yours figuratively.*

Shame clenched my stomach and heated my cheeks. I was not the type of person who believed the worst in people. I was a defender. I was the go-to person whenever someone needed help. I couldn't listen to the Scrooge in my head. There was no way Cassie would kill her father because she thought his interest in Bonnie caused the divorce. But would she if he forced her out of their house?

No. Samuel was almost six feet and weighed one hundred and eighty pounds. Cassie was a little bit of a thing. She barely weighed ninety pounds and was an inch shorter than me, and I was just over five feet tall. No way could she have dragged him into the trailer and shoved him into the bench.

Alone, a voice in my head corrected. Cassie had a lot of friends. Male friends. Large, muscular male friends. One, or two of them, could've easily carried Samuel into the RV and dropped him into the seat storage.

Stop it. First, you're accusing your stepdaughter and now you've come up with a conspiracy plan involving her high school friends. I rubbed my temples.

"Is there any way your ex-husband found out about your RV purchase?" The officer asked, drawing me out of my head.

My face was on fire. I dipped my head. "I bought it from his daughter."

"I think that explains it." The officer closed her notebook and settled a sympathetic gaze on me. "From what I've gathered, sounds like we might have a stalking situation on our hands. It appears your ex-husband died from suffocation. I didn't see any indication of foul play. It's likely he placed himself into the bench."

"Samuel hid in my RV?" My mind conjured up an image of Samuel, in the middle of the night, sneaking out of his hiding place and "surprising" me. My body shook. I wrapped my arms around myself. I was so, so stupid.

"That's what it looks like," the officer said. "At least you don't have to worry about that man bothering you. I'll write up your statement and you can come in tomorrow evening to read and sign it."

"What a horrible man!" Grace positioned herself so I could physically lean on her.

I knew Samuel hadn't been happy with the divorce, but I hadn't thought he'd try and hurt me. A week ago, he sent a text message asking if we could go out for old time's sake. I reminded him our old times were not pleasant and there was no reason I wanted to relive them. He kept calling, insisting I had to speak to him. I blocked his number after that. It took us months to finalize the divorce, and the splitting of assets was simple: I kept what was mine, he kept what was his. No alimony. Simple.

My mind floated going back to Cassie. Did she know her father was hiding in the RV when she drove it over to my house? She had to. Selling me the RV been a ruse for her father to see me again. He had told me he would win me back, or he'd die trying.

It looked like he accomplished one of those goals.

THREE

"We're all done in here." The forensic person picked up his last bag and walked out of the door of the RV.

There was a mess. Powder was everywhere. The dinette seat was left up. Pictures were taken of the seat from every angle, all the while assuring me that this was just standard procedure to cover all the bases. What bases were there to cover? Samuel hid in the seat. Samuel suffocated. He had wanted to hurt me and instead killed himself.

Tears flooded my eyes. Not for Samuel. I was angry at the man. Almost as livid as when I found out he spoke to my mom at the assisted living facility and convinced her she wanted to move. I couldn't believe he'd prey upon an eighty-seven-year-old woman with dementia. That ended our marriage. And it seemed he planned on ending me. I shuddered.

Grace draped a Santa throw around my shoulders. "Are you sure you want to stay here tonight? Abraham doesn't mind sleeping on the floor in my room."

"No, I'll be fine," I lied.

I didn't want to put them out any more that I already had, besides no matter where I was, I wouldn't be getting a good night's rest. I needed to do some therapeutic crafting before I fell asleep and I didn't want the churning and chugging noise of my die cutting machines keeping my friends awake.

Grace stood in the threshold of the RV, a hand resting on the latch. She didn't believe me and was hesitant to leave. Warmth and thankfulness flooded my heart. I had wonderful, caring friends. I would be all right. A true smile formed on its own will.

Relief shone on Grace's face. "If you're sure."

"I'm sure." I hugged her. "I'll do some crafting and crank up the Christmas music. Text me if it's too loud."

Grace hugged me back. "It'll add to the holiday atmosphere. If you need me, text. I mean it."

I shooed her out the door. "I know."

After Grace left, I took my Cricut out of its storage bag and went to place it on the table. My stomach flopped like a fish out of water. There was no way I could sit on the dinette bench, or even in one of the chairs of the dining area. I'd have to look at where Samuel died.

Quickly, I returned the Cricut to its carrier and hustled it down to my bedroom, putting as much distance as possible between me and where I found Samuel. Ebenezer whistled and screeched from his cage that was on the passenger seat.

I abandoned Ebenezer. I was a horrible pet parent. It would serve me right if Ebenezer gnawed on a cord.

"Forgive me." I raced back to the front of the RV and snagged the handle, scurrying back to the room with my companion and a rolling tote filled with crafting supplies. Ebenezer whistled as his cage swayed to and fro in my haste to leave the area of the crime.

I entered the room and shut the door with my foot. One of the things I had loved about this RV was it had a true door, not a pocket one. At the time, I had other reasons for preferring a real door, now it gave me a good separation from work and home. One of my plans was using the RV as a mobile store and set up my wares inside of it, allowing me to only need a parking spot on the grounds rather than a booth inside. I could stage everything in the main living space and have a space that always remained mine and mine alone. I hoped bringing my own "vendor space" opened a spot for me in one of the coveted and waitlist only venues.

Depositing the cage on the bed, I released Ebenezer then started arranging a work station. I pulled out the Cricut and placed it on the dresser. Not wide enough. If I turned the machine sideways, it hung off and, placed the correct way, there was no room for the 12x12 mat to move completely through the rollers. The other option was putting the Cricut on the bedside table and bracing the machine with one hand while using my iPad with the other. A good way to break expensive equipment.

I sat cross-legged on the bed, iPad on my lap. "I'll design tonight and cut in the morning."

Ebenezer flopped onto a pillow and closed his eyes, oblivious to my plight.

I unfolded my legs and leaned against the headboard, thinking of a design. A niche another vinyl designer wasn't selling at the craft show. I wanted to broaden my repertoire and not duplicate any products. One more wine glass design wasn't going to help increase my profits. And, I now needed money to renovate the RV.

A heaviness settled around me, almost like I was being pushed down. I fought the urge to lay down and curl up into a ball. I wouldn't let Samuel take away the happiness of this weekend. I had looked forward to this craft show for months. Squaring my shoulders, I sat up and studied the room, hoping to find inspiration. The room was blank. Devoid of any creativity. No Christmas spirit.

That was it. There was no Christmas in this vehicle since I took out the trees. Everything holiday related was in the underneath storage compartment or had been hauled into the Armory by Abraham and a security guard. Grace had been afraid my trees would get ruined if left outside.

With some vinyl, transfer tape, and Christmas designs, I'd turn the RV into a Christmas wonderland. I'd create a vinyl Christmas tree and ornaments. My mind raced with ideas.

I powered up the iPad and logged into my Design Space account. I'd cut out some decals in the morning, and during any slow times, add more into my shop and keep a few to spruce up my home away home. It was hard to concentrate with my mind flipping from one design to the next. Christmas tree. Wreath. Holiday sayings. Window decals. Santa Claus and sleigh.

A message popped up. Bright. I debated for a bit on ignoring her, but she was friend—my best friend—and her concerns had been valid.

I tapped on the message.

For a small animal, it takes a long time to bathe him. What did the little rascal get into? I'm sorry for lecturing you. I'm your friend not your mama.

Don't be, I responded, *I needed it. I get in my own way.*

Don't fret over it. Keep yourself in a happy place. You all tucked in for the night? Doors and windows secured?

I frowned. Bright wasn't a worrier. That was my role. She was a jump then look type of person. *Why the Nervous Nellie impression?*

The craft world is small. The business group is all agog about the police showing up at a Christmas Bazaar. In West Virginia. The rumors are a fight between two vendors, the theft of a vendor's trailer, and a body being found.

The rekindled Christmas joy spurted out of me. People were talking. Soon the whole truth would be out, and I didn't want to be internet fodder. Was there a way to squash it? Probably not. *One of those are true.*

Which vendors?

No, the last guess on the list.

A BODY! Bright added a whole row of exclamation points.

Yes. My fingers froze, refusing to type Samuel's name.

And you're still there? Alone? In the RV?

I'm safe.

Why aren't YOU concerned? It's not like you not to worry.

That was true. We were both acting out of character. Why was I being coy with the truth? *It was Samuel. He hid in the dinette storage seat. Suffocated himself.*

Oh my God! What was the man thinking?

That's what I'm trying to keep my brain from dwelling on.

You're right. Don't think about it. See if a security guard will come around every hour tonight. It'll be a comfort knowing someone is watching out for you. She sent me a GIF of a kitten offering a hug.

I'm safe. Nothing bad will happen.

You don't think Cassie will try and contact him and see how the surprise visit went? She sold you the trailer. She had to know he was in there.

My spirit plummeted even further. *We don't know that for sure. Samuel isn't one to get permission from anyone or fill them in on a plan.*

The girl is a hot mess right now. What if she blames you? Comes after you. Think about it, Merry, how's she going to feel when she finds out her dad died?

Headlights lit the area near the RV. I bolted upright in bed. Ebenezer whistled and huddled against me, seeking out the warmth that had left him. Footsteps crackled against the gravel outside the window. I gathered Ebenezer into my arms, holding my breath. With my free hand, I pulled my cell phone from the charger and placed it on my lap, tapping 9-1-1. My finger posed above the call button in case I needed it. My breath came in spurts. Ebenezer cuddled against me.

"I'll keep you safe," I promised in a whisper, dropping a kiss onto his furry head.

The phone played "Up on the Rooftop." I fumbled with it. Scotland. He'd know what to do. "Scot—"

He cut me off. "I saw movement in the back of the RV. Sorry for scaring you. I'm about to knock on the door."

What was my son doing here in the middle of the night? Second thought, I didn't care. I sprang out of bed, my feet hitting the cold floor. I stuffed my bare feet into my sneakers. The pants of my flannel snowman pajamas puddled around my shoes. Winter was not a good time for RV traveling. I needed to check into insulating the place better or my plans for the RV as a home away from home for craft events in November and December was a bust.

I opened the door. Before I could ask what Scotland was doing here, he stepped inside and drew me into a fierce embrace.

"I hate that man." My son's voice was tight with barely controlled emotion.

Scotland knew. I shouldn't be surprised someone on the force informed him of what happened. I hugged him back. My son was a good officer because he was a compassionate man. Even when he was younger, he was able to see the other side of an issue and had a forgiving nature. It was rare for him to dislike someone. He hated being the source of anyone's hurt.

"You'll regret saying that in the morning. I'm fine."

"Only because he killed himself." Scotland pulled back and studied me, frowning. "What happened to your face?"

I raised my hand and touched my cheek. There was a tender spot. "I tripped when I found Samuel."

"I'm so sorry, Mom." Scotland hugged me again. "That was a horrible experience. Are you sure you're okay?"

"Yes. What are you doing out here in the middle of the night."

"Checking on you. Isn't that obvious?"

"How did you know which RV I owned?"

"I was spotted driving around and had to go through an inquisition." He smiled. "Your friends are protective of you. Grace Turner pointed out which was yours."

"Grace was out patrolling?"

He nodded. "I advised her to ask the Armory to supply a security team and she said it wasn't necessary. She wanted to make sure all was quiet tonight as a lot of the campers were a little out of sorts because of the earlier police action. She told them there was nothing to worry about."

I still didn't like knowing Grace was checking out the RV park by herself. "I'd have kept her company."

"She had someone watching her back and told me not to be concerned."

"Abraham. Her son is never too far behind her."

"Can't fault a son for that." He smiled, the emotion reached his eyes. "Are you sure you're okay?"

"Yes. You should head home and get some sleep." I waggled my finger at him. "You told me you couldn't stop by the craft show because you were working. Off to bed young man. I'd offer a place here..." My gaze traveled to the dinette which also served as the extra bed. The table top could be lowered and used as the base for the bed. The bench cushions were then used as the mattress. I didn't want my son sleeping on the space where Samuel had died.

And from the look on his face, neither did he. "You remember Paul McCormick?"

I nodded. He was on the volunteer fire department squad with Scotland. Or had been as Scotland was no longer a part of it since he moved. I hadn't seen Paul since Scotland moved to Morgantown. The guy was more Scotland's friend than a family friend. "He's a friend of yours from the fire station."

"His hobby is working on cars and carpentry. He could knock that out for you and replace it with something better suited for your needs. Shelves for your machines and storage for your supplies."

"I don't want to inconvenience him. I'm sure I can find someplace that renovates RVs."

My son grinned. "Trust me, he'd love to hear from you."

Ugh. Not this again. My son had this insane notion that his friend, who was thirteen years younger than me, and I would make a nice couple. Apparently, I hadn't talked Scotland out of that idea. "Good night, Scotland."

"Sleep tight, Mom. If you hear anything call me or the police."

"Sound seeps through the windows. I don't want to bother—"

"Mom, don't ignore it. Call the police to investigate. That's what we're here for. To protect you. Tell the dispatcher you're Officer Winters's mom and he told you to call if you heard any strange noises in the RV parking lot at the Armory. An officer will come and check it out. It's not a bother."

"But..." My nerves were a little frazzled and my imagination was great at conjuring up possibilities.

"You're my family. Police are also my family. Which makes

them your family. We take care of each other. They'll take care of you." Scotland kissed the top of my head and strolled out.

FOUR

Jack Frost had visited last night. The small window over my bed was coated in a thin layer of ice, and the cold seeped through the wall. Ebenezer was pressed to my side, burrowed completely under the blanket and squealed his displeasure when I moved away from him.

"What are you complaining about? You wear a permanent fur coat." Leaving the bed to head to the bathroom was a giant struggle, but I wasn't going to sell anything if I didn't get out from underneath the covers.

I threw back the comforter and hustled into the bathroom, pausing long enough to grab a holiday-themed sweater and leggings. I was willing to contort myself into a pretzel to get dressed in the small bathroom and benefit from the steam of the hot water.

After showering and getting dressed, I packed up my Cricut then wrestled an annoyed Ebenezer back into his cage. He whistled and squealed at me. "Stop being a spoiled child. You don't want to be left in here. The only way to get you inside the building is in this cage."

My plan was to half-heartedly sneak Ebenezer in. After I set up the small table I used for my register, I'd put him in my folding utility wagon that I used to transport my items and place his cage underneath my register area.

Stepping outside, the cold acted like the first cup of coffee in the morning, straightening my shoulders and focusing my mind. Every task I needed to accomplish this morning fell into perfect order in my brain. Maybe the cold wasn't such a bad thing.

A hum filled the air and I spotted Abraham heading toward me in a golf cart. There was a small trailer hooked to the back. He stopped.

"I'm helping the vendors in the farther lots bring their items to the building. Mama said you'd be one of the first ones up." Abraham beamed.

"If you can take over the products, I can bring my cashbox and Ebenezer." I was excited. Less trips and I'd be able to get the set up finished sooner and have time to make some of the RV holiday décor.

"I can take him," Abraham offered, patting the empty seat beside him. "No one will be upset if I bring him into the Armory."

True. Most of the vendors knew about Abraham's condition. I felt bad taking advantage of him, so Ebenezer was allowed inside but it wasn't safe to leave my little pal in the RV all day. I retrieved Ebenezer and handed over the cage.

Abraham held the cage in front of his face. Ebenezer rubbed his cheek on Abraham's finger. "I don't think he wants to stay in here all day. He looks sad."

The little rascal was deliberately worming his way into Abraham's heart. I had no doubt Ebenezer figured out that Abraham had a soft heart when it came to animals. "Don't let him out. It's not safe for him to run around in the Armory and I can't leave him in the RV. It's too cold."

"Can I let him out in our RV? Mama lets me have a break from one o'clock to two thirty. It's my quiet time."

Routine was important to Abraham. Being able to retreat to a quiet spot helped him cope with social activities. "Ok. Just keep a close eye on Ebenezer so he doesn't do anything he shouldn't."

"I promise." Abraham secured Ebenezer beside him and slowly drove off.

I waved goodbye and hefted the handle of my tote bag higher onto my shoulder. At least I didn't have to carry Ebenezer's cage, my tote bag containing a water bottle, wallet, and iPad, and a cashbox. It was a major hike to the Armory. I should've asked

Abraham to return for me or given him the tote or cashbox. I adjusted the strap of the tote. Earlier, the contents in my bag hadn't seemed heavy, but now I felt like I was hauling a kitchen sink to the craft show. It was going to take a while to walk there lugging the heavy items. I should've put in my earphones and listened to an Audible book to pass the time.

My shoulder felt like it was about to fall off. Vendors passed me. I was slower than the last twenty-four hours before Christmas. The pain in my shoulder intensified. Hoping I could adjust the load some, I put down the cashbox and rummaged through my bag for anything I could transfer to the box.

Chapstick. Bandages. Old lottery tickets. Why did I still have these? A remnant of my life with Samuel. Occasionally, I had joined Samuel and his mom Helen on their twice weekly outing to a local convenience store to buy lottery tickets.

Where was my vendor badge? I shoved aside yesterday's newspaper I intended to use as extra bedding material for Ebenezer. I needed the badge to get into the venue without having to pay the admission fee. Closing my eyes, I pictured my packing process. I had placed the vendor packet in my suitcase—and left it there. Last night had thrown me off my battle plan, and I had slunk to bed rather than do my usual night before show hunting and gathering of items.

I looked longingly in front of me. I was halfway there and now I had to go back. Sighing, I picked up the cashbox, turned around and trudged back to my RV. With every step, the items grew heavier. Finally, I saw my RV and the sight energized me. Tucking the cash box under my arm, I awkwardly reached into my bag to retrieve my keys.

Of course, they were buried somewhere in the bottom. "Really should have done this earlier."

A movement caught my attention. I glanced up. There was a person dressed in blue jeans and a black hoodie fiddling with the door to my RV.

"What are you doing?" I ran forward with a clumsy gait as I

tried keeping hold of my box and purse.

The person jumped toward me. In that moment, I realized my stupid mistake. I should've walked away and called security, not confront the person. I spun. The cashbox slipped from my hands, clattering to the gravel ground. I left it and ran.

There was scuffling behind me. They were catching up. I scanned the lot, looking for someone to help me. There was no one. I started to slip the bag off, hoping dropping it caused the thief to stop and allow me more time to get away. Before it fell from my shoulder, I was tackled from behind.

A cry escaped me. I toppled to the ground. The force knocked my glasses off. Everything was blurry and wavy. A lilac scent wrapped around me. The purse was trapped under my body, the objects digging into my stomach. A hand pushed on my neck, clunking my forehead onto the ground as the other wrapped around the strap of my bag. Instinctively, I tightened my hold.

Let them take it, I scolded myself. My hand refused to obey the frantic order in my head.

The person grabbed my shoulders and lifted me up. Heavy breathing was in my ear. A hand moved from shoulder to the back of my neck. Fear raced through me. What was I going to do? I bent my knees, giving myself some height from the ground and tipped sideways, hoping to throw the purse snatcher off balance. My knee jammed into their side. I was free.

Description. The police would need a description if they succeeded in swiping my purse. Squinting, I tried to crisp up the image. I saw white tennis shoes, black shoelaces and bare ankles. One chubby ankle had a strip of gauze on it. Irrational thoughts slipped into my head. Why wasn't this person wearing socks? It was cold out here.

I scrambled to my feet, abandoning the purse on the ground. The hoodie slipped from their head, revealing blonde almost white hair. Their mouth and nose were covered with a bandana and sunglasses hid their eyes. The person took a menacing step toward me, fists clenching and unclenching. I was terrified.

Behind me, I heard the whirr of the golf cart. Abraham. Did I want to yell for help? I was conflicted. I wanted to be saved from the thief but also didn't want to place someone else in danger.

Abraham released a battle cry. "Merry Christmas, I'm coming."

Shoving me to the ground, the individual turned and ran. Once again, Abraham was my hero. I pushed myself to my feet, keeping my tote pressed to my body.

"Happy holiday to you," I yelled after the person.

"Are you okay?" Abraham glared at the tried-to-be criminal.

"I'm fine." I rotated my shoulder, working out the kink from carrying the heavy bag and the tug-of-war over it. It was getting chilly. The cold was seeping through the leggings. Looks like the thief wasn't the only one needing to dress more appropriately for the weather.

"You sure you're okay?" Abraham stared at my knees.

My holiday leggings were torn. Santa's sleigh was now flying over my knee instead of a house. That's why I was cold. Bah Humbug. It took me hours to find this pair that was the perfect complement to my reindeer sweater.

"Can you drive me back? I just need to change and grab my lanyard."

Abraham nodded and glared in the direction of the almost thief, picking up my glasses. "I won't leave you alone, Merry. I'll protect you."

Abraham pulled the golf cart to a stop and pointed out a guy standing in front of the doors to the Armory. "There's a guard, Merry. You should tell him what happened. I'll take your stuff to your booth."

The man looked rather bored as he scanned the necks of the people walking up to the door. Vendors wearing their lanyards were allowed in and shoppers were directed to the end of the long line forming.

I slipped my lanyard with my badge around my neck and

walked over.

The guard nodded and motioned me inside.

"Someone was trying to break into my RV," I said. "They knocked me down and took off."

The guard straightened, the bored expression fading from his face. "When did this happen?"

"A few minutes ago."

He took out a small notebook and asked me for more details. I told him what I remembered, and he scribbled everything down. "Anything taken?"

I shook my head. "Everything looked fine. I'm sure I caught the person trying to break in not leaving. They weren't carrying anything."

"Knowing the location you're parked at, I bet the would-be thief was on the start of their stealing binge. I'll make sure we have patrols driving around all day and tonight. Likely thought all the vendors were in the Armory setting up and it was time to start seeing what they could find a new home for. If we need any more information from you, we'll stop by."

"Should I report it to the police also?"

The guard shrugged. "It's up to you. Nothing was taken but you were knocked down."

Part of me said I should report it, but another part of me was done with talking to police for the weekend. I wanted to focus on the happiness of Christmas and the event. I had looked forward to this one for months. It was one of my favorites. Talking to the police would just take time away from selling.

"I'm good," I said.

"When you're ready to head back to your RV let a security personnel know, and you'll be escorted back."

"Thanks."

He opened the door for me. "We're glad to help."

The air inside in the Armory was suffocating. The heat was taking away from the cozy Christmas atmosphere they were trying to create. The inside of the one-acre Expo Center was converted into the North Pole. An eight-foot-tall candy cane decoration with a North Pole Headquarters banner hanging from it was placed near the registration table. Huge mounds of Poly-Fil fiber surrounded the table and was stacked in strategic places throughout the building. Christmas music drifted from the speakers.

In the west end corner of the building, there was a huge sleigh set up for photo opportunities, a Santa sack with door prizes, and in the back of the building, a Christmas inflatable featuring Santa's barn with eight reindeers. I was happy my booth wasn't near that blow-up decoration. I wouldn't be stuck answering the where's Rudolph question.

I was smack in the middle of the Armory building. Center aisle. Center booth. Not the choicest of locations as some shoppers' energy—and money—dwindled before they reached the middle aisles. Most people started at one end of the building or the other and worked their way to the other side. My spot was better than being in the back near the inflatables or near the food court. Every year, vendors suffered losses because of dripping food and spilled drinks on their merchandise.

I adjusted the drape of the cloth I used to cover up the portable table for my cash register. Ebenezer was stashed in the back and a small portable fan was plugged into my power cord. The air directed toward my little bundle of fur fluffed up his multi-colored strands of hair. Ebenezer was in bliss.

The place was abuzz with activity and gossip as the 185 vendors finished readying their booths for the onslaught of Christmas shoppers. The main topics of conversation was a man dying in the RV parking section and the twelve-million-dollar lottery winner from a nearby town. I placed my headphones into my ears and pretended I was listening to music on my cell phone. I didn't want to discuss what happened last night and hoped to keep questions at bay yet still hear the scuttlebutt going around the craft fair.

The cutting machine chugged in the background, my first vinyl Christmas tree was almost done. The glitter vinyl sparkled as the mat fed through the rollers. A nervous, giddiness danced in my stomach. When it was done, I weeded out the slivers of excess vinyl until only the tree remained. It was beautiful.

Santa's elves were putting the finishing touches on the North Pole while Santa gulped down some coffee and adjusted his black belt. Grace was arguing with a maintenance guy about the decoration attached to the ceiling. The snow garland made from felt and twine that was hanging from the rafters dipped lower. At the rate it was "melting," it would fall on Santa's head sometime during the event. Fixing it required dragging out a forty-foot ladder, and since the event started in fifteen minutes, the only thing to do was create a snowfall pool. I placed my bet for two thirty this afternoon.

The sign for my booth was tilted at an odd angle, so I adjusted the twine and straightened out our Merry and Bright Handcrafted Christmas banner. I arranged the final touches to my booth and stepped back. The eight-foot table was no longer crowded, and the prices were easy to read. There was nothing I disliked more than having to ask about prices and made sure mine were front and center. Plus, it helped cut down on inventory loss as people weren't picking up the breakables as often.

A rush of voices filled the center. The doors opened and shoppers, some decked out in holiday gear, stood in line to pay their entrance fee. One group of women was studying a map of the booth locations and marking places to check out. I hoped I was one of the must-see booths. Nothing made a handcrafter happier than knowing someone loved their work.

Showtime. I put away my headphones and used the camera function on my phone as a mirror and checked the placement of my Christmas headband. The silver fabric mesh material had a large elf bow attached to the side. It paired perfectly with my cream shirt embroidered with an oversized reindeer and Santa sleigh leggings, now with holes. I hoped I was able to patch them up.

The scent of coffee wafted toward me. Gingerbread spice. I inhaled the aroma and let it wash over me. It was pure comfort.

"Are you Merry Winters?" a male voice asked.

I turned. A young man was holding a cup of coffee and a bag from a pastry shop.

"Yes, I am."

He placed the goodies and coffee on the table. "Special delivery to brighten your day."

"Thank you." I tipped the young man and sipped my coffee.

Bright. She knew how frantic the morning of an event was and sent me breakfast. Warmth flooded through my heart. This was the type of feeling I needed to focus on, not the bad ones Samuel—and his death—generated. I wanted to think good thoughts about him, especially since he was dead. It felt horrible to think ill of him now, but the truth was Samuel had shown himself to be an extremely self-centered man—who wasn't as great of a father as I had thought. How could he allow Cassie to be thrown out of her home?

Unless it was a lie. The idea drifted into my head. Cassie could've known her father was hiding in the RV. If she did, it meant she told me a story. Fiction. She played on my sympathies.

My phone pinged. Bright.

Wanted to send you some Christmas cheer.

Gingerbread. Perks me right up every time, I typed back.

The caffeine probably also helps.

That it does. Thank you, my friend.

Anything to help the day be Brighter. She added a happy face.

The booth looks fantastic and I do believe this will be a much better day.

It should. You have one less problem in the world.

Bright... I didn't know what else to say. With what I learned yesterday, Samuel had planned on becoming a huge problem for me. I just didn't want to contemplate it now. It was Christmas craft fair time. A day for happiness and joy. There was nothing I loved more—except for my children—than creating and then sharing my crafts with customers. But, Bright had a point.

Christmas came early! I signed off.

*   *   *

Sales were steady. The weekend was turning around. If the afternoon was as good as the morning, I was on my way to clearing a nice profit for the day. By the end of the weekend, I might even be able to swing a small renovation to the RV.

Singing "We Wish You a Merry Christmas," I rearranged some of the product on the tables so there weren't any big holes. Customers were peculiar. They'd bypass a booth if there were too many products out as they presumed it meant your items weren't quality and no one wanted them, and they'd also go right by your table if you didn't have enough merchandise as it meant you were a newbie and your products weren't quality. It was hard to win.

The RV décor wasn't selling as well as I hoped, maybe it wasn't displayed properly. I needed to get some poster board and hang a sample for customers to see ways to use the product, even an old window that mimicked the shape of a RV window could hold some of the smaller designs. I slipped my phone from my pocket and emailed myself the idea.

During my lunch break, I'd do an internet search and see if there was somewhere nearby I could get something that would work and send Raleigh to pick it up. I was surprised she hadn't stopped by yet. She usually arrived with lunch and it was now approaching one in the afternoon.

A woman examined a vinyl decorated wine glass with *Win(e)ing Christmas* written in a script font, and grape vines twined underneath the phrase in the shape of a Christmas tree. I watched her carefully. She kept pulling her phone from her purse, glancing over at me, then picking up another glass. Either she was planning on stealing the glass or taking a photo to copy my design. I wasn't sure which option was the worst.

"Excuse me, are you Ms. Winters?" A male voice asked from behind me.

"Yes." I turned with a practiced customer service smile on my face. Not too big. Not too small. My smile faltered a bit when my gaze rested on the attractive man in his late thirties wearing a suit with a butt of a revolver peeking out when he reached inside his jacket. Shoppers didn't usually wear suits. Or had a gun attached to their belt.

He pulled out a small wallet and flipped it open. A police badge. "I have a few questions for you."

There were people milling around my booth. I didn't want to miss a sale. "My relief for lunch should be here in a few minutes."

Someone must've called the police about the thief running amok. Gathering my memory from this morning's almost theft, I pulled up the image of the would-be thief. What I recalled most was the no socks or gloves. Seemed silly to not to wear gloves, and not just because it was cold. It was a bad idea to leave fingerprints behind.

"Now. I have a few questions about a murder that occurred in your RV."

A customer gaped at me. The woman who had been examining my wine glasses stashed her phone in her pocket and scurried away. Murder. The word fully registered in my head. Samuel. Someone had murdered my ex-husband and the reason the detective wanted to speak to me was that I owned the RV where Samuel was found.

And, I discovered his body.

"Looks like you had an altercation with someone last night." He gestured toward my face.

I touched my cheek. With the steam clouding up the small mirror in the bathroom, I forgot about the bruise. I shouldn't have skipped my makeup routine. "I fell and hit the edge of the dinette table."

The detective made a sound and jotted something down in a notebook.

"I did," I defended myself. "After I—" Found Samuel's body. The rest of the words wouldn't come out.

The detective's head jerked up. All attention on me. "After you what? Please go on."

I whispered, "Found Samuel. I slipped." Customers were staring at me. I didn't want all this attention on me. Or at least not for this reason. "Can we discuss this somewhere else?"

"I just have some basic questions. Is there a reason you prefer this to be in private?" He jotted down some notes. The top of the page had Mary Winters written on it.

"It's Merry," I corrected. "Like Merry Christmas. Not Mary had a little lamb."

"I'll make a note of that." He flipped a few pages in his notebook and tilted it up, away from my gaze. "I want to clarify what happened last night. There are some discrepancies to clear up before I can close this case. May I?"

"I guess." I wrapped my arms around myself. It was getting a little chilly.

"Let's start back at the beginning." He offered me a sympathetic smile and flipped to a page in his notebook. "You called the dispatcher and reported that you found your ex-husband Samuel Waters hidden in the bench of your dinette seat in your Class A recreational vehicle."

"Actually, one of the RV owners called for me."

He jotted that down. "Is the rest of the information correct? You found your ex-husband in the bench seat of your dinette. Dead."

I nodded. "Yes."

"Why do you think your ex-husband hid in your RV?"

"To force me to talk with him."

"Was your ex-husband abusive?"

A sick feeling settled in my stomach as it did every time my marriage to Samuel entered my brain. I hated talking, or even thinking, about my marriage of fewer than two months. I was ashamed. I had always prided myself on being smart enough not to fall for a smooth-talking man and find myself in a heart-bruising relationship. Samuel wasn't abusive per se, but he had a way of speaking to me that made me feel less than. He wasn't like that when we were dating, but once we were married everything I did, said, believed, or wanted was criticized.

He'd make promises and then break them, blaming me for why he didn't follow through. There was always a reason I no longer deserved whatever he had sworn to do, whether it had been about spending time together or purchases. The only big promise he had ever kept was buying the RV, but I learned soon after that he didn't buy it for us to travel in together—it was to move my mother into so "we" could save money.

"No," I finally answered.

Abraham rushed over to me. "There's a police car outside."

"I know. I'm talking to the officer right now." I shooed at him. "You should go back to your mom."

The detective stepped toward Abraham and held out his hand. "I'm Detective Grayson."

Abraham placed his hands behind his back. He didn't like strangers touching him. "Are you here about the person who tried to take Merry's purse or the man Merry had in her RV?"

"Had in her RV?" The detective's eyebrows quirked up.

Abraham nodded. "Yes. In the seat storage."

"You saw the man?" The detective asked.

"Abraham, you should go back to your mom. She'll be worried about you." I tried to hold back the panic building in my voice. Abraham was doing a good job, without trying, to make me sound like a murderer.

He ignored me and continued talking with Detective Grayson. "Yes. Merry needed help to move things out of her trailer."

"You were helping Ms. Winters move items..." the detective flicked a narrow-eyed gaze in my direction... "from her trailer and saw the body of Samuel Waters?"

I was done for.

Tears filled Abraham's eyes. "The RV stunk and Merry said something might have died in there."

I cringed. "A cat. I thought a cat got stuck somewhere in the RV. I bought it yesterday afternoon."

The detective fixed a very ugly look on me. "Do not interrupt again."

Abraham continued explaining his understanding of the situation. "Merry had screamed for help and she looked at the seat. I thought there was a dead cat in there. I lifted it up and there he was. Dead. After I saw him, Merry told me I had to leave." He patted my arm. "She was so upset. Poor Merry."

The detective snapped the notebook closed and took a firm hold of my elbow. "You and I will finish this conversation at the police station."

Abraham's brows furrowed. "Did I say something wrong?"

The detective smiled at him. "On the contrary, you might have just helped me solve a murder."

FIVE

I stared at a blank white wall. The blank dirty-white cement walls of an interrogation room in the police station where my son worked. I hoped Scotland was out on patrol. The only sound in the room was Detective Grayson tapping a pen on the table as he awaited my answer to the question he asked and re-asked in a multitude of ways. I wasn't sure if I had been here for two hours or twenty minutes.

The metal chair was hard. My lower back hurt along with my derrière. I wanted to shift positions but was afraid any movement would cause Detective Grayson to jump up screaming, "Ah ha, you're admitting to killing your ex-husband." I never should've bought the stupid RV from Cassie. I crossed my arms over my reindeer sweater. It was hard for someone to take you seriously wearing a red-nosed Christmas animal on your chest.

"When did you say you bought the RV?"

"Yesterday. Early afternoon." For the umpteenth time, I explained to Detective Grayson what the lovely police officer had concluded last night. Was she on duty today? Could she explain it to him since he didn't understand a word I said? "Samuel put himself in the bench. No one killed him."

He did it to himself. I kept the last, unsympathetic thought in my head.

Detective Grayson leaned back in the metal chair, studying me. "Did you know it takes at least twenty-four hours for a body to start releasing an odor? I find it hard to believe that your ex-husband hid in the storage space twenty-four hours before he even knew you'd buy the RV."

A gasp flew out of me. I slapped a hand over my mouth. Someone *had* killed Samuel. What did Cassie know about her father's death? Did she know he was in there? Was she blaming me? Oh God, did she think I killed him? Tears blurred my vision. I blinked them away. Settle down. Deep breaths. You did nothing wrong.

"I bought the RV from my former stepdaughter. Maybe Samuel decided to test if he could hide in there and locked himself in."

Bang. The feet of the chair fell back to the tile floor. "And his teenage daughter, nor anyone else, thought to look for him? Was it usual for him to vanish for a day?"

"Yes." The answer came out quicker than I intended.

"And his daughter, Cassie, and his new wife would agree to that?"

I didn't know how to answer the question. The truth was yes, but I had no idea if they'd answer with the truth or lie.

"We'll move on to another question." He placed a picture on the table. It was from my RV. The box of my supplies: duct tape, rope, gloves, garbage bags.

Under these circumstances, those sure seemed criminal minded.

There was a knock on the door. Good, a disruption. The door opened, and an officer slipped inside the room. My heart thudded. I felt light-headed as coldness swept over me. Scotland had walked into the room and handed the detective a folder.

"I was asked to drop these off to you, Detective," Scotland said, quickly shifting his gaze from me.

"Thank you, Officer..." Detective Grayson looked at Scotland's name tag, "Winters."

My hands shook. I clamped them together then my whole arms trembled. Tears pricked my eyes. I was an embarrassment. Word would filter throughout the department that his mother was a possible murderer. Scotland should've stuck with his father's last name and not reverted to mine. He switched it his junior year of high school because he didn't want preferential—or prejudicial—treatment because of his father. I had reclaimed my maiden name after my divorce because I loved being Merry Winters. It fit me.

Scotland walked out. I sunk down in my seat. A useless movement because there was nowhere to hide.

"Maybe you had some help in 'hiding' your ex-husband?" Grayson's gaze drifted toward the door my son had exited.

"No!" I shot to my feet. "He had nothing to do with any of it."

He grinned like the Grinch stealing the last Christmas ornament.

Oh God, what did I just admit to? "I had nothing to do with my ex-husband dying. I did nothing, so no one else did anything for me."

He opened the folder and scanned the documents. He drummed a pen on the table and tugged a yellow notepad toward him. "You married a man, Samuel Waters, who liked to up and disappear and that was so annoying to you, you divorced him after two months."

"One month, three weeks, and five and half days," I broke in and immediately regretted it.

His eyebrows quirked up. "Is that what happened to your first husband too? Mr. Winters just up and disappeared one day?"

"Winters is my maiden name," I said.

"Your real name is Merry, like in Christmas, Noel Winters? And you have a business where you make Christmas crap and wear it."

I pushed down my anger. Yelling at the detective was a bad idea. "Yes. My parents named me that because they found me on church steps on Christmas Eve. I have always loved Christmas. Joy. Happiness. Love for one another." Something Detective Grinch knew little about.

The detective leaned back in the chair. "You really expect me to believe all of that?"

The door creaked open. "You should." The voice hit my spine

and shivered up to my head.

Frowning, the detective turned.

Joy danced through me and I suppressed a smile. I shouldn't be happy that my ex-husband Brett Calloway was leaning against the doorframe.

He aged well. Brett's hair was greyer than the last time I saw him, which was four months ago at Scotland's police academy graduation, but other than that, he looked like the Brett who had swept me off my feet twenty-four years ago. Too bad we were just too different to make it work.

I had a business that encouraged the celebration of Christmas. Brett was a partner with the law firm of Calloway, Demetris, and Perez that specialized in cases where people in authority abused their power. Politicians. Coaches. Professors. Law enforcement—the reason Scotland took my maiden name. Brett didn't believe in heroes, even though his children and I saw him as one.

He was a practical man. I was a dreamer. He believed in what could be seen. He searched for the lies hidden in people and hunted them down. It was why he was one of the best defense attorneys in the DC Metro area. Me, I believed good resided in every heart. In magic. Fairy dust. Santa Claus. Being opposites attracted us to each other and those same differences pulled our hearts from each other. One of the simple, and painful, truths of life was sometimes love didn't conquer all. Brett and I made better friends than husband and wife.

"Her name is Merry Winters," Brett said. "I can bring in the newspapers articles from forty-five years ago about her being found on the steps. And, she's not talking to you anymore."

"Who the hell are you?" The detective clenched his fists.

"Her attorney." Brett withdrew a business card from his wallet and placed it on the table.

My gaze settled on a person outside the door of the interrogation room.

Scotland leaned against the wall, a shoulder touching the wall, one arm dangling down while the other was crossed over his chest.

Just like his father's stance. It always twanged my heart when I saw him doing that. He had no idea he had picked up that mannerism from his father. Without a word, Scotland straightened and headed down the hall.

But not before I caught the small smile and the wink. My boy had my back.

Brett tucked my hand into the crock of his arm. "Let's go, Merry. We have some Christmas shopping to do."

"You should've called me." Brett opened the passenger door to his maroon Rogue Hybrid. He scanned the parking lot of the police station almost like he was expecting someone to jump out and start throwing out questions. If there was ever a tally done on what he spent most of his time doing, saying "No comment" was on his top ten list.

"And said what?" I slid onto the seat. "Hi, this is your ex-wife, the mother of your two amazing children, and I'm certain I'm the main suspect in my other ex-husband's death?"

With one hand on the car door and the other on the frame, Brett leaned in, grazing his fingertips over my cheek. There was a tiny flutter in my being. I reminded my heart I was not affected by it anymore. He wasn't mine. Brett was married. We were only friends.

"Hi Brett, this is Merry. The police are asking me questions about Samuel's death. I could use some help, would've sufficed," he said. "When did you get the bruise?"

"I tripped when I found Samuel." I buckled the seatbelt. "How did you find out?"

He pulled his cell phone from his pocket and tapped on the screen. Glancing down at the screen, he grinned and shook his head. "Sometimes I think that one is getting into the wrong profession. She cracks me up." He handed me his phone then shut the door.

Raleigh. What did she tell her father? On the screen was a

picture of the detective putting me into the back of a police cruiser.

I told Scotland to call Mom more often. She's now going to extremes to get some attention from her son. Got herself arrested. The devotion of a mother is so sweet—and a little creepy. Save her from herself, Daddy.

"The girl thinks she's a comedian." I placed the phone into the console cup holder. My daughter was one of those who used humor to cover up anxiety or hedge around the truth.

"And Scotland called me last night and asked that I come visit today. Said I might be needed. You'll be okay, Merry." Brett squeezed my hand. "I won't let that detective pin Samuel's murder on you."

"So, it is murder?" I had pretty much figured that out when the detective made a good point about the timing. There was no way Samuel would've hid himself in the seat a day before Cassie sold me the RV. Unless, he was trying it out first. But then why wouldn't she have looked for him? Or his wife Bonnie?

Brett started the car and pulled out of the parking space. "Yes. There's no question about that."

"That's not what the officer thought last night," I said. I fought the urge to turn around and see if the detective was standing in front of the station. The detective hadn't wanted me to leave. The man believed with all his heart he was a word or two away from getting a full confession. The dashboard clock said three. A little over two hours of my day was wasted by the detective. I didn't even want to contemplate how much money I lost.

Once we pulled onto the main road, some of the anxiety trickled from me. I hated being an anxious type, especially around Christmas time. It spoiled the holiday for me. I liked to surround myself with cheerfulness and love.

"She isn't the one who decides cause of death," Brett said. "The coroner does. There was bruising on Samuel's back, hip, and hands. They're running a toxicology report but that won't be back for at least a few days."

"The bruising might have been caused by Samuel trying to get himself out. The top of the seat could've fallen and was stuck."

"Or someone sat on it." Brett merged into the next lane. A police car was on our right side. My body slunk down in the seat and I avoided making eye contact with the officer in the cruiser. The cruiser pulled past us.

"Was Samuel's daughter interviewed?" My voice shook. I leaned forward and played with the vents. "It's a little cold in here."

The look Brett threw in my direction said he wasn't buying my little act. He knew I was upset. "She wasn't in a condition to answer any questions."

Tears streamed down my face. I wiped them away with the sleeve of my sweater. That poor girl. "I need to call her."

"No." The word was forceful.

My eyes widened. "No?" This time my voice trembled from anger. Who did Brett Calloway think he was, telling me no? "She needs me."

"She set you up, Merry."

I jerked sideways, my body hitting into the passenger door. "You think Cassie killed her father."

"Or knows who did. The facts are right in front of you. Samuel was murdered in the RV or led to the RV and then killed. He might have been talked into hiding in the bench seat and then it was kept closed until he suffocated." He nodded toward the back seat. "I have a contract I need you to sign."

"A contract?"

"Basic attorney-client contract. This way what you say is between us."

My eyes narrowed. "Why? Do you think I killed him?"

Brett laughed. And laughed. Tears slid down his cheeks. "You're a riot. At least we know who our daughter gets her sense of humor from because Lord knows she doesn't get it from me."

That was true. Brett was no nonsense almost to a fault. It wasn't what put a damper on our relationship. While he was an excellent litigator and defender in his job, he never stood up for me to his parents or siblings.

I pushed the past from my mind. They were no longer part of my life. No sense wasting emotion on it. And, I had enough trouble in the present.

"I'm not laughing at you," Brett said.

"I know. I just can't find any humor in this situation right now."

Brett's cheeks flushed a soft pink. "You're right."

"I should offer Bonnie my condolences. She and Samuel married a week ago."

"Even more of a no." Brett slid a look in my direction. "You and Samuel divorced two weeks ago and a week later he married Bonnie. That was a quick relationship."

"I'd been trying to divorce Samuel for three months. He wanted us to work it out even though his eye had already started to wander to Bonnie."

"Do you know why Samuel and Bonnie rushed into a marriage? Why did he fight the divorce if he was interested in another woman?"

"Because Cassie still wanted me as her mother. Samuel figured he could have the best of both worlds. Stay married to me, so Cassie had the mom she wanted. And have Bonnie as his mistress. He found out Bonnie nor I were interested in that arrangement. Now, Cassie has a stepmom who dislikes her. The poor girl."

Brett pulled into the parking lot of Panera bread. "I know your heart wants you to reach out to Cassie and Bonnie, but it's best you don't say anything to them."

"Because of the detective?"

"More like because anything you say can be twisted around."

True. I heaved out a sigh and closed my eyes. My body slumped into the seat. "But what if not saying anything also shows my guilt? What kind of person doesn't check on their former stepdaughter, an eighteen-year-old, after her father was murdered?"

"Good point." Brett drummed his thumbs on the steering wheel. "We've stumbled into a massive damned if you do, damned if you don't situation."

"This is my problem. I don't want you to get involved."

Brett unbuckled his seat belt and leaned over the console, reaching for his briefcase. "I am involved, Merry."

"You don't need to be."

Brett rested his briefcase on his knees and pulled out a stack of papers. "This is a standard client agreement with a few minor changes."

"This is standard?" I flipped through the sheets. Brett liked to cover all the bases.

"It lists who else will see your case file, work on it, who to contact in the event of an emergency. Proper protocol and behaviors for both sides. Expected time frames between updates, number of office visits expected, barring any new evidence or information I receive." Brett shrugged. "Standard stuff. I found that letting the client know from the start how much of my time, and how available I was for meetings and phone calls, saved all parties a lot of stress."

The retainer amount was a dollar. I frowned. The hourly rate for Brett's legal counsel was a dollar. I crossed my arms and ignored the pen he offered me. "A dollar? I know you're not this cheap."

"I have done pro bono work before. It's not unusual for me, but I felt it was important to put in some amount."

An ache developed in my chest. "I don't want to be a charity case."

"You're not a charity case." There was exasperation in his voice. "Can you please sign the agreement? You need a defense attorney. Do you think one of the attorneys in Season's Greetings is familiar with a murder case?"

"No. I'm sure I can find someone."

"Who will charge you a lot more than I will."

"I can support myself." I glared at him. "I've never asked you for more than what the court ordered."

"I know." Sadness filled his voice. "I'm not your enemy, Merry, nor am I a judge or jury over your life. I care about you. People help those they care about. If the detective builds a case against you, attorney fees could run in the tens of thousands of dollars."

"Tens of thousands?" I felt sick.

Brett nodded. "Depending how long it takes for the case to get on the docket, expert witnesses needed, filing of documents, hiring of PIs. It can get expensive. And that's without factoring in the hit to your income while the case is going on. You could be in court for weeks even months."

Every word increased the turmoil in my gut. How would it look? One ex-husband murdered and the other one defending me on his dime. "Could the detective use your helping me against me or you?"

"I'm sure he'll try but he won't get far down that road." Brett squeezed my hand. "Don't worry about me, Merry. Let me help you with this."

I still wasn't sure. I bit my lip and stared at the signature line.

"Our children will never forgive me if I don't handle your case. I will hear about it until the day I die. I'll be a disappointment to our children. I want them to be proud of me."

My eyes widened. I never considered he struggled with feeling inadequate. He was a successful lawyer. Great at his job. High in demand and paid very well for his skill and expertise. Why wouldn't his children be proud of him? Heck, he helped the downtrodden for a living and ensured justice was served.

"Your children are proud of you. Why would you even think they weren't?" Scotland and Raleigh enjoyed spending time with their dad. He was their foundation. Raleigh was a huge daddy's girl. "The kids brag on you all the time."

"And then there are times that they don't." Brett pointed at the papers. "If it'll make you feel better, I'll add a zero to the one."

"Two," I countered.

"Fine, two zeros to the retainer and no zeroes to the hourly rate." Brett wiggled the pen. "But, I'll add in two dozen glitter ornaments. I need an extra item to add to the staff gift baskets."

"You drive a hard bargain, Mr. Calloway." I took the pen and signed with a flourish.

He tucked the pen into his pocket and placed the contract into his briefcase. "I'll have a copy of the document sent to you. Also, keep a few of these with you at all times." Brett handed me a stack of business cards. "If a police officer, detective, or reporter asks you any questions about the case, refer them to me. Actually, if anyone asks questions about Samuel Waters' murder refer them to me."

Brett's stomach rumbled. He grinned. "Since we're in Panera's parking lot, how about we go inside and get some lunch? I know you love their sandwiches, and it's not like there's one in Season's Greetings."

There weren't many chain restaurants in our town, a fact I loved until I wanted Panera or Starbucks. "I need to get back to the craft show. There wasn't any time to find someone to man my booth so I'm sure I've made zero sales this afternoon."

"Then it's a good thing I placed an order for pickup." Brett opened the door. "I'll be back in a few minutes."

I should've fussed at him for ordering me food without asking what, or even if, I wanted anything, but I was hungry. I took out my cell. There was a message from Bright.

How's afternoon sales?

Wouldn't know. I've been at the police station. Samuel was murdered.

Murdered. Are you serious?

As serious as being on the suspect list.

That's bad. Real bad. You should hire an attorney. I should hire an attorney. Remember when I messaged you that I'd hire someone to kill him.

Oh no! Could the police get ahold of my text and Facebook messages? Of course, they could. I groaned and leaned my head back. How would they take the messages I sent to Bright that Samuel's death equaled Christmas coming early? Or hers about Googling mafia hitmen. Had I said anything worse about him? Ever? Could the detective subpoena my messages? *I'll ask my attorney what he recommends.*

It makes me feel better knowing someone is on your side.

Someone? Warning bells were pinging in my head. *What have you heard?*

Cassie has let loose on Facebook. She's worried the killer is coming after her next.

The poor girl was terrified and the only person around to protect her was her stepmother who disliked her. The stepmother. Had the police questioned her? Samuel loved his daughter. I couldn't believe he wouldn't fight for her. What if he refused to throw Cassie out of the house as Bonnie wanted and she killed him?

Brett was walking toward the car.

My attorney is returning, and I just thought of something I have to share. I know who killed Samuel.

I hope you're right because Cassie is telling all of Season's Greetings she has proof that YOU killed her father.

SIX

"What proof?" I asked Brett for the gazillionth time as we drove to the RV parking lot at the Armory.

"I don't know what Cassie has, but whatever it is makes the detective suspect you, though it isn't enough that he can arrest you."

"You knew this before you had me sign the contract agreement?"

"I knew it was serious when I drove out of Arlington." Brett pulled to a stop in front of my RV. "I have no details and couldn't get any until after you hired me. After we finish lunch, I'm heading back to the police station to see what I can get from them. They won't make it easy, but I know the ropes. That's why it was important to me—our children—that their mom had an attorney that was familiar with trying murder cases. Especially since you tend to allow your emotions to rule over common sense and self-preservation."

My eyes narrowed, and my mouth tugged down. "What does that mean?"

"That you'll say whatever is needed to protect Cassie even though she's the one who's putting the blame on you."

"Didn't you say Cassie hadn't spoken with the detectives?"

"I said she hadn't been interviewed by the detectives, but apparently she had unleashed a torrent of words against you when she was notified of her father's death."

I drew in a couple of deep breaths to control my anger. That was one of Brett's annoying traits, the semantics game he engaged.

It was a way for him to always be right. "Why would Cassie do this? She liked me."

"My guess is it's because it's either her or you. And for most people, if the choice is between themselves or someone else getting blamed for something, they'll pick the other person."

"Cassie knows I had nothing to do with her father's death. None."

Brett pulled to a stop in front of my RV. "The fact is Cassie is creating an alternative truth, or being fed one, where you killed her father. Talking to her isn't going to change her mind."

"Why not?" Tears clogged my voice. "She knows me. She knows I care about her. I love her like she was my own child."

I glared at the mammoth vehicle like it had personally betrayed me. It couldn't. It was an inanimate object, but I needed something to focus my churning anger onto, besides Brett, who was the bearer of the bad news, and also my saving grace. I couldn't contain the tears anymore. They ran down my face. I swiped at them with my sleeve.

Brett hugged me the best he could with a console between us. I rested my forehead on his shoulder as he rubbed my back with a circular movement. "I don't know why. I promise you, I'll find out."

I sniffled and moved away from his hug. I was a little too comfortable being in his embrace. Especially with my ex-husband having just died. I wanted to keep my and Brett's relationship totally in the professional realm: lawyer and murder suspect being defended.

"Let's go eat."

I placed a hand on his arm. "Can we just eat in your car? I don't want to eat inside."

Brett glanced at the RV, gaze scanning back and forth. "Have you checked the outside of the RV? See if any windows or a door was tampered with? We might be able to prove Samuel broke into the vehicle."

"He wouldn't have had to, it belonged to him, and he had gifted it Cassie"

"And yet, Detective Grayson finds Cassie's ownership to be of little importance. Why?" Brett asked.

"I don't know." The words choked out of me. This was all confusing. Why me? Why not Cassie? Not that I wanted the teen accused of her father's death.

"You have to trust me with everything. I need to know every ounce of truth about you and Samuel."

My brain spun with hurt, anger, and grief. "All of it? Like how I was missing our children so much, I ignored signs I shouldn't. I was lonely." Tears trailed down my cheeks. Angrily, I wiped them away. I was done crying over men who didn't deserve it. "You know what he wanted? A mother for his daughter. Someone to take care of his house. Clean for him. Cook for him. I didn't mind those things. Most importantly, he wanted money."

Brett stared at me. The expression in his eyes unreadable.

"We'd save money by moving my mother into the RV, and instead of my home becoming a crafting studio, he wanted to sell it and invest the money in a new business opportunity. I was such an idiot."

Brett took hold of my hand. "It'll be okay. I'll make sure it's all okay."

I allowed the comfort of his touch for a moment before I withdrew. I rubbed the tears from my face. "I'm fine. This whole situation is making me overly emotional. Especially remembering how Samuel treated my mom. I had to take out a restraining order so he'd leave her alone."

"What did he do to your mom?"

"It upset her when he'd visit without me and he'd do it anyway. My mom's dementia has gotten worse, and it confused her when I wasn't there. She was scared and yet he kept telling her he was going to move her. He was a stranger to her. She thought she was in trouble and was being locked up."

"Did the nurses ask him to stop?"

"Yes, and I did multiple times. He enjoyed agitating her, making her believe I didn't exist."

"Why would he do that?"

"Money," I said, disgust clear in my voice. "If I wasn't around, and he was, he could take over her finances." My heart froze. Was that why Samuel had hid in the trailer. To kill me? For money.

Brett hugged me to him. "I won't let him hurt you, Merry. I swear I won't."

"Samuel can't hurt me any longer." Or at least not in person. He could through the detective. And his daughter. "There's nothing the police can use against me."

"Nothing on your computer?"

"No." As soon as the word left an image flashed in my mind. The texts Bright and I exchanged. I groaned and buried my face in my hands.

"What did you do, Merry?"

It was no use even trying to play the "I didn't do anything" game. I pulled out my cell phone and opened my messages. I tapped on Bright's name and scrolled to the message I sent this morning.

"Yep, that might be a slight problem."

"How big of a problem?" I peeked at Brett through my fingers.

"It depends on the proof Cassie supposedly handed him."

"I swear to you, I had never written a threat to him or about him." I rummaged around in my brain, double checking my memory. "I'm sure of it. I never said anything that could even be taken as a veiled threat before. That's good? Right?"

"It's certainly better than you having made threats before. What about your friend Bright?" He held my phone out, tilting his hand back and forth. The phone rocked back and forth. "She ever made any threats on your behalf?"

"Well..." I told him what Bright told me this morning. His face said it all—that wasn't good. "But, she wasn't Facebook friends with Samuel. Nor did she follow him on any other social media platforms."

"Samuel used social media?" Brett reached for the glove box, his arm brushed my knee. A tingle shot through me.

Stop it, I told myself. He's your ex. He's married. And your other ex-husband just died. I felt like such a horrible person. I shouldn't react at all to Brett. We'd been divorced for sixteen years. Were my emotions a jumbled mess because of Samuel's death, which happened so soon after a tumultuous divorce? The last few months had not been pleasant ones in my life. Stress upon stress had been heaved on me, not to mention for the first time in...well ever...I was truly, utterly alone.

Brett sat back and opened a leather notebook. He tugged a pen from his suit jacket pocket. "What social media platforms did Samuel use?"

"Facebook and Twitter."

"Can you remember what he'd been posting the last few days? Maybe he ticked someone off or he planned on selling the RV and had someone come take a look at it."

"I don't know. I blocked him. He was calling and messaging me all the time, even after I told him to stop. I hired Milton, my attorney, because he had once been friends with Samuel and I thought it would make my soon-to-be ex-husband behave better. I was wrong."

"Last name of your attorney and Judge's name? I'll schedule a time to speak with them next week, hopefully I can get an appointment first thing Monday morning.

Uneasiness skittered around in me. "Are you trying to build a defense for me?"

Brett looked at me with wide brown eyes full of feigned innocence.

I frowned. "You are. You're planning on building a self-defense case for me."

The innocence was replaced by calculation. The quickness of the change chilled me. Small pieces of fence were built around my heart. I liked knowing he'd do anything to help me, but I didn't like being reminded that Brett didn't believe that the truth was enough. I liked living with the belief that good always won, dreams come true, and love at first sight wasn't just in Hallmark Christmas movies.

"I'm doing my job," he said.

"I'm not guilty."

"I know that. It doesn't matter."

"What do you mean it doesn't matter?" I was screeching. "Of course, it does. It's all that matters."

"Truth is fluid. It's more of an abstract than a still life painting. Truth is determined by who hears it and who sees it. What occurred is up for interpretation, it's dependent upon the person viewing the situation.

"I don't like your world."

"I don't want to argue with you, Merry. The food's getting cold. Let's eat."

There it was. The take charge, end of discussion man I had married. "I'm not hungry anymore." I reached for the door handle.

"I'm doing everything I can to help you. I don't want your life ruined because of Samuel and his daughter."

"It won't be because I didn't do anything wrong."

"In the real world, having done wrong matters less than someone being able to prove you could have done wrong. Trust me."

"I want you to believe in my innocence enough not to have a backup plan."

"That's not who I am, Merry."

"I know." I slammed the door.

Brett's voice carried to me. "Before this is over, you're going to be glad that I am the man I am."

SEVEN

I hurried into the Armory. It was three thirty. Ninety minutes of selling left before the event was over for the day. How much had the trip to the police station cost me? I conjured up visions of sugar plums, Santa Claus, reindeer, and Buddy the Elf. *Smiling is my favorite.* I repeated the quote from *Elf* until I felt a true smile on my face. A cheerful seller sold more gifts than a grumpy one, and I had ground to make up.

I scooted around the people waiting in line to buy admission tickets. "Vendor!" I called out to the young man and woman at the registration table that was now the information/ticket booth.

"Badge." The man stood and craned his neck, searching for the vendor badge that I had taken off earlier and left near the register.

"It's at my booth."

"Then you need to buy a ticket. Go to the end of the line."

A few of the people who I "cut" in front of snickered.

"I had to leave in a hurry or I'd have remembered to grab it." I pressed my hands together. "Please, I'll get it and bring it back to show you."

"Can't." The guy excused himself around the young lady sitting next to him and headed toward me.

I didn't want more time stolen from me by either standing in or line or chatting with security. Could this day get any worse?

"Merry, there you are." Grace hooked her arm through mine and led me away. "Abraham needs to have his break. I'd have found you a different replacement if I'd known your errand was going to take so long."

"I'm so sorry. I had to rush out and didn't have time to explain." Poor Abraham. He was probably frantic.

"Abraham told me. He's more concerned about Ebenezer. He didn't know if the little guy was missing lunch or something."

"I owe Abraham a huge thanks. Anything I can make for him?"

Grace grinned. "There is something you could do."

"Name it."

"Let Ebenezer sleep over at our place tonight. Abraham is smitten with him." Grace leaned into me, lowering her voice to a whisper. "I'm thinking about getting him a guinea pig for Christmas, and I'd like to see how he'd handle taking care of a pet overnight."

While I'd miss my furry companion, I couldn't say no to the request. "Of course. I'll even let Abraham take Ebenezer with him for his break. They enjoy each other's company."

Grace hugged me. "Thank you. I know Abe enjoys being with Ebenezer. He had a rough time sleeping last night and I hope with Ebenezer over, it'll be a better night for Abraham."

"Did something happen?"

"I think Samuel's death left him a little out of sorts. He's afraid whoever killed him is coming back. He was sure someone 'made the man dead' as he put it."

"Why did he think that?" Had Abraham seen something I missed? Did the forensic person see it?

Grace shrugged. "I don't know, and I'd rather we didn't question him about it. Right now, Abraham is handling everything okay, but I see signs that his anger is about to surface, and I don't want that." Tears shone in her eyes and I heard the tremble in her voice.

I hadn't seen one of Abraham's outbursts myself, but I had heard about them. Would the detective want to question Abraham more? What would the young man say? Would the detective stress the young man? I took out Brett's business card from my pocket. "Here."

She plucked it from my fingers and stared at it. She frowned, flicking the loosening flap of a bandage on the edge of the paper. "What's this for?"

"Just in case the police want to ask Abraham any more questions. It might be good if your son had an attorney in his corner."

Grace froze in place. I nearly tripped at the sudden stop. She glared at me. "What did you tell the police about my son?"

"Nothing. Abraham made some comments to the detective and I was taken to the police station."

"You're saying what happened to you was Abraham's fault?" Her expression was a mix of hurt and anger.

I was making the matter worse. "The detective likes to twist things around, I'm just afraid he'll talk to Abraham again and make him say something that sounds like Abraham knows something about Samuel's death. He tried it today."

"The detective did." Her eyes narrowed.

I nodded. "Like I had Abraham help me...do something to Samuel." I couldn't say the word murder in relation to me. It was all so seedy.

She pocketed the card. "I'll tell Abraham not to talk to anyone he doesn't know."

"He kind of knows the detective. I can see the man using their talk today as a way to get around it."

"Don't worry, Merry." She patted my arm. "I won't let anyone use my son to lock you up for that creep's murder. If I was the police, I'd look at some of his Facebook friends."

As we headed down the aisle toward my booth, I caught sight of another person in my area. A young woman with long brown hair streaked with blonde was sitting in my chair. My heart nearly burst with pride and love. Raleigh's head was tilted to the side, and if I was near enough, I knew I'd see her golden-brown eyes showing interest in what Abraham was saying. My daughter was tough and had a compassionate soul. People were her passion. Her goal was to fix the world, one person at a time by making sure they believed in the power of themselves and their worthiness.

Both of my children served the public in their own way, Scotland was a police officer, and Raleigh was on her way to becoming a certified counselor. She had just finished up her first year of her master's degree program. I was so proud of my children.

Raleigh saw me and smiled. She waved and rushed over, wrapping me in a hug.

I held my daughter tightly for a few moments before releasing her.

Another vendor waved for Grace's attention. She held up her finger and started walking in that direction. "Let Abraham know he can go on break."

"Will do," I said.

Placing her hand on my shoulders, Raleigh looked me in the eye. "Good day?"

"It's better now." I smiled at her, tucking a strand of her hair behind her ear. "A mom always loves seeing her beautiful daughter."

"Good thing I'm not ugly or you'd banish me to a tower." She shot me a cheeky grin before dragging me into the booth. "There have been a few sales this afternoon. Abe took care of ringing them up since I couldn't work your cash register."

Abe? And no correction? Abraham only let a select few people shorten his name, like his mother and Santa Claus, and after a few hours, Raleigh skated onto the list.

Abraham nodded. "I showed Raleigh, but she said I was better at it so I should do the money. I'm trustworthy."

I took stock of my inventory. Raleigh wasn't kidding when she said only a few items sold. All the wooden trees remained, along with the RV decals, and the ornaments Bright had made. What was going on? Bright's ornaments were usually sought after, and I had trouble keeping them stocked. Last year, I sold out of her hand-painted ornaments by the first day. Bright had sent a few more so I'd have some for Sunday.

"Were there any custom orders?" I asked as I flipped the book open. None.

"No." Raleigh draped her arms over my shoulders and rested her head on top of mine for a moment. "I'm sorry, Mom. I don't think I'm a good sales person. I tried getting some people over, but no one stopped at the booth for long."

Customer relations was a delicate art. It took time to know which customers wanted to chat and which preferred browsing without being acknowledged, and then there were the customers who were competing businesses who wanted new ideas or to undercut other vendor prices. The latter used to send me into a mini rage at the unfairness, but I didn't want the issue to ruin my attitude about my craft business or Christmas. I vowed not to worry about it. There was nothing I could do about other people's business model. I'd focus on mine.

The day was a wash. There wasn't a lot of time to drum up business, but I could get everything set up for tomorrow and sell, sell, sell without first having to reorganize the booth. The priority was displaying the RV Christmas décor better.

"I have to go, Merry Christmas." Abraham shifted from foot to foot.

My face heated. I was so excited to see my daughter, I forgot about Abraham. He was waiting for me to dismiss him and take Ebenezer. I lifted the edge of the fabric concealing Ebenezer's cage. "I'm sorry I was distracted."

"I'll get him." Abraham took the cage out from under the register area.

"What is that?" A woman stopped and leaned over the table displaying the decals and ornaments.

Abraham held out the cage. "This is Ebenezer. He's Merry Christmas's partner."

She squealed, a delighted not an I-saw-a-rat-and-must-flee sound. "Isn't he the cutest thing?" She cooed at Ebenezer and wiggled her finger at him. He wriggled his nose. "What do you recommend for my aunt? She's eighty-years-old, loves to decorate, but doesn't have a lot of space for storing items at the nursing home, nor does she have a lot of strength to carry items and she hates having anyone help her. Christmas was always her thing, and it breaks her heart that she's losing the ability to indulge in that happiness."

The decals. Why hadn't I thought of it before? The tree decals were perfect for people living in nursing homes, dorms, barracks, or any other small space. It allowed those who wanted Christmas around them to have it without it costing a lot or needing a space to store it. I quickly scribbled down "storage boxes" to remind myself later to create some labeled cardboard envelopes to store the holiday décor.

"A tree and some ornament decals are the perfect solution for your aunt. Currently, there are two sizes of trees. I can also customize one for her wall." I showed her the glitter vinyl tree I cut this morning.

"Does it peel off easily?"

"Yes." I lifted the tip of tree and slowly peeled it down. "I have a backing sheet that the decal can be stored on when not in use. I can also create a special holder for it to be stored during the rest of the year. It would easily fit on top of a closet shelf or underneath a bed."

"That's perfect."

Raleigh scooted some ornament decals closer to the potential customer. Pride filled my daughter's voice. "My mom is like your aunt, Christmas is in her heart year-round and she loves to share that joy and create items that help people display their love of the Christmas season."

My heart hummed with happiness. I always wondered what my children thought about their mother being only a crafter compared to their father's career. I had a lot of jobs: book store clerk, church secretary, tax preparer, shop pro at the golf course which consisted of pretty much anything that was needed as it was a one-employee-at-a-time job, and now crafter. Crafter was the one job I was working on becoming my career, and at times I felt like it wasn't a grown-up job. It wasn't everyone who could turn a love of Christmas into a career. I should embrace it rather than apologize for it.

The woman pulled out her wallet. "I am so glad I decided to stop at this booth after all."

After all? My curiosity got the best of me. I was here to sell and if the customer could explain to me why she hadn't been interested until she saw Ebenezer, I could make changes for tomorrow. I doubted the lack of my presence had kept people away from buying. "Is there something about the set up that wasn't inviting?"

"Oh no. Your display is lovely. Once I saw how much you love your pet, and Christmas, I knew you couldn't be a bad person."

"A bad person?"

"What's being said about my mom?" Raleigh clenched her fists.

The woman pointed down the aisle. "That young lady is telling people to stay away from your booth unless they want to buy stuff made by a murderer."

Raleigh's face turned bright red. Mine was Christmas snow white as I felt the blood drain from my face.

At the end of the aisle was Cassie. A look of pure hatred directed at me.

EIGHT

"How dare she." A fire gleamed in Raleigh's eyes and she marched forward, ready to battle her former stepsister.

"No." I snagged my daughter's arm, halting her charge. "I'll handle this."

"I don't think you should talk to her." Raleigh was glaring at Cassie. Cassie had the sense to look away. "She's accusing you of murdering her father."

"You talking to her isn't going to make matters better," I said. "Matter-of-fact, I think I'll keep a cooler head than you. It could hurt your job."

"No, it won't." Some of the anger ebbed out of my daughter as the truth sunk in past her denial.

It did my heart good to know how much my children wanted to protect me, but I was the one who should protect them—even from themselves. Yelling in public at Cassie wouldn't help my daughter in her quest to become a counselor for teenagers. Any fight she got into with Cassie had the potential to haunt her later in life.

"Finish up with our customer and I'll have a word with Cassie." I gave my daughter a gentle shove in the direction I wanted her to go, away from Cassie.

"Mom—"

I silenced Raleigh with a stern look. "No more arguing. I know Cassie better than you. If she's lying, I'll be able to tell."

"Dad wouldn't like it." Raleigh crossed her arms and tilted her chin up.

My eyes narrowed. Her I-got-you-now look hadn't worked when she was a child, and even less so now. "I really don't care about your father's opinion of this." I went to confront, or talk sense into, my former stepdaughter.

Cassie saw me coming. Spinning around, she hightailed it toward the door. I picked up my pace, not quite running but more pep than a fast walk. I wanted to settle this between us once and for all. I couldn't have her going around telling people that I murdered her father. It wasn't true. It hurt to know a girl I loved like my own thought so horribly about me.

She stepped outside. I followed, regretting it the moment the cold air hit my body. I hadn't brought a coat with me. I wrapped my arms around myself. "Cassie. Stop."

The girl stumbled as she flicked a gaze over her shoulder.

"I can—" I stopped my sentence. Yelling out "I can find you" to a teenager whose father was just murdered wasn't a good idea. Especially when you were the main suspect.

Cassie came to an abrupt halt. She spun around and glared at me. "You don't scare me. I won't let you get away with it. I won't." Tears ran down her face.

"I don't want you to be afraid of me." I kept my voice soft and level. "I didn't do anything, Cassie. You know that."

I refused to say anything that placed the blame on her, but I know she knew I had nothing to do with her father's death. She had sold me the RV—with her father in it. Had she known it? At this point I wasn't sure.

"Yes, you did." She swiped away her tears with the sleeve of her thin coat.

"No, I didn't." I stood a few feet in front of her. Her misery and confusion were almost touchable. My heart went out to her. She had lost her dad. The only parent that had loved and cared for her. "We both know when I bought the RV that you drove to my house, that your father and I weren't communicating with each other."

"You're trying to confuse me. I know what happened."

"I don't. How about you tell me?"

Cassie bit her lip and looked down at the ground. "I'm not supposed to talk to you."

"And why is that?"

"The detective said not to."

Grayson had spoken to Cassie. The detective convinced her that I had something to do with Samuel's death. I didn't know anyone else who would believe I was capable of committing murder even taking into account that I no longer had any tender feelings for Samuel. I avoided the man at all costs. Including no longer spending any time with Cassie. Not even a text message. An ache developed in my chest. I had abandoned her. At a time when she needed someone, she had no one. At all.

"How are you holding up?" I asked.

Cassie shrugged. Tears pooled in her eyes. "Why should you care?"

"Because I care about you. I can't even imagine how hard this is for you. You loved your dad very much." Life was cruel. I tucked a strand of her blonde hair behind her ear. Cassie closed her eyes, resting her chin in the palm of my hand. Tears blurred the image before me. I blinked them away. "I'm sorry I haven't been around for you. I thought it was best."

"Not for me." Her lips drooped into a trembling frown, blue eyes downcast. It was the expression she always had when she believed she was about to get into trouble.

At first, I had seen the action as a manipulation, but then I realized Cassie was afraid of getting in trouble—she didn't trust that a person would stick around for her. She believed all her mothers left because of her.

"It was for me. And Bonnie," I said.

"I hate her." She clenched her fists. "You wouldn't have divorced my dad if it wasn't for her."

It wasn't because of the affair that I divorced Samuel, but now wasn't the time to explain it to Cassie. If ever. There was no reason for her to see her father in a different light than she did. He had shown her some flaws, but not the true nature of his character toward others, and I refused to be the one to reveal it to her. She didn't need to know.

"Honey, it wouldn't have worked between your father and me. Even without Bonnie in the picture." Because there would've been another woman. I just wished I had paid attention to Samuel's wandering eye before we got married. It would've saved me a lot of grief and being suspected of murder.

"It would've. I would've made sure." There was determination in Cassie's voice.

I fought back a smile. Only a teenager believed they could control the lives of the adults around them. "Honey, there was nothing you could've done. It wasn't your fault."

"Bonnie hates me. And you." Cassie peered at me through her lashes. "She said you were going to ruin her and dad's life."

"I wanted nothing to do with either of them."

Now there was someone who had the potential to kill someone: Bonnie. Not Cassie. The woman's scowl was a permanent fixture on her face like her tattooed eyeliner. I was always surprised she was a nurse. I always expected them to have more pleasant personalities.

"She said Dad was meeting you. You shouldn't have been anywhere near him."

I gaped at her. Meeting him? "When? Where? Why?" The one-word questions tumbled from me.

Cassie shrugged. "She didn't say." Her downcast gaze lifted to meet mine for a moment before returning to the ground. Her body swayed slightly, left and right, as she rubbed her left ring finger and thumb together. Cassie's signal. The girl was lying, but even more than that, she was scared. Who was threatening her? And why did it involve blaming me for her father's murder?

NINE

Dots of white drifted from the night sky. I waved goodbye to the security guard who escorted me and stepped into my RV. I slipped off my coat and immediately put it back on. An RV wasn't a good wintertime vehicle. I was I glad I hadn't left Ebenezer in it all day. It was only a few degrees warmer in the RV compared to outside.

Okay, maybe a slight exaggeration. I rubbed my hands together and searched for the source of the cold. I hoped it was an opened window rather than lousy insulation. Purchasing the RV was turning into one of the worst decisions I had ever made. Cold air seeped through the closed door of the RV. The windows nor the door were sealed properly, small drafts of cold worked their way in from the sill. It also didn't help that the door leading to outside refused to close all the way. I might have to shove a towel between the door and jamb to keep winter outside where it belonged.

I paused and studied the door. Had this morning's burglar damaged the door? I didn't remember it being quite so cold last night. Then again, the temperature had dropped about fifteen degrees from yesterday. I knelt and carefully ran my hand under the door frame, feeling for any chips or mars in the door. None.

What if the person trying to get into my RV was the murderer? What if they were coming back to retrieve something they left behind? The cold seemed to increase in the RV and I shivered. I should've called the police this morning as the security guard suggested. That decision was a huge mistake. I had been so scared this afternoon, it had slipped my mind to tell the detective. If I called now, would the detective think I was trying to explain away any evidence that had been or might be found in the RV? I wrapped my arms around myself.

Had the police found the item, and that was why the detective believed I killed Samuel? If so, why were they allowing me to stay in the RV? But, what could the killer have owned that tied to me? Something Christmas related? Something related to the weekend event? Craft related? It was hard for me to wrap my mind around the idea that Samuel's killer had something in common with me. Especially since the killer had placed Samuel in the RV in Season's Greetings. His murder had nothing to do with the holiday bazaar. It had everything to do with our hometown.

My gaze flicked to the dinette area. The only connection between Samuel, the RV, and me was Cassie—and Bonnie. Were they trying to set me up? Or was that an unintended consequence because I bought the RV from Cassie? Had Bonnie threatened the teen and that's why Cassie was pointing the finger at me? She wanted to save herself by taking the suspicion off Bonnie. No. Cassie hated Bonnie. She was more likely to scream to the world it was Bonnie if there was a hint of evidence her current stepmom killed her dad. It would get her stepmom out of her life and house.

Bonnie had the most to lose if Samuel came to his senses and picked his daughter over his new wife. Bonnie worked at Season's Living, the assistant living facility my mother lived at, and ironically had been my mother's nurse. Samuel met her when we went there to tell my mother of our upcoming nuptials. I guess it was love at first sight for Bonnie and Samuel. Wished he'd mentioned it before we said our I dos.

There was one place to check—where Samuel died. Steeling my nerves, I approached the dinette bench cautiously, like one does an unfamiliar dog. My hand shook as my fingertips grazed the seat. My heart thudded, breaths came in spurts. *Settle down. Deep breaths. Nothing in there can hurt you.* I eased open the seat. Samuel's face flashed in my head. Unstaring eyes. Hands raised as he tried to escape. Bile rose in my throat. I jumped away from the seat, trying to settle my breathing and stop the churning in my stomach. I couldn't do it.

I collapsed onto the floor, drawing my knees toward my chin and resting my forehead on them. Maybe tomorrow I could bring myself to do it. What else could I do? I had to do something to figure out why the detective had me on the suspect list. I lived a very rule-abiding life. Drove the speed limit. Paid my taxes on time. Didn't cut in line. My customer service was superior. It was why Bright and I had a popular Etsy shop. We were the queens of customer service. Now, I found myself on the list for most likely to have murdered my ex-husband. The only one who knew why I was on the list was the detective and that man wasn't planning on being forthcoming with me.

My phone pinged. It was a Facebook message from Bright. I swiped my finger across the screen. My heart plummeted at the words: *A detective contacted me.*

Detective Grayson? I typed. *What did you say?*

Nothing yet. Bright responded back immediately. *I was working on orders and my phone was on silent. I just listened to his message. He has some questions for me and it's of utmost importance. What do you want me to do?*

No doubt, putting his chief suspect in jail was the highest priority. Had the detective gotten ahold of our messages? I know what I wanted her to do—ignore him. But, I knew what Bright had to do—call the detective back. I didn't want to drag her into this anymore than she was by being the business partner of a murder suspect.

You must call him back. My hands shook as I pressed send, doing the right thing was scary. On the bright side, maybe Bright would learn why the detective believed I killed Samuel.

I don't want to. Bright added a crying face emoji. *What if something I say hurts you?*

It won't. Maybe you'll be able to find out why I'm number one suspect on Grayson's list. I can narrow down which of Samuel's friends and acquaintances is the most likely culprit and pass the information onto Brett.

Why not ask Brett?

He's looking into it. I don't trust him to keep me in the loop. He wants me to stay out of everything because he fears my involvement makes me look guilty.

Men are always trying to save us from ourselves. Okay, I'll do it. For you.

I sat in one of the recliners and propped my phone up on the arm rest and stared at it, willing a message from Bright to pop up about what the detective said. Time inched by. Enough. I had to do something besides sit here and look at my cell phone. The detective sure wasn't waiting by his phone for someone to tell him that they saw Merry in the RV with a candlestick.

A wonderful snarky crafting idea popped into my head. It was a different style than my other products as I steered clear from innuendos and crude, and it was totally not in keeping with my mindset of keeping Christmas well or pure, but sometimes a woman had to shake things up. I bet there were plenty of customers who'd like one of their own. I just hoped others didn't get the wrong idea. Of course, I'd sell more if some ladies had wickeder ideas about my new holiday shirt. One must do what they could, legally, to increase their profit margin.

I set up a die cutting machine on the floor, wanting to avoid crafting at the dinette table. It felt a little heartless to work away in the space where my ex-husband died. I pulled out my iPad and designed my shirt. I typed I'm On the Naughty List, using a font that swirled at the ends. I created a pair of handcuffs and dangled them from the "y" then switched the cuffs over to the "g" to balance the decal. Perfect. Sometimes all you could do was have a sense of humor or a situation would break you.

The containers of vinyl were in the living room area, placed in order of neutrals then the Roy G. Biv system. I found keeping my vinyl and paper organized using this system helped lessen the time it took to find the correct color. The first container was violet. Where was the white? I must've inverted the order and put the neutrals on the right-hand side instead of the left. I went to the last one, yellow. The containers were all in a haphazard order. Good thing I labeled them, though it was more helpful to have the label facing out, not toward the wall.

"Next time no rushing," I scolded myself. In my defense, I didn't have long to load the RV before I had to head out. I picked out a glitter black sheet and placed it on the mat and took out a white t-shirt from a plastic container.

While the Cricut chugged away, the blade appeared to flow over the vinyl rather than cutting it, I pulled up Cassie's Facebook. I had to know how she was even if it meant reading the horrible things she was saying about me, and I hoped I might find a clue on what she told the detective.

I cringed at the venom in her posts. Cassie was stating it plain and clear: she blamed me for her father's murder. It was my fault. She was careful not to say I murdered him, but I was responsible for it. If it wasn't for me, he'd still be alive. My vision blurred. Tipping up my glasses, I wiped away the tears. Why did Cassie believe that?

More hurtful were the people in my community agreeing with the accusation. Some were my friends, others were teenagers I looked after and fed—people I helped in their times of need. Even a co-worker at the tax preparation place I worked. So many willing to believe the worst about me without a shred of proof. A flashflood of emotions rushed through me. Hurt. Devastation. Anger. Determination.

The machine was quiet. I turned my phone screen off. After I was done with my sample shirt and adding the design to my Etsy shop, I'd aggravate myself and read more of Cassie's posts and see what Samuel had been up to the last couple of days. Maybe there was a hint on his Facebook page of what he had wanted to tell me.

I took off the vinyl still attached to the backing sheet and placed it on a tray I used for weeding. Bracing my back against the chair, I removed the white spaces of the design from the backing sheet, leaving only the portion that I wanted to iron onto the shirt. It was a tedious process. This design wasn't so bad except for the tiny slivers of vinyl that needed removed from the links in the handcuffs. If I didn't, it looked like two round circles were attached with a curved line and the whole design would fall flat.

The muscles in my back ached. I'd regret this decision in the morning. I pulled away the last unneeded part of the vinyl and the design was finished. The weeding process was kind of like trying to find out who and why someone wanted to blame me for Samuel's murder. I was having to start with a big old blob of information and pull out what didn't matter to leave me with only the details that showed me the way to the truth. The issue for me was I didn't have a diagram to know which pieces needed weeding out.

There was one way to start sorting things out. Look into Samuel's last few days. My finger paused over the button that would let me back into Samuel's social media life. How much of a risk was I taking? Would I be proving my innocence or establishing my guilt? Was the risk worth it? Was there another way?

No. I was the only one who'd be able to know what was a piece that belonged in this situation and what was a distraction. Samuel's body being in the RV fit into Samuel's death, but not in his murder. Grayson was looking at the wrong building, so to speak. If he wanted to know who killed Samuel, he had to look beyond the RV.

And so did I.

Closing one eye, I unblocked Samuel. My heart pounded. There was no reason to be afraid. Samuel couldn't hurt me. At least not personally.

No more drama queen antics or blaming the dead. It's not keeping Christmas well, I scolded myself. I was allowing bitterness to invade my spirit, and if I wasn't careful it would change me, and not for the better. Scrooge allowed bitterness to make him selfish, keeping everything that belonged to him, including his heart, and begrudging even the tiniest kindness a person needed.

Samuel's smiling face greeted me. It was a punch in the gut. The cover photo was Samuel and Cassie standing in front of the RV. Cassie's head rested on her dad's shoulder. He was smiling broadly. He was gone. Forever. Sadness enveloped me. The anger I held against him slipped from my soul. It was no longer important. A man I had loved was gone from the world.

Rest in peace messages filled his page.

"I wish the same for you Samuel. We had some good memories. I'll try to keep those in my head." Thinking ill of the dead never helped a soul. There was nothing that could change the past, only cloud up the future. "Samuel, who wanted you gone?"

I scrolled through the messages for Samuel and found the last two posts he wrote. The first was the morning of November fourteenth: *Things are looking up for Samuel Waters. Watch out Season's Greetings. Life is about to get exciting for one local boy.*

Samuel was one for dramatics. I wasn't surprised about the vaguebooking. Samuel liked to lead people on and have them beg him for information. Unfortunately, I discovered this after the I dos.

You can't play a man who knows all the games. Samuel wrote. Followed a few hours later by, *If you're trying to steal home, make sure no one is looking.*

The last post he ever wrote was late afternoon on the fourteenth: *Can't wait till they find out the jokes on them.*

It was like he was taunting someone. Or he was fed up with people trolling him. There were tons of Go Fund Me links posted on his page. I scrolled and counted, giving up after I reached fifty. The messages started right after Bonnie posted on Samuel's timeline that the day was their one-week wedding anniversary and including a link to a ten-day Caribbean cruise out of Baltimore. *Perfect way to mark the occasion, Sammy! Book it.*

One week and it's time to celebrate with a trip? I snorted. Cassie must've loved knowing her dad and new stepmom planned on celebrating every passing week of their nuptials.

At least I knew the reason for all the donations requests—they were veiled jabs at Bonnie asking her husband publicly to purchase a trip for them. Most people in Season's Greetings squeaked by every month and mentioning your income, especially in such a brazen way, was uncouth. I wondered how Bonnie felt when she peeked into their family checking account and realized Samuel didn't make quite as much as he'd been bragging about. Of course, at the time he started bragging, Samuel thought I had quite the stash of cash from having been married to Brett. He found right after our wedding that the fantasy he created was just that.

A message from Bright blipped onto my screen. I switched over to Messenger.

The detective didn't come out and say why he suspected you. He was interested in when you told me about the RV. There's your clue. I bet Cassie told him a different date.

That's easy to prove, I typed back. *I have the bill of sale and the title.* Yesterday's text from Cassie took up residence in my head. Was that what she wanted from the RV? The bill of sale.

Give a copy to Brett and he can shove it under the detective's nose.

I wanted to shove it under the detective's nose and then laugh in his face when his evidence against me vanished. I reveled in the image for a moment before I returned to the present. The only bad thing about that scenario was it turned Cassie into the most likely suspect.

Thanks. Need to finish up an order for tomorrow.

Put the documents in your tote. This way if the detective shows up, you can just show them to him.

I'll ask Grace if I can use a copier. Don't want to give the detective the original.

Good plan.

I went to the glove compartment and moved my CDs out of the way to get the title and bill of sale. Evidence of my innocence. I grinned. It slipped from my face. The date. It was wrong.

Cassie had dated the bill of sale November 14, the day before I bought the RV from her. With that error, she placed the RV in my possession around Samuel's time of death. Was this the item Cassie wanted from the trailer? Either to prove I was guilty or to hide the fact that she wrote the wrong date—either deliberately or accidentally.

For the first time, I studied the signature. It was a mush of letters. I rummaged around in my equipment box and pulled out a portable OttLite and turned it on, hoping the natural light bulb helped me read the signature. Something I should've done when I bought the RV. Even before knowing what it said, I was kicking myself. I was so intent on helping Cassie and fulfilling a dream, I rushed into buying the RV and ignored common sense. My stomach plummeted to my toes then jumped up and lodged in my throat. The signature, under my untrained eye, was a mix of Samuel and Cassie's signature.

Under a trained eye, like Detective Grayson's, what would it look like? And more importantly, what would that mean for me—and Cassie?

TEN

The next morning, I sat in my vendor's space, my leg twitching as I roved my gaze from my phone screen to the empty aisles of the Armory. It seemed liked I spent so much of the weekend staring at my phone, and I wasn't even getting any orders or updating my Etsy shop. I'd have plenty of products to add to it tomorrow. Shoppers were non-existent as a fluffy, accumulating snow had started right around the time the doors opened. I needed shoppers to take my mind off what I discovered.

A few attendees had been in line and quickly made their way through the venue, wheeling and dealing with the vendors. The bargain shoppers usually arrived Sunday afternoon as they believed a vendor would rather sell low than cart items back home. With the weather, I wasn't sure they'd arrive.

Early this morning, I had texted Brett a picture of the registration and my interpretation of the signature. Still no response. Where was the man? Wait. It was Sunday. Family day. A day devoted to his mother. I wouldn't hear from him for a while. I pocketed my phone.

"This isn't a good day." I plopped myself into my chair and adjusted the hem of the t-shirt I made last night on the spur of the moment. My long white t-shirt had the phrase I'm on the Naughty List emblazoned on it with black glitter vinyl.

Ebenezer squealed his agreement. Or at least I was taking it that way. For all I knew he was arguing with me. I leaned over to move his cage further under the register and caught a whiff of him, or rather his cage. Drat. I forgot to give Abraham extra bedding for the cage last night. Good thing I still had the newspaper in my purse. I pulled it out and raised it up, preparing to shred it when a front-page article caught my eye: "Winning Lottery Ticket Sold Here."

I read the article. The gas station/convenience store, One Stop, in Season's Greetings had sold the lottery ticket. It was a place on Samuel and his mom's list for their weekly errand date. Every Monday, Samuel took his mom to the bank, post office, and One Stop to buy lottery tickets. They both got an Easy Pick and a ticket with their lucky numbers on it, though I always wondered how lucky the numbers were considering they'd been doing it for twenty years and neither of them had won more than two dollars.

A woman stopped by my table. Quickly, I shoved the paper back into my bag, giving her my full attention. "Welcome to Merry and Bright."

She adjusted my price list, squinted at it then poked at a few of the decals before wandering off to another booth. A deal searcher. Maybe I should drop my prices a bit. Or cut my losses and leave early. There was a lot on my mind. The sooner I was back home, the quicker I could clear up some of the confusion in my head about Samuel, Cassie, and why the detective thought I was a murderer. There was nothing here that would help me.

The organizers hated for vendors to leave early but I had a ninety-minute drive back home—in the snow—in the RV, which I wasn't quite that proficient at driving yet. I really should've checked the forecast for the entire weekend not just Friday. It likely wouldn't have done me any good as I swore the weather app on my iPhone worked like a Magic Eight Ball. If I didn't like the forecast, check again in a few minutes and it changed. No other vendor had bailed, and I didn't want to be the first.

Slower than molasses, the minutes inched by. Vendors wandered up and down the aisles, half-heartedly looking at products in other booths and hinting they might buy some. A vendor who sold paracord jewelry had wandered into my booth a few times, eyeing some of the wine glasses. Maybe I should offer a trade. I was thinking a paracord bracelet was a nice stocking stuffer for Scotland. He wasn't much of a jewelry wearer, but he enjoyed geocaching and hiking.

I rearranged the ornaments on the vinyl sample tree. I had two cutting mats with me and vinyl sections cut into the sizes I needed for the trees. The plan was to cut the trees to order based on the size needed so I wasn't stuck with any trees. The vinyl trees were hard to ship. Rolling them up might damage the vinyl and laying them flat required a large box, and the postage made it cost prohibited. Customers weren't too keen on buying a product that the shipping was almost, or more than, the item.

The wooden trees hadn't sold. I should've made less trees. Last year, it had been a best seller. I had also hoped I'd get some returning customers from that sale to pick up extra ornaments, or a tree topper, for their wooden tree.

The piped Christmas music was not lifting my mood. I turned on my Bluetooth speaker and played some of my favorite Christmas music. Something had to turn the day around. I lifted up the corner of the fabric covering the register table and peered at Ebenezer.

His dark, soulful gaze settled on me for a moment, then he made a production of turning his back to me in his waddling way. Great, now I was getting attitude from my guinea pig. "It's either under here or staying in the RV. I know you don't want that. Too cold in there."

Ebenezer plopped down on the bedding material. I wasn't sure if that meant he agreed with my assessment or didn't care. Likely he didn't care. This day was turning out to be a bust.

Sighing, I scrolled through the apps on my phone. I clicked on my messages. There was one from Scotland.

The weather is getting bad. If you leave now, I can help you load.

I'm thinking of packing up early.

Don't think, Mom. Do.

I don't want to be the first to bail. If I leave, I'll text.

"My goodness, how cold is it outside?" The vendor's voice next to me was awestruck.

A woman, or at least I guessed so from the white boots with beige furry trim she wore, headed in our direction. She was decked out from head to toe like a winter mummy. White crocheted hat. White scarf wrapped around her face, only two blue eyes visible. White mittens. White coat. The mittens were pulled off and shoved into the pocket of the coat. She peeled off the coat, revealing a feminine-cut, white sweater with white pearls decorating the neckline.

The woman loved white. She unwound the scarf from her neck. Around and around, her hand went. How long was it? Her features appeared. Bonnie. Samuel's wife. I so did not need this today. Shouldn't she be in black instead of white? Heck, even her pants were white. Who wore white after Labor Day, and after her husband was murdered? I wished I had snapped a picture of Bonnie for the detective. He might have found it interesting. Or if not Detective Scrooge, then Brett could add it to his arsenal in case the truth didn't set me free as he feared.

Of course, not too many people in Season's Greetings could afford different colors of coats. A person bought one to last the whole year through, for at least five to ten years. Coats weren't one season wear. No one, or at least not many, had the income for that kind of extravagance.

"I'm glad you're still here." Bonnie dropped her garments onto the table holding my products.

Remaining silent, I removed them, placing them on my chair. I didn't want melting snow to ruin anything. It was easier to dry my pants without damaging them than our products. Her head tilted, she read my shirt. I had felt a little snarky last night and this morning and was now regretting my choice of holiday wear. I hoped the detective didn't show up today.

"I take it you heard about Samuel." The tone of her voice was a cross between snide and questioning.

I continued remaining silent, not sure where the snark intended to take her, or how my words might be used against me.

Other vendors glanced over, curiosity on their faces.

"What do you want, Bonnie? I know you didn't drive all this way, in the snow, to see if I heard about Samuel's death."

"Murder. You do mean murder. Correct?" Her left brow arched up as she studied my face.

Take the bait or not was the question. She wanted something from me. A reaction of some sort to prove—I didn't know what. Had Detective Scrooge sent her? Cassie hadn't tripped me up, so he went with Plan B. Bonnie and I were neutral toward each. Switzerland. I knew Samuel's sexual urges for her hadn't been the cause of the divorce, and matter-of-fact, I had hoped Samuel's wandering eye toward the well-endowed and sexy Bonnie would have him wanting to divorce me faster. Bonnie made it clear she wanted a ring on her finger before any hanky-panky happened.

"That is one of the avenues the police are exploring." I fixed my attention on my table, tapping vinyl decals into neat stacks.

Bonnie placed her hands on the table, long scarlet nails drumming on top of a stack of decals. I tried to pull them away, afraid the two-inch long pointed tip nails would leave an indent. Bonnie rested her nails on the decals, digging in just a bit. "What is the other avenue as you so quaintly put it? Because I know for certain someone killed Samuel."

"Do you now?" I crossed my arms. "How would you know that? Did the police tell you something or...?" I trailed off, saying the last word in an ominous tone. If she wanted to come here and blame me, I could launch the suspicion right back at her. I wouldn't take it from her. I'd be danged if I'd allow her to ruin my business by starting rumors. If I didn't show a backbone, the accusations would be spread all over the internet.

"I didn't come here to argue with you, Merry." Bonnie shifted more of her weight onto her hands. The transfer sheet protecting the decal buckled. Darn it. I lost that one.

"Then why did you?" I asked. "I doubt you came all this way for Christmas shopping." A list of reasons popped into my head, and none of them fell into the category of goodwill toward me.

A deep sadness replaced the anger in her gaze. Tears pooled in her eyes, brightening the blue, making them look like crystals. "I need a copy of your divorce papers."

I drew back. Not what I was expecting at all. "Why?"

She heaved out a sigh. Tears trembled down her cheeks. "Because the idiot at the insurance company doesn't believe my marriage license is authentic. He wants proof that I am the current wife. Apparently, Samuel never changed his policy to add me by name. All it says is wife, and the adjuster only has a copy of your and Samuel's marriage license."

That was another reason the detective suspected me. Insurance money. Why hadn't Samuel added his wife's name onto the documents rather than wife, and what kind of insurance person allowed him to do that? Never mind. I knew the answer to the last part of the question. A cheap one. Samuel liked to spend as little as possible for any service.

Unless it came to his daughter—then cost wasn't an object. Cassie dressed impeccably. Hair professionally cut and colored. Nails manicured. Then why had Samuel conceded to Bonnie? I was having a hard time believing Samuel would kick his daughter out, but the fact was Samuel had signed over the RV to someone. Cassie. Instead of his daughter signing the registration card, she left it blank and sold it to me, writing over her father's signature. Had Bonnie tricked Samuel into signing the document, killed him, and told Cassie the RV was her new home, thereby getting rid of Samuel and his daughter. But why? The two-word question drummed itself in my head.

Bonnie cleared her throat and a glint flickered in her eyes. I didn't know if she read my thoughts or if she was wondering what was taking me so long to answer her. Bonnie wasn't a woman who like being ignored.

"I'm taking it the silence means no," Bonnie said.

"I was thinking of all the places that would require a marriage license. I'm surprised it didn't come up earlier for you and Samuel. Did the insurance agent say what was wrong with it? Something typed incorrectly?" The truth was I didn't have a copy of my divorce decree. Samuel signed it after me, and I had been wrapped up in completing enough crafts for orders and the craft show that I hadn't made it a priority. I was divorced. That was all that mattered to me.

"I guess now that I actually want to get the life insurance benefits, the agent is double checking all the documents."

"Chances are he's trying to find a reason not to pay out. Especially if it's a large policy." I tried to sound nonchalant. Uninterested. But I really, really wanted to know how much insurance we were talking about.

"I'm hoping I won't have the same problems with Samuel's employer. That's why I'd like a copy of the divorce decree. I looked everywhere for Samuel's and can't find it. You could make me a copy." She crossed her arms and stared into my eyes. It was calculated.

Had her tears been real or fake? The quickness of it evaporating and the anger returning had me thinking Bonnie was up to something. "I don't travel with it."

"You are going back to Season's Greetings tonight. Right? You can call me when you get home."

Now I was even more suspicious. Why tonight? Were a few hours going to make a difference? Why not wait until morning rather than driving ninety minutes, during a snow storm, to ask your husband's ex-wife for a copy of her divorce decree. "It won't be until late. I'll be tired. I'll look for it in the morning."

"How about the RV? Maybe it's in there. Samuel was haphazard with his paperwork. I wouldn't be surprised he placed it in the glove compartment or somewhere else."

So that was it. She wanted to get into the RV. Was she hoping to find something, or plant evidence against me? I was no longer buying she needed the divorce decree. The woman thought I had such a soft heart that I was an idiot. The person with the opportunity to kill Samuel—and motive—was Bonnie. I had to get Brett to make Detective Grayson see it.

"Cassie and I made sure there wasn't anything of Samuel's in the RV when I bought it from her."

She opened her mouth to speak.

"I triple checked," I added. "The last thing I wanted was a reason for Samuel to see me. We both made sure there was nothing that belonged to him in the RV."

"Cassie might've left it on purpose." There was disgust in her voice when she said her stepdaughter's name. "She'd do anything to get you two back together."

Involuntarily, my hands clenched. "Cassie wouldn't have deliberately left something important in the RV. She'd never do that to her father." And yet, I was contemplating if she'd killed him. Who had Samuel intended to give the RV to?

"A piece of paper she hated? I wouldn't put it past her. Matter-of-fact, I wouldn't be surprised if the girl found the divorce decree and ripped it up. Nothing she'd like better than to make my life difficult."

A bitter laugh escaped me. I pressed my fists into the table. "Your life is difficult? Her father just died. She has no idea where her mother is. Cassie is now an orphan."

Bonnie waved her hands in the air as if my concerns for her stepdaughter were of little concern. "She's eighteen."

"And her stepmother dislikes her," I continued speaking, my hands turning white with the pressure I was placing on them. I hadn't hurt Samuel, but I wanted to physically hurt the woman in front of me with every fiber of my being. "You are responsible for her well-being. She's your child now. Step up and do right by her."

Bonnie stepped back, face whitening. "She's not mine."

"Yes, she is. The marriage certificate with your and Samuel's name on it says so. She's legally your responsibility." I wasn't quite sure about that, considering Cassie's age, but I'd ask Brett. The idea of Bonnie collecting insurance money and leaving Cassie penniless enraged me. Someone had to protect the teen's interest. She needed Brett's help more than I did. If he couldn't help her because of me, conflict of interest, I'd fire him. There was no way I'd leave her unprotected.

"No, I'm not." Bonnie said, voice even and deadly. "I married Samuel. His adult daughter isn't my problem."

Problem. Another word I tucked away to share with Brett. The woman was a real piece of work, a shoddy pieced together handcrafted item: crooked, peeling, and made from inferior materials. "You married a man with a child so that makes that child yours. That house is just as much hers, maybe even more so, than yours."

"She can move in with her grandmother."

"Or her grandmother can move into Cassie's house." I decided I wasn't going to bother with getting a copy of my divorce decree. If Bonnie wanted it so bad, she could ask the judge for it. I smiled at her.

Bonnie stepped away from me. I couldn't see my expression but something in it chilled Bonnie. I saw the fear in her eyes. I pressed my lips together, wanting to force the look from my face.

"I won't help you," I told her. "I don't care if you get the insurance money, bury Samuel, or whatever else you need to do for him or for you." I dusted my hands. "I'm releasing this. It's yours."

She stomped forward, rage turning her face red.

This time, I stepped back. Away from the pure hatred, and terror on her face.

"You think you're helping but you're not. You have no idea what evil that girl hides. How hateful she can be. You'll find out. You left her. You told her you loved her, mothered her, and then left her. Don't you dare judge me. At least I didn't pretend to like her, give her hope, and then smash it."

Sorrow wrapped around me. She was right. I had. I chose myself over Cassie. Now the girl was left with a stepmother who loathed her and a grandmother who was just recovering from a battle with cancer.

"You think Samuel played you and your mother," Bonnie continued. "Just wait until the truth smacks you. He wasn't the only one."

I snagged her arm as she turned away. Fear gripped my heart, twisting it painfully in my chest. "What do you mean by that?"

Bonnie laughed again, a high-pitched, bitter tone. She raised her hands, placed them near my nose and copied my earlier motion of dusting them off. "Not my business anymore. We could've helped each other, instead you wanted to pick sides." Bonnie tugged her coat back on. "Good luck navigating whatever Cassie has in store for you. Defend her all you want, Merry, all that's going to happen is you're going to suffer for whoever killed her father."

ELEVEN

A mechanical screech filled the air. I grimaced and covered my ears. Bonnie tugged her hat down to her chin and glared in the direction of the speaker. The sound stopped then started again, a pulsating static that gripped onto your spine and tensed your muscles. The few shoppers in the venue stopped milling about and looked up.

Grace's voice floated throughout the building. "Good morning shoppers. The organizers have made the decision to end the craft show at noon. The Governor plans on declaring a state of emergency around 4 p.m. today, and we want our vendors to have plenty of time to pack up and arrive home before the worst of the storm hits."

Shoppers scattered, not toward the exits but to the booths. The woman nearest me had a telltale gleam in her eyes. Sales. The bargaining was about to get intense.

Bonnie sent a sympathetic glance in my direction. She picked up the stack of decals she had branded with her nails. "How much are these?"

"Those are all the same."

"They'll make great office gifts." She smiled at me. Kindly.

The mood shift baffled me. What was she up to? I fought back a frown. She was a customer. Not my dead ex-husband's wife who thought I had something to do with his murder. I fixed my customer smile on my face and quickly calculated the total on my phone and then knocked off a few dollars for a bulk sale. "Twenty-five dollars."

She pointed at my sign. "That's less than the price states. I can afford to pay full price."

I drew in a deep breath to steady my temper, nearly choking on cloying flower perfume scent. "I'm not insulting you, Bonnie. I usually give a discount for bulk items."

"I think a business should be paid what they're worth." Bonnie took a small wallet out of the coat of her white coat. "I'm able to afford it."

"Fine." I told her the full price total. "Cash or credit?"

"Cash. I hate using credit cards." She handed me two twenties.

"It's easier to keep records with a card." I gave her change.

"Exactly." She pocketed the money and twirled around, tossing the end of her twelve-foot-long scarf. It trailed down her back as she glided away.

"Would you take twenty for the tree?" A woman was hunched over, her hand possessively around the base of one of the wooden trees. Her blue wool trench coat puddled around her feet. Her gray hair was pulled back into a severe bun and her heavy, bold makeup choices distorted her features rather than enhanced them.

I swallowed down my ire. Half off. I'd have been willing to bargain if she asked for a reasonable discount. Now, I'd rather lug the thing through the snow than offer a price break. "No. It's forty."

"Do you really want to take it home?" Her eyes gleamed behind her tinted glasses, making it hard to tell her natural eye color. "You do have a lot of them still available. Isn't it better to sell one?"

Not at that price. "I have other craft shows coming up. It takes a long time to perfect those trees."

She stood, eyebrows raised. "Perfect them? Really? There's one that has a slight blemish on it. Would you sell that one at a discount?"

"Which one?" I had inspected the trees before I loaded, and when unloading, and hadn't noticed any damage. Then again, it had been dark during the removal of the trees and finding Samuel dead had thrown me off. I wouldn't be surprised if I missed something. I choked back a cough. The heavy flower scent lingered in the area.

Someone was generous in the perfume department, or the essential oil vendor was scenting the air with lilac, trying to sell some of her product. She should've chosen pine, matched the Christmas theme better.

"The one with the red splotch on the tip of the tree." The woman walked into the booth and tapped the spot. "I noticed it yesterday."

Yet, she hadn't mentioned it. This was one of the bargain hunters who browsed and took notes on Saturday, then asked for large discounts on Sunday on imperfections they saw or created. Last year, an attendee was caught scratching up vendors items, or snipping threads, and then requesting discounts on the "inferior" items, as a favor to the poor crafter who hadn't noticed the flaw before putting the product out for sale. It was why the organizers had requested all vendors keep track of discounts for damaged items, noting them on a sheet that was included in our packet. They wanted to investigate if vandalism was becoming a huge problem at the show. Some people were willing to do anything to get a deal.

"That's interesting." I kept my voice in neutral. "I didn't use any red paint when I was making the trees."

"It's right here." She pointed, using her cherry red painted nail, at some pin point size drops of red on the top of the tree.

I wondered if there was any red nail polish in her purse. For touch-up purposes. "Let me take a closer look at it." I leaned forward, first trying to sneak a peek into her large bag, then examining the spot she indicated. There were four tiny spots on it. I frowned. It was a blackish-red color.

The color swirled in my mind. Red. Blood. My stomach clenched. How in the world—I slammed the question down. Not now. I'd think about it later. If I contemplated too much now, I'd either break down crying or throw up all over the customer's tennis shoes.

She poked me in the shoulder. "Do I get a discount or not? I don't have that long to shop."

"That's my tree, Merry Christmas. I put it in the back. Please don't sell it." Abraham's beseeching voice came from behind me.

Abraham was shifting from foot to foot, biting his lip. "Mom told me to remind you that you promised a tree. I got first pick. That is the one I want." He pushed past the woman to guard his tree. He covered the spot with his large hand.

I frowned. Abraham had declined the gift.

"I was here first. You can pick another tree." The woman placed her hand on top of Abraham's. He flinched and jerked back, nearly knocking down the wine shelf behind him.

He straightened, panic clear on his face. "It's mine. Not yours."

"I'm discussing purchasing it with the vendor."

"My mom told me to get it. She's in charge. You're not." Abraham challenged the woman. His voice growing angry. A flicker of concern crossed the woman's face.

I wasn't sure what was causing Abraham's distress, which was coming out as anger, but I needed to calm him down. I faced the woman. "I can give you a discount on one of the other trees."

The woman shook her head. "No, I want that one."

"A discount on an undamaged tree. Why pay full price for a tree with an obvious imperfection on it?" I asked.

"Why can't I have it?" The woman crossed her arms and glared at me. "I was here first."

"I did promise my helper he could have the first pick of trees. I bet he marked the trees with those dots. I just hadn't noticed it. He's been very busy helping his mother who's one of the organizers."

Abraham nodded furiously.

"I don't care," she said. "We were making a deal on that tree."

"No, we weren't." My temper was sparking to life. "You wanted me to sell you a handcrafted wooden Christmas tree for half price, and when I said no, you then said I had a damaged tree you wanted a discount on. A tree I know for certain wasn't marked with a red color similar to your nail polish." My voice rose with every word. Okay, the red on the tree had a darker hue but I wanted her out of my booth and the quickest way was to offend her.

Instead of leaving, she hunkered down, planting her feet apart and jamming her fists onto her hips. Her eyes snapped with anger. "Are you saying I marked it?"

"Is there a problem here, ladies?" A security guard stood near my booth.

Abraham clenched his fists, readying to defend me. I had to stop this. Now.

"Someone has been vandalizing items to get a discount," I said, moving in front of Abraham. If nothing else, I'd slow him down for a bit.

The woman blushed and looked away.

"I am aware of that. The organizers asked me to keep an eye out for it." The guard crossed his arms over his massive chest and stared at the determined customer.

"My helper reminded me that I gifted him choice of tree and that was the one he picked. He must've marked it."

"Yep, that's it. I marked it. With those dots. My tree. Mom said it was okay. To say it was mine," Abraham spoke in a halting manner.

Compassion shone on the guard's face. "It's a good choice."

"I offered the customer a choice of another tree at a discount," I said. "For some reason she wants the one that belongs to Abraham."

The guard smiled and winked at the woman. "I'm sure there's another tree to your liking. As a bonus, I'll carry it to your car."

She blushed. This time it was a slow pinkening of her cheeks rather than a rush of red. I do believe the customer was developing a crush on the kind-hearted, and rather cute, security guard.

"I'll buy one if you carry it for me." An elderly, gray-haired lady scurried into my booth. She wrapped a hand around the officer's bicep and squeezed. "With those guns I bet you could carry two trees. Mine and hers."

The guard's cheeks turned a dusty rose. Poor guy. He came over to help and was now being pawed at by a woman old enough to be his mother.

"I have a helper. I'm sure he..." Before I offered Abraham's service, he fled, heading for his mom.

"Not a problem," the security guard said.

"Wonderful, because my daughter wanted one of these and there just wasn't a way for us to carry it. Her having a broken arm."

The insist-on-a-discount shopper rolled her eyes. She wasn't happy that she was being ignored for the older woman. "I changed my mind." She huffed out a breath and stomped away.

"Sorry for losing you a sale," the older woman smiled at me. "I'll make it up to you. I'll buy two of your trees since this officer can carry them. One for me, one for my daughter. There she is." The woman raised her hand in the air. "Over here, darling girl. Have I got a surprise for you."

A pretty blonde woman wearing skinny jeans, a long sleeve top, leather jacket and brown knee-high boots waved using her left arm. The right one was in a sling. The guard perked up when the blonde walked in our direction. He heaved up two trees, one under each arm.

The older woman beamed and gave me her credit card. "Add in two sets of decorations. I like contemporary, my daughter prefers an old-fashioned Christmas style."

I rung up the sale.

"You handled that well." Grace draped an arm over my shoulder. "Abraham told me people were yelling and touching him."

"An insistent discounter spoke in a very demanding tone and placed a hand on his. He didn't like it."

Abraham hated being touched. He had once explained to me that it was painful to him. It was like a flame getting closer and closer to his skin the longer someone touched him, until it felt like fire was consuming him.

"I sent him with my friend to unhook our car and tow cable from our RV to attach to yours." Grace pulled a box plastic storage container out from under the product table and started placing the decals inside. "I'm driving you home. It's terrible out there."

"I know how to drive." I removed the wine glasses from the shelf, wrapping them in bubble wrap before storing them in their container.

"In two inches of snow. In an RV." Grace removed her cell from her back pocket and sent a message.

Two inches. Already. "I'll manage."

"Now you don't have to. I've been granted permission to leave early, but the others on the organizing team must stay here until the last vendor leaves. Don't let it be you."

My phone pinged. A text from Scotland. *Let Grace drive.*

I narrowed my eyes on Grace. "You called my son."

"I called your ex-husband and told him to pass my number onto your children. This way they'd know someone was looking out for you."

"I can look out for myself."

Grace centered a soft look on me. "Oh honey, your kids adore you. They worry about you. Embrace it. It's a blessing to have children that look out for you."

She was right. I was lucky. Some parents had children who turned on them even when they treated their children with love and affection and provided everything they could afford. My children understood the financial limitations I had and never made me feel guilty over it or pitted their father and me against each other. My children were kind and compassionate adults who believed looking after their mom—their family—was just done. No other reason needed. It was cruel to turn down that gift.

"Thank you, Grace. I appreciate you reaching out to my family and offering your driving services."

She laughed and hugged me. "I would've asked you outright, but you can be stubborn at times. You cling to your independence too much."

"I'll finish packing up. I can meet you at the RV when I'm done."

"There's not much left for me to do," Grace said. "I do want to explain the situation to Abraham again. I have my significant other driving Abe home, but this wasn't the original plan. You know how my son is about change."

Abraham didn't like it. Matter-of-fact, most people didn't like change though were able to adjust. Abraham, on the other hand, had his whole day, if not world, thrown into chaos and it set him on a mood roller coaster for days. "Your guy can always drive me."

"But you don't know him. I would hate to put you in a situation that was uncomfortable," Grace said.

"You trust him with your son. That's enough of an endorsement for me."

Grace crossed her arms. "You'd be perfectly fine with housing a man you don't know in your house overnight? The accumulation could reach eight inches in some parts of the state."

Overnight. I covered my mouth and faked a cough to hide my grimace. I wasn't so keen on that part. "It'll be fine."

"Merry, I'm not going to argue with you anymore. We're wasting precious time. I'm driving you. That's it. You might not have any problem taking a strange man home, but I do. I'm thinking about your reputation, not your comfort. Your ex-husband was just murdered and a detective thinks you're responsible for it. How would it look for a man to spend the night at your house?"

"It'll be easy to explain." My voice trembled. She was right. It wouldn't look good and as Brett liked to say, truth was determined by the eyes of the beholder, not by—well the truth.

Grace looked directly into my eyes. Not saying a word. The twitch of her lips told me she knew I was relenting.

Santa walked over, placing a large luggage trolley in front of my space. "Abraham asked me to deliver this to you. Says his mom is driving Ebenezer and you home. Have to keep you both safe."

Grace grinned at me. "I knew my son would come around."

I laughed. That young man would do anything for my guinea pig. Including giving up his mom.

"I'll bring the RV out front," Grace said. "Easier than pushing the cart through the snow."

TWELVE

The cold wind penetrated through my winter coat, mittens, and hat. I lifted a corner of the cover from Ebenezer's cage. He was huddled under a pile of bedding. I stomped my feet, trying to get the circulation going again. What was taking Grace so long? She went to get the RV thirty minutes ago, and I had texted her ten minutes ago that I was waiting outside. Please don't tell me the dang thing wouldn't start. Or the hoses had frozen and the RV was still plugged into the utilities and sewage lines.

"Come on, Grace. We're freezing." I sent her a text, asking if everything was all right. *Should I walk to you?*

"We're a Couple of Misfits" played from my phone. Brett. Since he was likely calling me between family conversation time and lunch, I jumped to the point. "Does the document I texted you help or hurt me?"

"Can't say until I see it in person," Brett said. "There's a chance that the detective will interpret it as you wrote the wrong date to prove the vehicle wasn't in your possession when Samuel was murdered in it."

"The signature. Cassie wrote over her dad's name."

"Or you wrote Cassie's name over his to prove you didn't get it from him. You're in a proverbial he-said-she-said situation. We have no idea what Cassie has been saying, and whatever it was, it has the detective believing you're the prime suspect."

My phone pinged. I pulled it away from my ear and glanced down.

All is good. Be there soon, Grace responded.

"My ride will be pulling up soon."

"I'm glad you're letting Grace drive you home."

"Thanks a lot for giving her our kids numbers."

"I passed on the message to them. Our children are the ones who contacted her. As soon as I hear anything, I'll let you know. I plan on being in Season's Greetings tomorrow morning but there's another case brewing and I might be delayed. Talk to you then."

I pocketed my phone and lifted the corner of the blanket and peered at Ebenezer. "Sorry, Ebe, I didn't think we'd brave the elements for this long."

I should've stayed in the large foyer of the building. I had wanted to save Grace some time and speed up the loading process so we didn't tie up the front of the building for so long. Unfortunately, I was bringing home most of the product I crafted. Between the snow and my trip to the police station, my selling time was short.

There went renovating the RV. I was stuck with the dinette until at least the beginning of the year. I shivered again. This time more from the having to live with the place where Samuel died than the weather. I was glad Grace was driving me home, or rather keeping me company. It would've gotten creepy driving home alone knowing that right behind me was the spot where my ex-husband took his last breath.

Something akin to dread skittered along my spine, an evil that lurked around me and wanted to invade my bones. Not like the ghosts of Christmas past, present, and future at all. Images of Samuel floated in front of my eyes. Stupid Samuel. Ruined everything.

There was a twinge in my spirit. Shame flickered through me. It wasn't nice to blame the dead for the way the police conducted their murder investigation. If I thought about it in a practical manner, of course I was a suspect. Who was the most likely to kill someone? The ex-wife and current wife.

"Stop it," I scolded myself. "Don't get morbid. No dredging up Halloween into your head. You're a Christmas girl." I started singing "The Twelve Days of Christmas." The song would occupy my mind for a while and conjure up more pleasant images. Like partridges in pear trees and twelve lords a leaping. Lords that looked very much like Chris Hemsworth. Dressed as Thor.

This whole weekend was a huge bust. Maybe Samuel had been right, crafting was a nice hobby and a way for some pocket change, not a career. *Never take advice from a man who puts money in front of people,* Bright's advice zipped through my head. She was right. Samuel was only concerned about his best interests. How did I know what I was capable of doing if I didn't try? When I left this world, which I hoped wasn't for a very long time, I didn't want to leave behind a list of regrets. It was now or never to try and live my dream.

A horn bellowed. About time. My RV pulled to stop a few feet from me, making it easier for other cars to get around us.

"It's time to head home." I grabbed the handle of Ebenezer's cage and shuffle-walked my way to the door. The sidewalks were icing over. I wanted to arrive at my destination without breaking me or Ebenezer.

The door opened. I stepped inside. Blessed warmth. The temperature was at least thirty-five degrees warmer. "What took so long?" I carried Ebenezer to the couch and strapped the cage in.

"Had to let this baby warm up first. Your RV likes to wake up slow."

"I hope it wasn't too much trouble unhooking everything. I didn't even think about doing that this morning."

She waved off my concern. "No biggie."

"I hope your hands didn't freeze."

"I had on work gloves. It shouldn't take long to load up, then we can hit the Interstate. Hopefully, the crews are keeping the roads cleared."

The snow was accumulating faster than predicted. With the help of some of the organizers, and other vendors, my items were loaded into the RV in record time and we were on the way.

I settled in the passenger seat, casting an appraising gaze at

Ebenezer. He was still under the pile of bedding. "You'll be toasty warm before you know it."

"He's wearing an amazing fur coat. A little bit of cold won't harm him. Type your address into my Waze app and we'll be on the way. I'm looking forward to this little venture." She beamed at me. "I can't remember the last time I had a girl's day. This will be fun."

I never thought much about Grace's day-to-day life. There probably wasn't much time for her to have a social life, even with Abraham being twenty-four. He still required a lot of care. Abraham's father ran out on them when he was a toddler, right around the time Grace realized Abraham didn't see or react to the world like other children. The man went to work one day and never came home. At first, she thought something horrible happened to him until the day the divorce papers arrived in the mail.

Grace swore it was the best thing for her and Abraham. She moved forward, never giving the man another thought. She never even shared the man's name, not wanting to give him any power in her life. It was her and Abraham.

"We'll turn it into a slumber party." I took off my gloves and placed my hands near the vent. Warm air flowed around them. My fingers tingled. I stretched them out then curled them back, repeating the process a few times, encouraging blood flow.

The snow crunched under the wheels. The middle lane had a light dusting of snow while the outside lanes had a couple of inches on it. Semis whizzed past us. I gripped the door handle, making sure it was locked.

"Want to sing some Christmas songs?" Grace asked.

"I'd rather not." I checked my seatbelt. Buckled. I knew she was trying to keep my mind off the snow.

Grace eased the RV onto the Interstate. "How about we listen to the news for weather updates."

"We can see the most accurate weather update by looking at the window."

Grace laughed. "That is true."

The snow was thicker. Visibility was getting worse, and we still had about an hour to travel. I slumped in the seat. My friend was risking her life for me. She'd be safe at home with her son right now.

The wipers swiped back and forth in a quick beat, still doing little to increase our visibility. I turned on the defroster and prayed it cleared up the windshield. Would it be best to find a place to hunker down for the night? I opened a browser on my cell and searched for a nearby RV park or a Walmart. You could usually find one of those and most Walmart stores allowed RV parking and some even had places to hook up.

"It's going to be okay, Merry." Grace flicked a gaze in my direction before returning her full attention to the window. "Are you checking Samuel's Facebook page to see who wanted him dead?"

"I'm looking for a place to overnight. The snow is getting worse. I think we're in a full-fledge blizzard."

Grace laughed. "Honey, this is a little snow."

I gaped at her in an exaggerated manner then pointed out the window. "That's more than a little snow. We can barely see."

"It's the wind blowing that's causing that. These are tiny flakes. They're not even sticking to the wipers. It'll be safer for us to get home than exit off to one of these smaller towns and find a place to lodge for the night. The exits ramps on some of these are twisty and with the roads being slick, will be hard to navigate. It's easy to make a mistake and end up in a ditch."

I crossed my arms and settled back into the seat. "We should've stayed in Morgantown. We could've extended our stay by a day."

"And then have to deal with frozen water pipes? Not a good option."

"Frozen?"

"Yep. Water can freeze in the lines and do considerable damage." She let out a dramatic sigh. "Don't ask me how I know."

The last thing I needed was another repair I couldn't afford. At least the renovation I needed, removing and replacing the dinette, didn't render the RV unusable while a busted water wipe would garage the vehicle until I earned the funds to pay for it. The expenses for the RV kept adding up, and that was without considering the fact I found the body of my ex-husband in it.

I clasped my hands together and placed them in my lap, the only way to stop myself from clutching onto the door handle for dear life. Grace was keeping the RV steady, but I was still heading straight for full-fledge panic mode. I drew in a deep breath and slowly released it.

"How about we talk about the craft show. Get your mind off the drive," Grace said.

Good idea. "How were your sales? Mine weren't so good this year. I had too many distractions during this event. I hope the situation with Samuel didn't create such a problem I won't be allowed back next year."

"As long as you send your paperwork in on time, you're fine. You didn't cause any disruptions for the other vendors," Grace said. "I did okay even though I had to spend too much time away from my booth."

Shame heated my cheeks. Grace's pottery was amazing, and a Christmas cookie platter was still on my wish list, but without a vendor or helper at the booth, it was hard to make any sales. "You didn't have Abraham there to fill in for you because he was at my booth."

"That had nothing to do with you." She smiled at me. "He was enamored with Ebenezer and Raleigh. He bounced back and forth between our booths all day. I think it helped him not being stuck in one place. If he started feeling overwhelmed, he went to the other booth. I have an idea of creating volunteer positions for associate help for those vendors who come alone and don't have family nearby that can spell them breaks. It would be great for Abraham. He'd be able to work on his social skills."

"Won't that be overwhelming for him?"

"No, because he'd know that he'd only be there for thirty minutes. I'd make sure his shifts were short unless he was at a booth of a vendor he knows well. Like yours."

"He loves being there because of Ebenezer."

She grinned. "My other idea is adopting a guinea pig for him. It can be his emotional support animal."

"He'd love that."

"I just have to make sure the other craft shows don't mind us bringing an animal."

I winced. "Sorry about that. I should've asked you beforehand.

"I'd have let you."

"I'm sorry I forgot about promising Abraham a tree. I thought he didn't want one, or I'd have made sure to set it aside."

Grace's cheeks reddened, and she tightened her grip on the wheel. "That was my fault. Abraham knew I wanted to look at that tree. He overheard me and another organizer discussing a potential vandalizer. A couple of other vendors had called me on their cells to report red drops being discovered on their products, and a deep discount being demanded. I had said we needed pictures of the so-called damages to determine if they were similar in style."

Relief rushed through me. The tightness in my shoulders wasn't from the drive, it was from my imagination. "She was a scammer. Her insistence on buying the tree after I offered one of the perfect trees at the discount now makes sense."

"Do you remember what she looks like?"

"Gray hair. Wore it pulled back from her face in a tight bun. Blue trench coat. Heavy handed in the makeup department."

"Anything else? Eye color? Did she have a limp? An accent? I'm going to ask the other vendors for a description and see if they match."

"She also wore bright red nail polish. The color caught my attention because it was the same as the red drops on the tree."

Grace nodded. "I bet that was what she used. I hope we can track her down."

"Can you prove she's been vandalizing items?"

Grace heaved out a sigh. "Unlikely, but I can let her know we're on to her. It'll at least keep her away from our event. Crafters struggle hard enough to earn a living. We don't need scammers skimming off the profits we do make."

"Ain't that the truth."

The snow continued to fall. The roads were turning slick. I felt the wheels slide. Panic welled up in me. I glanced at Grace's phone. Forty-eight more minutes. A groan slipped out.

"We're fine, Merry." Grace flipped on the blinkers and merged into the middle lane since it was clearer. "Turn on some Christmas tunes. I love singing carols and usually I can't."

"Why not?" I opened the glove compartment.

She laughed. "Abraham loathes my singing."

Where were my Christmas CDs? I put some in there this morning in case the Bluetooth and my phone decided they weren't compatible. Now not a one. I rummaged around in the mess. It had been well organized this morning. What was all this paper in here? When I took possession of the RV, there was the bill of sale, RV registration, insurance card, and some print outs of how to hook everything up, along with my classic Christmas and Pentatonix CDs.

"Something wrong?" Bonnie asked.

"My CDs are gone."

"Maybe you put them somewhere else."

I shook my head. "I wanted them near me when I was driving."

"You wouldn't be able to reach them from the driver's seat. I always put items I might need while driving in the holder on the door. They're usually pretty deep." Grace reached down.

"I'm positive."

"Are you sure?" Grace held a CD out to me.

I took it, frowning. "Yes."

"This weekend hasn't been kind to you. It's natural if you misremembered something."

"I know it was in here. And I wouldn't have shoved these scraps of vinyl into the glove compartment either. I have a trash can." My stomach plummeted.

Bonnie. She was at the craft show. She never attended craft

shows as she preferred more sophisticated items, basically store-bought items. Samuel had told me that when I asked if he wanted me to leave any of the décor. I thought Cassie would've like some and I wanted to be kind to her. I hated that my leaving hurt her.

"What's wrong? You look sick." Grace flicked a concern gaze at me. "Need me to pull over?"

I shook my head. "Bonnie came today to see if I'd check the RV for a copy of my divorce decree."

"Whatever for?"

"She couldn't find Samuel's and believed he stored it in the RV. I told her I was too busy."

Grace hummed a knowing sound. "Bonnie broke into the RV and looked for it after you said no."

"Or used a key." I sighed. "Cassie gave me one key. She said the other one was lost."

"So, Bonnie came in here and searched through your stuff and put everything back where she thought it went."

I scowled. "Yes. I told her the decree wasn't in the RV. Cassie and I made sure nothing of Samuel's was left in here. I was diligent about it. The last thing I wanted was for him to have a reason to see me." Tears filled my voice. Again, I was crying because of him. I promised myself I'd never do it again.

"Honey, I'm so sorry. I'll help you put everything back in order when we get to your place. Make sure there are no traces of Samuel anywhere in here."

A new dread washed over me. "What if she left something?" My voice was barely above a whisper.

"What?" The concern on Grace's face deepened.

"What if Bonnie planted evidence against me? To prove I killed Samuel."

She sucked in a breath. "Do you really think she's capable of that? That she'd set you up for Samuel's murder?"

The image of the registration flittered into my brain. What if Samuel's signature had been forged? Cassie knew her dad didn't sign it and decided to get rid of the RV by selling it to me before

Bonnie was able to convince Samuel that Cassie wanted the RV. "If she killed him she would."

A muscle in Grace's jaw twitched. She gripped the steering wheel and turned on the blinker. "We'll search this RV from top to bottom."

My head was spinning with gratitude and confusion. "What do we do if we find something?"

"Put it back where it belongs."

THIRTEEN

Grace parked the RV in front of my cottage styled house with gingerbread trim. Large trees framed the house. The white picket fence was more for decorative than containment purposes. All the houses in the neighborhood had the same old-fashioned charm. Quaint. Simple. Homey. I had loved the house and the neighborhood the moment I saw it fifteen years ago. I house-shopped the first week of December because it was important to me to know how the neighbors decorated even though I had agreed that the children and I would stay in Virginia until June, allowing the children to finish out the school year. Brett had wanted me to stay in Virginia but knew that it was important for me to move closer to my mother as my father was extremely ill. My father died two weeks after the kids and I moved to Season's Greetings.

"Abraham would love to visit here. It's so charming, like a town you'd see in a snow globe."

It was a quaint town. No large buildings, franchise stores, or eateries. Everything reminded me of Christmas and times past. Like I had stepped into a Norman Rockwell painting or *It's A Wonderful Life*. A town with a Christmas name without an over-the-top Christmas feel. My mother never told me why her and my father retired to this particular West Virginia town. I loved it from the moment I saw it, so maybe the Christmas feel also drew them to it. Christmastime was their favorite time of the year too. Plus, they'd know I'd fall in love and would be tempted to move there. My mother had been concerned, almost frantic, when I moved out and started college. She had feared it would crush my spirit. I only stayed for a couple of semesters as finances and love got in the way.

I didn't need to live in Christmas Wonderland, but I didn't want to live in Scroogeville either. The brick buildings on Main Street were all decorated with garland and lights. The houses had a mix of timeless Christmas décor: wreaths, red ribbons, garland and white lights. Along with a few houses that were a contender for a crazy, Christmas house label: multiple inflatables, hundreds of thousands of multi-colored lights, Santa displays, laser light shows. It was perfect. The only holdout on our street was Cornelius who lived across the street from me.

The houses were still undecorated though some of the neighbors had taken their big pieces from their garages and storage units and placed them in the driveway, waiting until Friday, the day after Thanksgiving, to set up. It was considered uncouth to start the display until after Thanksgiving. Season's Greetings liked to give every holiday its due.

"Want to search today or wait until tomorrow?" Grace asked. "There's still some light out. I'm sure I can back this up into your driveway. We can load directly into the garage."

"We'll unload tonight. Keep the RV parked here. It's too long for the driveway. I tried it earlier and the front stuck out and I was blocking the road. I was a trending topic on the Season's Greetings Facebook page, and it wasn't because people were admiring my new vehicle. Someone had posted a pic and the police arrived just as I parked at the curb."

"You rebel you." Grace grinned at me and turned off the engine. "I'll unhitch my car and park it in your garage. Don't want to block your driveway."

I stepped out into the cold. Ebenezer whistled and huddled into a corner of the cage. With my luck, an emergency would pop up and I'd be delayed with moving the RV. There weren't many spaces to park the massive vehicle on the road that wouldn't tick off the neighbors. I was sure they wouldn't be happy if I left the RV permanently in front of my house.

One, it ruined the Christmas ambience, unless I decorated it, and the vehicle took up a lot of curbside parking. Tomorrow, I needed to check around for options for parking, something I should've considered before I bought it. Would've saved me a whole bunch of angst.

Under the door knocker, there was a note attached to my door. Darn. UPS must've stopped by with my order of wine glasses. I should've left a note for the delivery guy that it was okay to leave it. We didn't have a lot of package thefts on our street. Had more to do with Cornelius scoping out everything and everyone rather than no crooks in Season's Greetings. Every town had their share of crime. I shoved the note into a front pocket of my jeans.

"A few more moments, Ebe." I fumbled with the keys, finding the lock on the third try. The door creaked open. We walked inside.

Comfort wrapped around me. The tension in my body and my misgivings faded. I was home. It always brought me joy.

A large brick fireplace stretched almost from one end of the room to the other. It was the focal point of the living room. The Christmas tree would go to the left, in front the large picture window. A couch and two recliners filled up the space, a white rug with swirls of green, gold, and red pulled the conversation grouping together. There was no TV in the living room. It was the crafting, reading, and board game space. I always wanted to make it an electronic free zone, but I knew that would encourage my children to live in their rooms, and I'd have to ditch the old record player console the previous owner had left. I loved listening to records on it. The slight scratching sound of the needle going over the grooves of the album was a lovely sound. It recalled memories of my childhood, dancing to Christmas albums with my mom and dad. Trimming the tree with popcorn and cranberries. Love and peace. That was what my childhood had contained.

The moment I opened the cage, Ebenezer ran out. He raced round the living room, lapping it a few times before doing a step-hop up the stairs. The first day I brought him home, I had set up a guinea pig zone in the living room. There was large plastic toddler swimming pool filled with bedding, a large wheel and some tubes for him to play in. I had wanted him comfortable and entertained at night. I was a light sleeper and hadn't wanted Ebenezer's possible loneliness to keep me up. It hadn't. The critter whistled and squealed until I brought him upstairs. He figured out how to get into my bed and curled up into the crook of my neck and slept there all night. Since I had slept better than I had in years, I allowed it to become a habit.

"Behave yourself while I make sure no one is trying to frame me for murder." I shut the door and went back into the RV.

While I sorted through everything in the glove compartment, Grace checked around the dinette and in it. "Want me to open it?" She asked as she raised the storage seat.

I shuddered the moment I heard it open. It creaked, like coffins in old time horror movies. I kind of expected Samuel to fling up, cackling like a crazed clown. I edged toward the dinette. I felt a little guilty making Grace look in there. She had insisted, believing her nerves would handle it better than me. She was probably right. It still wasn't nice to do to a friend.

Trembling, I stood behind her and peered in. There a slight blackish brown stain in the corner of the dinette. Scratches on the inside of the lid. My stomach rocked. Then rolled. "I'm going..." I flew out the door.

My side banged into the edge of the door. Pain shot through me. I'd have a bruise tomorrow. I stepped away from the RV, drawing in breaths of the cold air. My lungs burned, and my limbs started to freeze. The sick feeling in my stomach evaporated.

Grace handed me a coat. "Thought you could use this? Feeling better."

"Much." I slipped on the coat. "Sorry about that."

"Merry, don't be sorry. This has been a stressful weekend for you, and now Bonnie has made it worse. Call Brett and tell him your suspicions." She wrapped a scarf around my neck and handed me a pair of gloves. "Let's check the underneath storage compartment."

"Do you really think she'd hide something in there?" Bonnie

loved her white attire. I couldn't see her mucking it up when she had better options, like hiding spots inside the RV.

Grace used my keys and unlocked the compartment. "If she didn't think you'd look in here until later. It's easy to mix in some incriminating evidence with your craft supplies."

"It was empty," I reminded her.

"Then she wouldn't have had to climb inside. Just toss something in there and hope it found its way into a corner. She wasn't expecting you to figure out she was in your RV."

True. It was cold and snowing when we loaded up. The temperatures were frigid, and my items risked getting damaged by the snow. It would be a quick process. She'd also assume that I'd leave everything packed up until the weather cleared. Plenty of time for her to send the police my way with an anonymous tip to check the RV before I discovered whatever she left behind.

"Let's start moving everything out. I don't want to be convicted of a crime I didn't commit."

"With two of us, it won't take long at all."

I opened the garage. "Let me grab a tarp for the trees. I like putting the trees in last, so boxes aren't crushing them." I snagged one that was bundled up in the corner and spread it out.

"I have an idea," Grace said. "I'll go inside the compartment and hand everything out to you, it'll take less time and you know where everything goes. No sense in you having to rearrange all the boxes and trees tomorrow." She scrambled inside and pushed out trees and boxes. I had no time to think, just catch.

I placed tree after tree on the tarp. There were a lot of trees. I should've sold one for fifty percent off. It wasn't a win to have to haul all of them out and wrestle them into the garage and then back to the RV.

The sound of tires crunching over the snow grabbed our attention. We stopped working and looked over. A police car parked behind the RV. An officer got out of the cruiser and walked toward us.

"Evening, Merry." Officer Orville Martin adjusted his utility belt and tipped his chin down at the items on the tarp. "Had a report of a junk yard sprouting up."

I didn't have to look far to know who reported me. Cornelius. The man needed a hobby besides tattling on people in his neighborhood. "I'm just unloading my items from the craft fair. You can tell Cornelius that I'm not leaving the trees in the front yard. I don't want them stolen."

He peered into the storage compartment. "You got a lot of stuff in there. Let me give you ladies a hand."

"No, we're fine." I said. "I'm sure you have more important things to do." It would be hard getting rid of planted evidence with a cop nearby.

He smiled at me. "It's no problem, Merry. I can help you until I get a call. It's better than Cornelius staying riled up. You know how the old guy gets. Next, he'll be calling the chief or posting on that dang town Facebook page."

True. Cornelius had a love-hate relationship with everything and everyone in Season's Greetings, including the town's Facebook page. He used it regularly to air his grievances and ranted how others used it to criticize his behavior.

I ran through a multitude of options to get rid of Orville, but none of them seemed probable or prudent. The more I fussed that I didn't want his help, the more insistent and suspicious he'd become. I doubted the local police didn't know about Samuel's murder, especially with Cassie talking about it on social media.

"Thanks, Orville, I appreciate it."

"Just tell me where to put them." Orville picked up a tree and headed for the garage.

Oh well, I'd just put all the boxes inside and sort them in the morning. A lot of them belonged in my craft studio anyway.

With Orville's help, we unloaded the RV in record time.

Grace stayed inside the compartment, making a production of placing bungee cords into a plastic box. "We have it under control, Officer. Thank you for your help." Grace's voice echoed from the chamber.

Excitement and dread raced through me. She must've found what Bonnie hid and didn't want the officer watching while she brought it out. "Yes, thank you." I smiled brightly at him.

"I'll let Cornelius know I gave you a warning and watched you put everything into the garage. That'll make his soul happy."

Grace slid out of the compartment and closed it.

"Did you find anything?" I whispered.

She shook her head. "If she hid something, she hid it good."

FOURTEEN

Grace nearly tripped over Ebenezer when she walked into my house. The critter was zipping all over the place. "He sure does have energy." Grace placed her overnight bag by the front door and glanced around the living room, disappointment tugged down the corners of her mouth.

I looked at my house with a more critical eye. My decorating style was flea market mixed with craft projects and understated Christmas that I kept out year-round. Christmasland house didn't appear until after Thanksgiving. It was a promise I made to my kids when they were youngsters and I kept it even after they moved out.

"Scotland's room is set up as a guest room," I said.

Grace peeked around the corner into the dining room. "No Christmas? I was looking forward to seeing your Christmas display. I always imagined it was a sight to behold."

"I start decorating on Black Friday. It's my break from crafting. Bright and I know how many orders we have to fulfill by Christmas, and while I'm decorating, she's putting together our battle plan on how to divvy up the orders."

"Bright isn't a Christmas person?" Grace plopped onto one of the recliners and stretched out. Her eye lids drooped. Driving the RV had been more stressful than she let on. My heart went out to her.

"She enjoys Christmas. Her husband is a Christmas lights fanatic and has a blueprint of where everything goes. Bright says the task of the front of the house, living and dining room are his domain and she takes care of the other rooms. She's learned it's best to wait until he's done before she decorates elsewhere. She never knows, until his vision is created, what he plans on using."

The wind howled outside. Fortunately, I had a house of stone. No worries of the big, bad wolf wind blowing it down, though it rattled the windows.

"How about some hot chocolate? Or would you rather call it a night?" I asked.

Grace bolted upright. "No. This is the first girl's night I've had since Abraham was born. No way am I sleeping now."

"Our movies and television are in the family room downstairs."

Grace hopped up. "I can't wait to see your holiday movie collection."

As the house was built on an incline, the left side of the house wasn't underground and there was a set of patio doors that let in a lot of natural light. There was also a brick fireplace downstairs. It was one of the reasons I fell in love with the house. I loved having two mantels to decorate with evergreen boughs and lights.

When Samuel and I married, I had kept my paid for house to convert into a craft studio and shop. A small bedroom downstairs would be turned into my administration office with a small desk, a desktop, and file cabinets with tax records and receipts. I hadn't wanted to keep my personal and financial information on the laptop as I brought it to shows. The den was the area I planned on doing classes. Samuel and I were still in the process of deciding whose furniture would go into "our" home when I realized the marriage wouldn't work, and I hadn't started reinventing my house after I moved back in. It was too hard on my heart. I liked the comfort it brought me having the downstairs exactly the way it was when Scotland and Raleigh lived at home. It was enough at the time that I changed their empty bedrooms into a crafting room and a guest room. I just couldn't do anymore.

Maybe it was time.

I prepared the hot chocolate and took out the air popper, making sure to line up the bowl properly as the last time a quarter of the popcorn landed on the floor. Between the popcorn, butter, and hot chocolate, my kitchen smelled amazing. I couldn't wait for Sunday. Holiday baking time. Or at least my first round of it. Though, with Scotland having to leave Sunday, I might start a day early. There was no way I'd send a child of mine off at the start of the holiday season without a couple batches of Christmas cookies.

There was a skittering sound at my feet. Ebenezer settled himself onto the hardwood floors near the popcorn bowl. He remembered the fiasco from Thursday night and was hoping to benefit from my mistake again.

"Sorry, Ebe. None for you."

The phone vibrated on the counter, bouncing a little on the Formica countertop, and pinged. Bright.

Home safe?

In my haste to start the sleepover, I forgot to text Bright. It was part of our standard procedures. I texted Bright when I left a show and on my return home.

Yes. A friend drove the RV home. Having a movie night.

Male or female?

Female. Of course.

You are an adult. And divorced. You can have fun.

The last thing I wanted to do right now was venture into another relationship. I was divorced, not very long, and my ex-husband was dead. *Said ex-husband was recently murdered. Not the best time to start seeing someone new.*

True. I just want you to be happy. You deserve it.

I am happy. I typed, keeping one eye on the popcorn bowl. It wasn't overflowing yet. *My children are happy and living their dreams. I'm at my full-time crafting season. And it's Christmastime!* I also sent a row of smiling emoticons.

There's more to life than Christmas.

Blasphemy! Popcorn's done.

Have fun and keep safe.

I sent an emoticon rolling their eyes. I was home. I was safe.

Our snack and drink were done. I walked into the kitchen and took out two of my Christmas mugs, choosing the first day of Christmas and seventh. The seven swans a swimming had been Raleigh's favorite. Swans to her were romantic and regal creatures. One year, she had placed a swan on her Christmas list. It took weeks for Brett and me to find a largish stuffed swan for Raleigh to sleep with. Her bed was piled high with lovies. The following year, she wrote: *Swan—live one.* It was a heck of a time explaining to our daughter why she couldn't have a live swan when her friend had a pet duck.

I placed the bowl of popcorn and mugs of hot chocolate onto a breakfast tray and carried our treat downstairs. Ebenezer hopped down the stairs, right by my feet.

"Quit it." I narrowly missed stepping on the little guy. "You're going to trip me up or become one with my shoe."

"I think he's hoping to trip you." Grace ran over and plucked him off the stairs. He screeched before settling into her arms.

"He has a thing for popcorn." I placed the tree on the coffee table. "What are we watching tonight?"

I was hoping for *Christmas with the Kranks* or the Hallmark movie *Naughty or Nice* with Krissy Kringle. Those were my go-to movies when I needed a laugh. No matter how many times I saw them, they still cracked me up. Samuel and Cassie hated them, which had the added benefit that there were no memories of them tied to the movies.

"I couldn't find one." Grace sat in the plush love seat, curling her feet under her. I handed her a mug.

I looked over at my Blu-Ray and DVD storage unit. I had romantic Christmas movies, funny ones, black-and-white classics, more current classics like *A Christmas Story*. It might be a little overwhelming to have so many choices. "What type of Christmas movie are you in the mood to see? I'm sure I'll have something that would work."

Grace smiled over her mug. "I'm sure you do. You have quite the collection. Abraham would be in heaven."

"Maybe one day, you could both visit. I have a guest room." I blurted out the offer, regretting the words the moment I finished the sentence.

While I liked people, I was an introvert. It was why crafting was the perfect job for me and my best friend and I communicated through messaging and text. We were in each other's lives but not *up in* each other's lives. I liked that we still had private parts of ourselves and could answer when it was convenient for us rather than right away like talking on the phone. My parents had been homebodies as well. Most of our weekends were spent together in our home.

"I'm sure my son would love it. For a little while anyway. Maybe an afternoon visit, this way his routine isn't changed too much." Grace blew the steam rising from her cup. She looked sad.

"Missing Abraham?" I asked.

She smiled sadly and nodded. "Sometimes I can't help but wonder what will happen to him when I'm no longer here. How will he support himself? Take care of himself? The truth is he's just not capable of it." Tears pooled in her eyes. "What will happen to my son? It breaks me thinking about Abraham alone in the world."

I moved from the upholstered chair to sit beside Grace. I wrapped an arm around her shoulders and hugged her. A deep, dark feeling welled up in my gut. "Are you sick?"

She shook her head and patted the tears dry with her fingertips. "No. It's just a thought that creeps in now and then. I've been thinking about it more. Probably because of Samuel dying."

My thoughts turned to Cassie. She was alone. Who was supporting the teen through her father's death? I knew Bonnie wasn't a source of comfort for the girl. For all I knew, the woman locked the girl out of the house. Who would Cassie turn to? Her grandmother was back and forth between her small house and the hospital. When Samuel and I were married, I had nagged him to fix the water heater and the front steps of his mother's house. The water heater was on its last legs and the steps were crumbling. Shame flickered through me. I should've paid to fix those items myself rather than buy the RV.

It wasn't Samuel's mom Helen's fault her son was a bad husband. Helen had always acted like Samuel was a gift to her. She bragged on him. Told stories of his generosity. At first, I thought Helen hated me because we never dined at her house. We always met at a restaurant or ventured out on shopping trips. Never visited at her home. I stopped by one day as a surprise and learned why she kept me out of her home. It told the truth of Samuel. He didn't take care of her as he bragged. For Helen it was a source of embarrassment. For Samuel, it was just another layer, a coverup for another deception.

I hadn't done my homework well. I trusted what I was told rather than look myself. My motto from now on was actions spoke louder than words. "I should call Cassie. See how she's doing."

"Merry, you know that's not a good idea."

"She's basically alone. Bonnie won't take care of her, and Helen can't."

"She's eighteen."

I almost reminded Grace that Abraham was twenty-four, and she worried about him. Instead, I took a sip of my cocoa to settle my ire and stop myself from talking. Those words would hurt Grace. Abraham had a different situation than Cassie. The truth was he'd likely never be able to live alone. His brain worked in such a way that he needed reminders on basic tasks and didn't process situation as others did.

"She's still in high school," I said. "Samuel doted on her. She's never had to deal with day-to-day stuff. Paying bills. Buying groceries. Cooking. Laundry."

Could Cassie even get money from Samuel's bank account? Had Samuel taken me off? If not—*No. Don't do it!* My brain screamed at me. Bad idea was written all over the plan of pulling money out for Cassie. Taking money from your murdered ex-husband's checking account fell onto the checklist of "evidence you're a murderer."

Grace leaned over, placing the first day of Christmas mug onto the coffee table. "If I were you, I'd see if someone would contact the high school for you. The teachers will keep an eye out for her."

"That's a good idea, but school is closed until the Monday after Thanksgiving."

"That's right. I forgot about that." Grace leaned back and heaved out a sigh. "Sorry. I thought I had the answer."

My sigh accompanied hers. *Don't we all.* The two mugs placed side by side drew my attention. The partridge in the pear tree looked forlorn. The poor bird was always alone. The turtle dove had a buddy. Why couldn't an inanimate object had been first, the one to stand alone, instead of a living creature. On the first day of Christmas my true love gave to me, one bright red sled. Or even one golden ring. Who needed five?

There had to be a way to help Cassie. Make sure she was okay. Rachel. My friend and Cassie's boss would know something. Right? I slipped my phone from my pocket and texted her, asking about Cassie.

She responded back immediately. *Haven't seen her since Wednesday. Worried about the girl. Tomorrow, I'll stop by her house.*

"I'm going to call it a night." Grace stood, stretched and yawned. "I'm more tired than I thought. I'm sure that's why I couldn't pick a movie."

"Once you get upstairs, the room is the second one on the right." I stopped in mid text. That was no way to treat a guest. "I'll show you."

Grace hugged me. "I can manage to find my way upstairs. I know you're worried about Cassie and need to have someone check on her. See you in the morning," Grace said, collecting our empty mugs.

"The upstairs bathroom is at the end of the hall."

Keep me updated? I want to see her but not sure it's a good idea.

I'm sure it's not a good idea. I'll let you know what I found out. Sorry you're going through this. No matter what others say, I know you're innocent.

FIFTEEN

I curled onto my side, Ebenezer snuggling against me, and tried to sleep. My mind fretted about Cassie. How was she doing? Should I call? I didn't want to come across as I was stalking her or considered her a murderer. No, listen to your friend's advice. Don't contact Cassie. It would make things worse.

Reaching out, I snagged my cell from the bedside table and clicked on the Facebook app and brought up Cassie's page. Her last post was Saturday morning when she accused me of being responsible for her father's death. Friends posted condolences and asked if she was okay and if she needed to talk to contact them any time day or night. Cassie remained silent. Or at least was quiet on her page, she might be messaging them privately.

I popped over to Samuel's page. More rest in peace message. I scrolled down some more and stopped, moving back up. *Told you, man, trouble follows.* Gary Meadows. The name was unfamiliar. I clicked on the guy's name and all I saw was his name and no other identifiers. The only way for me to learn more about Gary, and his connection to Samuel, was to friend the guy.

I hoped Gary Meadows was intrigued enough by the name of Merry Winters he'd accept it. I switched from his page to my main page and changed my icon to something a little less Christmassy so I didn't frighten the guy. One might not want to friend a grown woman who was wearing light up antlers.

Exhaustion washed over me. My emotions had been up and down all day, grieving Samuel then angry at him. Feeling sorry for him then wondering what he did to deserve his fate. Some of those thoughts weren't nice at all. I needed my brain turned off for a few hours. I switched off my phone and placed it on the bedside table. Rolling over, I curled myself into a ball and Ebenezer snuggled into my stomach. The warmth of his tiny body was comforting. Tension drained from my body and my eyes fluttered closed.

Scritch. Scratch. I bolted upright, clutching the pillow to me. Disorientated. My heart pounded. Ebenezer screeched and scrambled into my lap. *Scritch. Scratch.* He heard it too. Instinctively, my gaze went to the window. The branches outside the window were bare and nowhere near the pane. Had the wind knocked a branch against the pane? Placing Ebenezer onto the bed, I quietly made my way to the window. Nothing moved outside.

Scratch. Thump. With wide eyes, I stared at the ceiling. It was coming from above. The roof. What was going on?

I slipped on my jeans. Something crinkled in the front pocket. The note on my door. I snagged the paper and placed it on the bedside table. First thing tomorrow, reschedule a delivery.

I shoved my feet into my faux fur lined suede slippers and headed for the door. Another bump. Another scratch. This time it was in the hallway. My hand trembled, pausing, almost frozen above the doorknob. Was someone sneaking around my house?

How could a person move from the roof to the hallway in a matter of seconds? That was impossible. It was too early for a visit from Saint Nick. Was I mistaken on where the sound originated? I tiptoed my way back to my bed and unplugged my phone from the charger. The screen lit up. The paper I took from the door wasn't a slip from UPS. It was a sheet of notebook paper with red writing. I unfolded the notebook paper. The lettering looked like slashes of lines. Bright red slashes. In all capital letters. *Murderer.*

My legs gave away. I sank to the bed. The noise repeated itself in the hallway. Clutching the phone in my hand, I quietly made my way to the bedroom door, feeling like a thief in my own home. I twisted the knob. Carefully. Inch by inch. It creaked. I held my breath, counting in my head to twenty before I leaned over to peer out the slight gap.

This is a bad idea. A voice, sounding very similar to my son's, popped into my head. *Someone threatened you.* My gaze drifted to the note on my bedside table. The handwriting had a familiar quality to it. Or was I trying to convince myself of that? Should I call the police?

There was a shadow near the stairs, coming or going I couldn't tell. My heart slammed in my chest. Sweat dotted my forehead. I had to call the police. I eased back, so the intruder didn't see the light from my phone screen. Something brushed against my ankle. I yelped, slapping my hand over my mouth, and the phone slipped from my grasp. Tears filled my eyes. Ebenezer had squeezed through the gap and ran out into hallway.

"No!" I flung the door open. I had no choice. I had to save Ebenezer.

"Merry, you okay?" Grace hissed from the hallway.

I sagged against the doorframe. There was a practical explanation for the noise. My houseguest was going to the bathroom. "Yes, I'm fine. I thought I heard something and scared myself with possible scenarios."

"I was downstairs getting a glass of milk and heard something." Grace wrapped her arms around her waist and moved closer to me. "I also saw lights outside. I was coming back upstairs to get my phone and go out and investigate."

I frowned. "The sound I heard was overhead."

"Snow falling from the trees?"

"That makes sense." What had Grace heard outside? I linked my arm through hers. She was cold. The heater must've clunked out in the guest room again. Another item to add to my mounting repair list. "Let's go see what's going on outside."

"Let me grab my phone. We might need to call the cops."

I looked around the hallway. Something felt...off. Goosebumps prickled my skin. The hairs on the back of my neck rose. A coldness griped my scalp. Frowning, I cased the room. Where had Ebenezer ran off? I'd have to find him later.

"Ready?" Grace whispered.

I nodded, and we crept down the stairs.

Grace paused in mid-step. I almost tumbled down the stairs. "I'm second guessing this decision. Maybe we should just call the police. Your ex-husband was just murdered. What if whatever he did that angered someone so much was somehow tied to you? It could be dangerous."

My eyes widened. I hadn't thought of that. Had Samuel put me in danger because of a choice he made—was Cassie in danger? Had something happened to her? "Okay. Call them." Once the police arrived, I'd ask them to do a welfare check on Cassie.

While Grace called the police, I tiptoed to the window, in case someone lurked outside. I hooked a finger around the curtain and tugged it back an inch. No cars on the street. Near the door to RV, there was a fluttering movement. I pressed my nose to the glass, straining my eyes to see what, or who, was causing it.

"Everything okay?" Grace looked over my shoulder.

"I think someone's by the RV." I pointed.

She placed a hand on my shoulder and leaned forward, squinting into the night. "I see it too."

I ran to the front door and yanked it open. "The police are on their way."

Grace tugged me back and slammed the door shut, leaning against it and turning the lock. "Are you crazy? What if they try to bust in here? How fast are the police in your town?"

"I don't know. I never had to call them before." I was regretting my not so smart moment. This situation was so foreign to me, I didn't know how to respond correctly.

We stood with our backs to the door, hoping the police came before a lurker beat down the front door. It might be better for one of us to act as look out but neither one of us wanted to move. Fear had us in a stronghold.

After what seemed like hours, flashing red lights bounced off the walls. The police were out front. A relieved breath whooshed out of me. I waited for the knock on the door before I opened it.

Orville nodded. "Someone called in a report of a lurker around your RV. The door was open. I looked inside, and no one is in there now. Can you come with me, Merry?"

"I locked the door." Orville's no-nonsense tone and serious expression rattled me more than the figure I saw by the RV.

"That's what I thought." He smiled reassuringly. "You're safe. I'm here and Officer Myers is on her way as well."

He called for backup. I was more worried.

Grace took hold of my hand. "We'll go out together."

"This way ladies." Orville clicked on a flashlight and swept the beam back and forth over my driveway. The bright lights showed every cracked piece of asphalt and bounced off small patches of ice scattering on the driveway.

The door fluttered open then closed. Then back open again. Was that what I saw from the house? "Someone broke in," I said.

"I remember the door being closed when I left earlier this evening." Orville used his night stick to push open the door. "And...well...you'll see. Don't touch anything. Myers will get prints."

I stepped inside. The place was trashed and slashed. Uneven cuts ran down each cushion on the couch and the dinette bench. The contents of the refrigerator and the cabinets were on the floor. The driver's seat was turned toward the main living space and a jagged scar ran down the length of the seat.

Tears dripped down my cheeks. My dream had been torn to shreds. Why? The note flittered into my mind. *Murderer.* "They hate me."

"Aw, Merry, no one hates you." Orville handed me a handkerchief.

I wiped my eyes and face and told him about the note I found on my door. "This was done because people think I'm a murderer."

"No one thinks that. Can you get the note for me? I'd like to take it and see if we can get any prints from it."

"Yes, they do. Look at the RV. There's also a detective who's really interested in my whereabouts when Samuel died. Want his name?" Bitterness was laced in every word. I took the note from my pocket and shoved it at him.

"I already know it." Orville scribbled down something in a notebook then retrieved a small paper bag from his squad car. He opened the bag. "Place the note in here. Did anyone else touch it?"

At least the local police weren't considering me a suspect, not that it mattered since they weren't investigating the case. "Just me and the person who wrote it." I couldn't keep the bitterness and fear out of my voice.

Grace had her arms crossed and was rubbing her hands up and down, warding off the cold. "I'm glad the police are taking this seriously. I know where I live they wouldn't waste police resources to try and get fingerprints from a note or a trailer that had been vandalized."

"Normally we wouldn't be so concerned about it," Orville said. "But Samuel was killed in there. Someone might have come looking for something they left behind."

A sportscar pulled into my driveway. Paul McCormick, Scotland's friend, hopped out. "Are you okay, Merry?"

I frowned and stepped back. How did he know I was in trouble? My son teased me that Paul liked-liked me. I told him that wasn't possible. The man was thirteen years younger than me.

"I called him," Orville said.

I wasn't happy with Orville's decision. Why did he think I needed a man to help me? I narrowed my eyes. "Why?"

"Because I couldn't get hold of the fire chief. McCormick has keys to the station."

Paul dangled the keys from his lean fingers. "I brought them with me."

"My chief says it's best we get this vehicle into a secured location while we search for evidence on who did this," Orville said. "The only place we can think that'll fit it is in the fire station. You have an open bay right now?"

Paul nodded. "One of our trucks is out for modification. We're having lights added to the ladder thanks to an anonymous donator."

"Is that okay with you, Merry?" Orville asked.

"I'll get the keys." I trudged toward the door, feeling older than my forty-five years. My spirit felt broken, like I finally believed there was no Santa Claus. There was a hint of a thought weaving into and out of my mind. I was too tired to grasp it or even care to know it.

I pushed the front door open. A scratching sound was at the stairs. Ebenezer was at the landing, gazing down at me and wriggling his nose. He hopped down the stairs, heading for me. Some of the despair in my heart left at Ebenezer's anxiousness to get to me. I scooped him up and he rested his face on my cheek.

"I'm glad you're here."

"Anytime you need me, Merry."

I spun around. Paul was at the door, smiling at me.

I held out Ebenezer. "I meant him."

Paul's smile slipped. I grimaced. Probably shouldn't have corrected his interpretation. It didn't hurt for him to think I was talking about him and not a guinea pig.

"I'm sorry," I said. "That was rude. It's been a long weekend. I can't seem to say anything right. My brain is so scattered."

"Apologies aren't necessary. Once the police are done getting evidence from the RV, would you like me to clean it up?"

I should say no. Though the prospect of having to drag out the damage items was rerouting my Christmas spirit into Grinch territory. "I'd appreciate that."

I placed the keys on his palm. For a moment, his fingers curled, a gentle caress of my pinky and ring fingers. Our gazes meet. He relaxed his fingers.

"Thank you." The words come out as throaty whisper. I blushed.

He excused himself past Grace and left. She shut the door and fixed a curious gaze on me.

"Ebenezer and I are calling it a night." I fled upstairs before any of the questions in her eyes came out her mouth.

SIXTEEN

I slept fitfully, dreams and nightmares merged, settling an other-shoe-will-drop feeling over me. Not the best way to start a day. The strongest impression from the images wrecking my sleep was Cassie beaming at me through a thick pane of glass, both of us holding a landline phone to our ear. I couldn't see what we were wearing so no idea who was the prisoner or the visitor. Yawning, I stumbled out of my room.

Grace joined me in the hallway. "Good morning, Merry."

"Are you a breakfast girl?" I asked, "Or do you normally skip it."

"Abraham is a picky eater, so I make sure we have three meals a day this way I know he gets enough to eat."

"How does blueberries pancakes and bacon sound?" I wanted to keep busy, giving myself less time to obsess over troubling dreams.

"Wonderful. Do you get the morning paper? I love reading small town papers. There are usually more unique news stories in them."

Or at least they were news worthy here while not so much so in a larger town. "Yes. It'll be in the newspaper holder at the end of the driveway. Right next to the mailbox."

"Thanks, I'll get it."

Humming a Christmas tune, I went downstairs and whipped up the batter while the griddle warmed up for the bacon and pancakes.

Grace sat at the dining room table and flipped through the

newspaper. "This is what I love about small towns, the most pressing news is if the pool will open for the whole summer or just a part of it."

"It's the biggest controversy in Season's Greetings." Or was. Samuel's murder ranked higher than it. "Is there anything about S...S..." His name locked in my throat.

"Samuel's death." Grace scanned each page, a frown growing deeper with each page. "Nothing. Maybe there was a mention in Saturday or Sunday's paper."

A man was murdered, and everyone was going on with their lives without any closure. Like it didn't matter. What about his daughter? His wife's feelings? Samuel always feared not mattering to people. It was why he opened businesses and became a friend to everyone and anyone. If there was a party, Samuel was there. Needed a public favor, Samuel volunteered. It was why none of his relationships worked, he wanted to be the hero to the masses even if it meant being the villain to the women who tried loving him. The love of one was never enough for him. All the people he helped, all the ones he gave money and time to now carried on as he was nothing. My heart ached for my Samuel. He wasn't the best man, and was a lousy husband, but he was a decent enough man who thought too much about money and deserved better than having his death ignored.

"Nothing? Are you sure?" I asked.

"The big story is the lottery winner still hasn't claimed the twelve million dollars yet." Grace fixed wide eyes on me. "The winning ticket was won in your town."

The word ticket bounced around in my head. Could it be? Was that what Cassie was looking for? Or why Bonnie was so desperate to get her hands on the divorce decree? Had she lied, and it wasn't the insurance agent that questioned the marriage license but someone at the lottery commission? It was twelve million reasons for Bonnie to kill Samuel—she didn't have to share the money with Samuel or Cassie.

"You haven't heard any rumors about who it might be?" Grace

asked.

"You know how it is before a craft show. All your focus and attention are on preparing items to sell. I don't get on social media during that time. Don't want any distractions. Can I see the paper?"

"Sure." Grace handed it to me. "I wonder why they haven't stepped forward yet?"

I read the article. My heart beat faster. Four out of the six winning lottery numbers meant something to me—and Samuel. His birthday. His mom's birthday. The other two numbers didn't register. Was it Bonnie's birth month and age? With shaking hands, I placed the paper down and shrugged, trying not to let the thoughts in my head show on my face. Samuel had won the lottery. "They might be getting their affairs in order before they tell anyone. Probably scared unknown relatives will start beating down their door."

My gut encouraged me not to share my theory. Most of the reason was fear. If it got out, the homicide detective would have one more reason to suspect me. The recent ex-wife wanting a share of the money, especially after all the grief Samuel put me through. The detective didn't believe me now that I had nothing to do with it, he sure wouldn't change his mind with this potential truth.

"If I won that amount of money, I'd take Abraham on a Caribbean cruise. He loves the beach. Buy a house near the ocean with a pool and invest most of it for my son's care. What would you do with that kind of money?" Grace doctored up her coffee with creamer and a lot of sugar.

"Pay for Raleigh's master's degree. Go on a cruise with my children. Buy a new RV as I'm not so fond of mine anymore."

Grace smiled sympathetically. "Can't say I blame you. What are you going to do with it?"

"I have no choice but to keep it. It'll look bad if I sold it now. I used most of my savings to buy it. I have to keep it if I want a mobile studio." And not have to deal with the fact I threw away a lot of money. I couldn't afford to do that either.

"My boyfriend renovated our RV. Things are slow for him at

work right now. I can see if he can come out and fix yours. It shouldn't take too long to remove the dinette and add in a new one. The police shouldn't take too long dusting it for fingerprints and whatever else they'd do."

"I was thinking about converting it into a desk area for my cutting machines. Some proper storage for my vinyl."

Grace grinned. "That's a great idea. I'll talk to him tonight about it."

"I don't know."

"Come on. It'll be good for you to get the bad mojo out of there. Maybe even Christmas it up a bit to match your business. Think of the awesome photos for your Instagram and Facebook page."

True. But the cost. One way or another, money always inserted itself into situations. "I can't afford it right now." Scotland had volunteered his friend Paul to fix up the RV, but I wasn't comfortable with that plan. Last night, I had a strong feeling that Paul was interested in me as more than a friend and it was complication I wasn't up to handling. My life right now was a huge obstacle course and I didn't want one more item to navigate.

"How about a trade of services? Let Abraham visit with Ebenezer and my boyfriend will fix up the RV. He's been bugging me about taking a few hours for us as a couple."

"How will you guys spend time together if he's working on the RV?"

She grinned and waggled her eyebrows. "Day is for work, night is for fun. If you don't mind Abraham bunking at your place for the night."

Smooth. Grace went from me keeping an eye on Abraham during the day and evening to having her son spending the night. Considering what I'd get out of it, it was a good trade. It was hard for Grace to have time alone or private time with her boyfriend. She didn't want to hurt her son's feeling by hiring someone to look out for him. This was the perfect solution. He'd be visiting with Ebenezer. Raleigh was coming down Wednesday night after work for Thanksgiving, and Scotland hoped to spend a few hours on Thanksgiving at home. I had thought of bringing Thanksgiving to the kids, but right now I wanted to spend as little time in Morgantown as possible.

"Deal," I said. "You guys can stay for Thanksgiving."

"I don't know."

"It's a good excuse to give Abraham. I know Abraham enjoys decorating. Tell him I need some help getting Christmas up and am feeling a little down."

Grace nodded. "That will work. I hate reminding Abraham that he has different needs than others his age. This way he's helping you."

With that settled, we dug into our breakfast.

My cell phone sang "We Wish You a Merry Christmas." Season's Living Retirement Community. I jumped up and snagged the phone from the kitchen counter.

"This is Merry." My heart pounded. The assistant living facility usually called in the morning if my mother had a bad night.

"It's Holly. Doctor Yielding wanted me to give you a call and let you know your mom is dealing with a heavy case of the Christmas blues. She'd been binge watching Hallmark Christmas movies and is sad she can't have a tree."

Last year, it was decided not to have large decorations in my mom's room. She loved a large Christmas tree but would forget it was Christmas time and demand it be taken down. Only to insist a few hours later it be put back up. It placed an undue burden on the staff. The doctor probably reminded my mother that she couldn't have a large tree in her room. We were telling her it was because Christmas tree lights overloaded the facility's power grid. I hated lying to my mom but the truth, her memory was slipping away, turned her combative.

The Christmas tree decal. "I have the perfect solution." I told Holly about my Christmas décor vinyl decals.

"That's perfect." There was a smile in Holly's voice. "If you have any extras, bring them with you. I know a few other residents who would benefit from some good old Christmas cheer."

"Absolutely." I was called Merry Christmas for a reason. Nothing lifted my spirits more than bringing Christmas joy to the masses.

"I hate to end girl time abruptly, but I have a Christmas decorating emergency."

I took a quick shower and dressed in one of my tamer Christmas outfits: a long sweater decorated with tiny Christmas wreaths along the collar and hem and paired it with jeans and winter boots as it looked like snow was coming our way. I had found my weather predicting ability during the holiday season was more accurate than any weather apps and reports. My body just knew when snow was coming.

I snagged my keys from the kitchen counter. I liked storing my keys as far from the door as possible, believing it stopped people from breaking in. At times, I questioned that reasoning as if someone was in my house to steal the keys, they'd wouldn't need them to get in. It was one of my false sense of security habits that my children teased me about. Since it gave me peace of mind, I just went with it.

Grace had left, leaving me a note thanking me for my hospitality and a reminder that she'd be back on Wednesday along with her guys. I emailed myself a reminder to ask Paul about getting my RV out of lock down. It would be hard to renovate the RV if it was still residing in the fire station.

There was movement on the right-hand side of the porch, near my one-person wooden swing. Cats liked to perch there at night. Like other areas of Season's Greetings, stray cats were becoming an issue. I was more worried about it freezing and starving to death than I was at a homeless cat claiming my porch as a resting place.

A figure lunged toward me. It was not cat-sized.

I screeched and lurched backwards, the keys and phone slipped from my fingers and clattered to the wooden porch.

Cassie grabbed my arm. "Where's the RV?" There was venom in her voice.

Her anger brought out mine, shoving out common sense. "Why was the registration dated for the wrong day?"

Her grip fell from my arm and she stepped back. "What are you talking about?"

"I checked the registration for the RV. It's not dated for the day I bought it." I almost mentioned the signature, changing my mind at the last moment. I didn't need to let Cassie know everything I discovered.

Cassie rubbed her left ring finger and thumb together. "What are you talking about? You watched me date and sign it. Everything was legit. You're trying to switch the topic on me. I told you I needed to get my ticket. You said I could get it today."

A ticket consisting of six numbers was my guess. At least I didn't have to worry about her well-being anymore. She was feisty as ever and dressed quite nicely, if not warmly. Her feet were shoved in sparkly canvas shoes without any socks. I spotted a faint hint of black and red on her left ankle. I squinted. Was it a tattoo?

She glanced down and blushed. She used her right ankle to block her left one.

"The RV was secured by the police," I fibbed a little.

Her eyes widened and her face paled. "They took it because of Dad's murder?"

Tears filled my eyes. The truth sounded eviler and bleaker coming from his daughter. I drew in deep breaths and brought my emotions under control. Cassie needed my support.

I took hold of her hands. They were ice cold. "It was vandalized. The police thought it best to have it moved to a safe place."

Tears welled in her eyes and her mouth and body trembled. She was ready to crumble. "What did they do?"

"Cushions were ripped. Whatever I had in the refrigerator was on the floor. Just trashed."

Like the culprit was searching for something—a ticket. I was positive my suspicion was correct. Everything added up. Bonnie asking for a trip. All the Go Fund Me requests on Samuel's

Facebook page. Samuel *had* won the lottery and apparently a lot of people in town knew, except me.

Cassie tucked her hands under her arms and wandered away, looking devastated, hopeless, and scared. She knew her dad won the lottery and counted on finding the ticket. Now, someone else had it. I prayed Samuel had signed it to protect himself and his daughter, making it useless to anyone else.

Except for possibly his wife, who I doubted would share it with the stepdaughter she loathed.

The frosted glass doors of Season's Living parted, and I tugged my utility wagon into the lobby. The pale blue walls added a hint of color, giving the room some warmth and cheer. Plush gray chairs were staged throughout the lobby in conversational groupings. The area was used for open houses and parties for the residents. Most residents stayed in their care units, especially the memory care resident-patients like my mother. The staff had wanted functions that allowed the residents from all the special care units time to mingle together so they hosted special get togethers four times a year.

The wheels of the cart sailed over the honey-colored laminate oak floor. I waved to Holly. "Here to spread Christmas cheer."

She tapped a pen onto the clipboard at the reception counter. "Merry, you have to sign in. Every time."

"Alright." I scribbled my signature down. Right above my name was a barely legible one. William Grayson. My heart dipped. What was he doing here? Heck, I knew what he was doing here—talking to my mother.

I raced down the hall, the cart banging into walls.

"Merry," Holly called out to me.

I ignored her. I reached the end of the hall and smacked the button that opened the main doors to the memory care unit. There were four apartments down this corridor, my mother's place was at the end of hall on the left side. At the very end of the hallway was a window with a locked bar keeping it secured so a resident couldn't slip out. Every staff member in the unit had a key to unlock the window if there was an emergency. Everything was built with safety and comfort for the residents.

I punched in the code to unlock my mom's apartment door, violently twisting the knob and throwing the door open. It banged against the wall.

Grayson spun, hand on the butt of his weapon.

"You want to shoot me?" I stalked toward him, scanning the room for my mother. Masking tape marked off the floor around my mother's kitchenette. "Arresting me isn't enough for you?"

"You broke in here." His arm dangled by his side.

"I belong here." I jabbed a finger toward the detective. "You don't."

My mother was huddled in a corner of her living room, squished between the couch and the wall. A nurse sat on the couch, trying to coax my mom to sit next to her. The detective was lucky my mom was my main priority because the other instinct rolling through me was to punch him in the jaw.

Tears flowed down my mother's cheeks, dipping into the deep lines on face. "I did it. He said I did it."

Rage roared through me. What had the horrible man accuse my mom of? He was worse than a Grinch. Worse than Scrooge. He was like a parent who took away Christmas from a child and made them watch their siblings enjoy the holiday. I kissed the top of her head, running my hand over her white hair. "I don't care what he said or told you. Mom, you did nothing wrong. He's an awful man. A liar."

"Watch what you're saying, Ms. Winters." The warning in Grayson's words came through as clear as ringing Salvation Army bells.

I didn't care. No one messed with my babies. No one messed with my mom. I knelt beside her, drawing her trembling form into my arms. "You're the one who should watch themselves. How dare you come here? You have no right." I'd contact everyone I could think of and tell them how a detective treated my mother. The mayor. The newspaper. Television. Brett. Twitter.

"The nurse allowed me in." The man was too pleased with himself, increasing my ire.

"He said he had some questions about your divorce." The nurse wrung her hands. "There was a little confusion about it."

She was new. I looked at her nametag. Evelyn Graham. She was around my age, mid-forties, and had dyed bright red hair falling in a tangled mess of faux curls to her shoulders and was makeup free. I couldn't recall seeing her around Season's Greetings, although we were a small town, it wasn't so small everyone knew each other.

"He tricked you. He wanted to question my mother about me, and you gave him the opportunity to do so."

"I was doing what I felt was right."

"Strangers are not to visit my mother. It's in her chart." Why did they pair this nurse with my mother?

"He's a police officer," Evelyn whispered, looking at the ground. "Why wouldn't I trust him?"

My anger toward the nurse ebbed away. She was right. We were raised to trust law enforcement. Heck, I usually trusted those with a badge. My son always adored police officers and the job they did—protect and serve—it was why he became one. The person who was in the wrong was the detective for lying to the nurse and bullying my ailing mother.

"Nurse Graham, can you please get Doctor Yielding and call the local police. I want this detective removed from this facility. He has no right to interrogate my mother."

"Your mother," Grayson's voice rose, "admitted to seeing Samuel Waters Thursday afternoon, she is likely the last one to have seen him alive."

"He came here?" I leaned away from my mother, checking her eyes for clarity.

My mother nodded though her brows were scrunched together. Her gaze roamed around the room. She was trying to place herself, figure out where she was—and when. What Grayson didn't understand was that Thursday to my mother might not have been the Thursday that just passed. Time had no meaning to my mother anymore.

"He said he had happy news for you. Your life was going to change." My mother stroked my cheek, a shaky smile developing. "You'd get everything you ever asked from him whether you changed your mind about him or not."

Grayson sneered. "What was Mr. Waters' net worth?"

I ignored him. What the detective didn't want to understand was the only thing I had wanted from Samuel was a divorce. "I think it's time you left, Detective."

"It's important to retrace the final moments of Samuel Waters. It will help determine who might have information about motives and give us some viable suspects. I'd have thought you'd want that Merry Winters."

If I wasn't mistaken, he drew out my last name. Why? There was a reason for everything he said and did. Like visiting my mom. Grayson talked to someone else who sent him to my mother. But who? Everyone in town liked my mother and even me. Some residents found my Christmas love a little over the top and my usual normal cheerfulness hard to take, but no one disliked me enough to hurt my mother.

I aimed my foot to nudge Evelyn's and missed, kicking her ankle instead. She sucked in a pained breath and speed-limped out of the room.

"This situation doesn't involve my mother. I want you to stop harassing her."

"Harass?" A bitter laugh erupted from him. "So, that's the way you want to play this. You want to claim this situation, investigating Samuel's murder, is improper police behavior. It's my job to find the truth when someone is killed. Murdered. Someone is guilty. And no one," his gaze settled on my mother, "is off the hook."

I enclosed my arms around her and glared at him. "You're threatening my mother."

"I'm not the one trying to get away with something," Grayson said. "Someone in this room is."

A breath hitched in my mom's throat then more sobs shook out.

I tightened my hold on her and glared at Grayson. Why was he tormenting an eighty-seven-year-old woman? "My mother did not see Samuel on Thursday. He was instructed not to visit her."

"Why was that?" Grayson asked.

"Because he upset her," I said.

"That's true, Detective," Doctor Yielding entered the apartment and the conversation. She pulled my abandoned utility cart into the room. "We were instructed not to allow Samuel Waters to see Gloria Winters as he was a source of agitation. His visits upset her. Almost as much as yours."

The detective had the good graces to blush. He pulled out a pen and a small notebook from his pocket. A bit of relief flowed through me. He hadn't been taking notes when he talked to my mother, or at least not when I arrived. "When was Samuel banned from seeing Mrs. Winters?"

"About three months ago, if my recollection is correct," Doctor Yielding said, "though I'd need to check Mrs. Winters records to confirm. I do know it was within a day or two of Merry making that request that she filed for divorce."

"Why was that?" Grayson asked.

I answered the question. "He was a jerk to my mom."

"That's interesting because Mrs. Gloria Winters told me she saw him on Thursday. November fifteenth. She was quite insistent on the date being correct. I asked her numerous times if she was certain. She said yes."

"Of course, she agreed with you. She knew that was the answer you wanted, and it stopped you from asking again." My body felt heated. I fidgeted as a flashflood of emotions rushed through me. I knew it was anger and not the onset of hot flashes. The detective's questioning convinced my mother of her rightness. If asked a question multiple times, my mother responded with the same answer. She never liked her memory questioned, even more so now when it was slipping away from her day by day.

"It was an important detail to the case." Grayson snapped the book closed. "Samuel Waters is dead. You don't seem to care about that."

I took some deep breaths, hoping to settle my anger. "I do care. I care that his daughter is basically an orphan. I care that Bonnie Waters is now a widow. She and Samuel were married a week before he died. It must be heartbreaking for her. I'm also saddened for Samuel as he likely had finally found his true soulmate and he died right after."

"Why do you keep changing the truth? There is a distinction between died and was killed. Samuel was murdered. Someone ended his life. It wasn't natural," Grayson said.

My mother wailed, a sound from the soul. Heart breaking. If terror and hopelessness had a sound, it was like the one coming from my mother. Her body quaked. Eyes were cloudy as if she was far away. Some other time or place. She was leaving the here and now. Leaving me. Going to a place in her mind where she felt safe.

I grabbed onto my mom, desperate to hold her together. Terror and rage pulsed through me. I had never disliked a person as much as I did Detective Grayson.

Doctor Yielding knelt beside my mother, checking her pulse. "Detective, I insist you leave."

"Leave my mother alone," my voice cracked. "I'll answer anything you want. Just leave her alone. She doesn't understand what you're asking. She has dementia. She doesn't know when November fifteenth was, you could've asked if she saw him on October thirty-first, or November sixteenth and she'd have said yes."

For the first time since I encountered Detective Grayson in my mother's room, he looked unsure of himself.

"If you'd done all your homework, Detective Grayson," the doctor's voice was colder than the North Pole during a massive blizzard, "you'd know this assistant living facility specializes in memory loss issues. Gloria resides in our memory care unit."

"Is that true?" Instead of the rage that was usually in my mom's voice when her diagnosis was mentioned in front of her, there was hope.

I gazed into her widened eyes.

"So, I might not have seen him just a few days ago? I might not have killed him?"

Shock rendered me speechless and immobile. Frozen. Detective Grayson wasn't trying to prove I killed Samuel, he had a new suspect. My mother.

SEVENTEEN

I fisted my hands and stood, turning to face the detective. First, he tried to use my son against me and now my mother? Hate churned inside me. I was unaccustomed to the raw, blistering emotion and it unsettled me. "She did not see Samuel. You will not railroad my mother."

Our gazes clashed. My mom opened her mouth, struggling to her feet.

Doctor Yielding shushed her and helped her stand. "Don't say anything in front of that Detective, Gloria. He's trying to blame a death on you."

"But I—" She started.

"Don't!" I screamed. "Don't talk."

My mother cowered away from me. Shame filled me.

"Mom, he's tricking you." I gentled my voice.

Detective Grayson let out a dramatic sigh. "I do not think Mrs. Winters murdered anyone. I highly doubt she'd been able to kill him, sneak him out of this building, and place him in a RV that her daughter bought. Your mother misunderstood what I was saying."

My mother looked at me, confusion clear on her face. "Merry, why did you bring this man to visit? Do you need my help deciding if he's the one?"

Heat blasted across my face.

She sized up Detective Grayson. "I don't like him. You can do better, Merry. You need a nice Christmas man. This one isn't a holly jolly type."

She was correct. Grayson was more a Scrooge than Bob

Cratchit.

There was a knock on the door of my mother's apartment. The detective answered it and Drew Harrison, a local handyman around my children's age, entered carrying a piece of carpet and a roll of duct tape worn like a bracelet.

"Want me to come back later, Gloria? You have a lot of visitors right now." The young man looked worried.

Then again, Drew's natural expression was eagerness with a hint of did-I-do-something-wrong. He had hung out with Scotland a few times, though Scotland always said it was because the guy had a crush on Raleigh.

"For what?" My mother's voice was hesitant.

"To lay down the rug in the kitchen area. You said the tile was slippery and you almost fell three times. You were afraid you'd break your hip." Drew ping-ponged his gaze around the room. "Remember?"

She shook her head.

"On Thursday." He looked to us for reassurance.

"Did my mom call you?" I asked.

"No, Samuel did."

"You saw Samuel Waters on Thursday?" The detective broke into the conversation.

"Yeah. Who's he?" Drew dropped the rug and let the tape slide from his arm.

"A detective." Why hadn't my mom told me she needed a rug? Why had she called Samuel? "Mom, you never told me you were having trouble with the tile floor."

"Or the staff," Doctor Yielding said.

Gloria listened to every word. Her brows still furrowed but she was now nodding. "I do remember talking about it, but I don't remember Samuel. Someone told him."

"Who else has been visiting you?" I asked. How many times had my ex-husband visited my mother? Something he was forbidden from doing.

"You. Raleigh. Scotland. The new nurse and Cassie. I don't like the new nurse. I liked Bonnie." My mother fixed an accusatory glare onto me. She kept forgetting that Bonnie was now married to Samuel and that meant my mom's former nurse was no longer trusted.

"Evelyn has only been here for a couple of days, Gloria," Doctor Yielding said. "You have to give her more time."

"Samuel Waters was here on the fifteenth." The detective interrupted.

"Not when I was here." Drew jotted down the measurements onto his hand. "He Facebooked me about the job. I had posted on the town's group page that I was looking for handyman jobs."

I turned my mother to face me. "Mom, why did you call Samuel for help? I would've fixed it for you."

She tilted her head to the side, confusion clouding her gaze for a minute before she smiled lovingly at me and patted my cheek. "It must've been because you were busy with your business, Baby Girl. I know how important it is to you."

A heaviness entered my heart. I blinked to stop the developing tears from sneaking out. "Not more than you. I would've made fixing your unit a priority."

"The staff would've taken care of it for you." Doctor Yielding was as upset as me.

"Samuel said he knew a young man who needed a job. I love to help people and there's not much I can do now. This was something I could do." My mother's voice was strong. "I will not be a burden. I am a capable woman."

Independence. That was why my mom reached out to someone who wouldn't make all the decisions for her. "Don't you like it here?" My voice was soft.

"Don't be sad my Merry Christmas." My mom kissed my cheek. "All is well with me. I agreed to live here after your father died. It was what I wanted. I'm not a pushover. I can go to the library, or the movies, or get my hair done when I want. I don't have to wait for someone to take me."

Gloria Winters was a strong woman. The first sign my mom's

health was declining was when she grew anxious about everything. She called me numerous times a day from a hiding place in her house telling me someone was trying to force themselves into her home. My mother hadn't wanted to live with me as stairs were hard for her to navigate, and she wanted her own place—not to live in someone else's, even her own daughter's house. The unit she lived in had efficiency apartments rather than hospital rooms, though that option was available for residents with those needs.

Drew used the toe of his leather work boot to move the tape away from the detective. "I hope I'm not causing any problem. I asked Samuel's lady friend if it was okay that I was here, and she said it was."

Bonnie. I shot a glare over at Doctor Yielding.

"Why did you ask her?" Doctor Yielding asked. Unlike me, she wasn't willing to jump to conclusions.

Drew withdrew a tape measure from his back pocket and measured along the sections of tape. "Because she works here."

"You were here on Thursday talking with Gloria Winters and Samuel Waters?" Detective Grayson asked, trying to reel us all back to his topic of conversation.

"I was here in the apartment with Mrs. Winters. She showed me where she needed the rug. I taped out the area on the kitchen floor then measured it."

"You talked with Samuel and Mrs. Winters on Thursday. Just not at the same time in the apartment." The detective was trying to make sense of Drew's statements.

Good luck with that. Drew was a rambler. The few times he visited my house, Drew hung out in the kitchen with me while I cooked dinner. I found out that he preferred to chit chat with me rather than play video games with Scotland. I also wondered why my son didn't check on his friend. I had my answer soon enough; Scotland's ears needed a break from the constant chatter. Drew talked about everything and nothing all at the same time. It was a unique gift.

"When did you talk to him? Was it Thursday morning?"

Grayson asked.

My mother rubbed her temples. "You're confusing me with all the questions. What day? What time? Who else was here? I don't know. I thought I spoke to Samuel on Thursday. This young man says no."

Sometime during our loopy-loop conversation with Drew, Evelyn walked back into the apartment and handed Doctor Yielding a red folder, dipping her head and causing her hair to cascade over her face before scurrying out of the room. The words "visitor's log" were stamped on the front.

"I can clear this up." Yielding opened the folder and flipped back a few sheets. She frowned. "Samuel was here that day."

"Bonnie let him see my mom. She should be fired." I clenched my hands.

"Merry, I promise, I'll check into this incident and find out exactly who allowed Samuel to visit with your mother," Yielding said.

"Samuel said he'd pay me today." Drew unfurled the rug, continuing with the job as if nothing was going on around him. "I'm meeting him at Wing King tonight. Said if it was done before you found out, Ms. Winters, he'd give me a big tip." Drew sat back on his heels, sad puppy-dog eyes on me. "You won't tell him? I just found out my girlfriend is pregnant. We can use the extra money."

"Haven't you been following the conversation?" Grayson asked.

"Probably not," I muttered, "Drew is a talker not a listener."

"Sure. You wanted to know if Mrs. Winters saw Samuel on Thursday. He wasn't here when I was in her place. I talked to him outside, in the parking lot. I don't know why everyone is upset about him being here. He didn't come into her apartment."

"He signed the guest book," Doctor Yielding said.

Drew adjusted the rug by an inch then sat back on his heels to study it. He tugged it back a millimeter. "Maybe once he signed his name someone checked it against a list and told him he couldn't visit Mrs. Winters. I'm telling you, he met me outside in the parking lot. Said it was best he didn't go in after all."

"What time was this?" Grayson asked.

Drew heaved out a sigh, scratching his head with the tip of a pencil. "Right before lunch time, I was ticked because I had plans to meet my girl for lunch at my mom's diner and Samuel said no. He said how could a man feed his girl if he didn't have money. I can't mooch food off my mom forever."

"The time." Grayson's irritation was obvious.

"I was here for probably about an hour. Maybe two. Mrs. Winters made me lunch." He smiled fondly at my mom. "Great old gal."

"What time did you talk with Samuel on Thursday the fifteenth?"

"Why do you need to know that? I thought you wanted to know if he was talking to Mrs. Winters not me."

"Because I'm trying to find out who saw Samuel last."

"The police?" Drew offered a guess.

"Samuel's dead. Someone killed the man." My mother, on the other hand, was tired of Drew's cluelessness and had no qualms blurting out the truth. "You might have been the last person to see him alive."

Slowly, Drew's eyes widened, comprehension finally smacking him upside the head. "I can check my phone. I got here about fifteen minutes after he called me."

"Do that." From the expression on Grayson's face, the last thread of his patience was almost completely unraveled.

Drew swiped his finger across and up and down. "Samuel texted at 11:14. I probably got here around 11:29. It takes me fifteen minutes to get here from my house. Unless there's traffic. He told me he had to get to the post office before it closed for lunch and I don't remember Samuel yelling at me for being late, so I had to have gotten here at that time."

"Then you worked in Gloria's apartment for two hours. Putting tape on a carpet," Grayson said.

"And eating lunch," Drew added with a helpful smile.

"Yes, and lunch. It took you quite a while to accomplish one small task," Grayson said.

"The boy loves to talk. Like the rest of you. My head is aching." Gloria rubbed her temples.

Her face was pale. Dark circles were under her eyes. "Let's get you to bed, Mom."

She opened her mouth to argue then closed it, a protective gleam in her eyes. "Yes, help me to my room. If the detective has any other questions, he can ask me later."

"I don't think that will be necessary," Grayson said.

"It never was." I cupped my mother's elbow and led her down the hall. The front door opened and closed. I let go of the anger I clung to, knowing the detective was out of my mother's apartment

She paused in front of her bedroom door and frowned at it. "Why would I do that?"

My mother never closed her door. Never. Even when I was child, she left it open. It was the one disagreement she had continuously with my father. He preferred a closed door at night, for privacy. She wanted it open. She hated feeling caged in. The compromise was that my door was closed at night and a walkie-talkie was on my night stand in case I needed them in the middle of the night. Though, there was one reason my mother closed a bedroom door.

"I bet your clean laundry is sorted on the bed like you always do before you put it in the drawers. You closed the door when the detective knocked."

My mother narrowed her eyes on me. "I don't need you to tell me how I like to do my laundry. Stop reminding me about everything."

I lowered my head. I had embarrassed her today by telling the detective and Drew she had memory problems. I was glad her fighting spirit was back, but saddened I hurt her. It wasn't my intention.

She sighed and hugged me. "I'm sorry I snapped. This is hard for you. It's hard for me. I don't like the new me. I don't like forgetting."

"I love you, Mom. Always."

"No matter what." She pressed her forehead to mine. "You promise?"

I blinked back the tears and wrapped my arms around her. "I promise. No matter what."

She stood, squared her shoulders and walked into the bedroom. Her clothes were laid out on the bed. "I have to finish hanging my clothes before I nap." Her voice was lighter. There was a normal, true-to-her reason for the door being closed. Her clothes, including her unmentionables, were displayed on the bed. My mom liked to lay out her bras and underwear as if she going to wear them.

"I'll help."

She shooed me toward the closet. "You hang, I'll put away my garments into the drawers."

Even at my age, my mom didn't want me seeing her delicates. Holding in a giggle, I picked up an armload of blouses and slacks and went to the closet. Slacks on the purple hangers, blouses on the pink. In the corner was a laundry basket filled with crumbled clothes. Men's clothes.

Gloria hummed "Silent Night" as she arranged her lingerie in the drawer. Quietly, I knelt and looked through the clothes. I yanked my hand back. I recognized one of the shirts. Samuel's. Why was my ex-husband's laundry in my mother's closet? I snagged a pillow case from the top of the closet. I was moving on instinct, not rational thought, every fiber of my being screamed to get the clothes out of my mother's apartment before the detective saw them and made something of it.

I shoved the clothes into the pillow case. How would I get them out? My cart. I'd leave the Christmas décor here and take out the bag of clothes.

"Mom, I brought a Christmas tree to put up. Would you like me to do that today or tomorrow?"

"I don't have space for a tree," her voice was wistful.

"It's a vinyl decal, Mom. It'll go on the wall of your living room. I also have ornament decals to put on the tree."

Gloria clapped her hands. "That sounds wonderful, Merry. Can we do it tomorrow? Or on Friday when the grandchildren are visiting. Let's make a whole day of it. Bake cookies. Decorate the tree. Craft each other a present. Just like when you were little."

Mentally, I rearranged my decorating schedule, planning to do my house tomorrow and Wednesday. "Absolutely. I brought everything with me, so I'll just unload it now. Can I leave it in here?"

"No, the living room." My mother walked over to me and whispered, "Things keep moving around in here."

"Moving?"

"Dresses on the pant hangers. Things just aren't where they should be. I couldn't find your father's picture on my table this morning."

Frantically, my gaze went to the bedside table where my mother kept her favorite framed photograph of her husband. She wanted the first thing she saw in the morning and the last image at night to be my father. The love of her life. And right there, near the edge of the table, was my father's photo. His mouth curved in that special smile of his that said he adored you above all else.

I adjusted the picture. "Here it is."

"Thank you so much for finding it for me." My mother sighed in relief as I fought back tears. "Since the day we got you, you've always been the one who made our lives better."

EIGHTEEN

I yanked open the front door of Season's Living and stepped outside. The cold air cooled my heated skin. The detective had riled me up good. *Cha-ching*. The sound made me smile. It signaled that Merry and Bright Handcrafted Christmas received an Etsy order. I hadn't heard the noise all weekend. I was certain word was getting around about my alleged felonious behavior. I pulled out my phone. Wine glass order. *Need before Christmas* was in the note section. The date fell within our two-week time frame for completing orders. Good. I hated having to message customers and letting them know their order wouldn't reach them by the date they requested unless they purchased the rush option. Most felt it was a way to nickel and dime them rather than considering that they weren't the only open orders on our books.

Pausing on the sidewalk, I texted Bright. *Have an order. My phone has been silent since this incident with Samuel started. Starting to think shoppers were avoiding us.*

A few moments later, Bright responded. *Honey, we were on vacation mode. We voted to put the shop on vacation when either of us are doing a vendor event. Especially during the high season. Since it was a slow event, I knew it was safe to open for custom orders as we didn't have to replenish stock for the event in two weeks.*

Being accused of murder had my brain in a tailspin. I headed for my vehicle. I totally forgot the shop was shifted into vacation mode, thereby not allowing us to receive orders. It was the best choice for us. *Can't believe I forgot.*

Understandable. Hope we get some more cha-chings today. Me too.

I dropped my phone into my pocket and folded up the utility cart. I started to wrangle it into the back of my SUV when I felt someone breathing down my neck. Jerking around, it slipped from my hand and landed on my foot. I yelped and glared at my potential stalker. Bonnie. My big toe throbbed. A tip of the folded cart had smashed onto it. Thankfully, I was wearing boots, or my toe would've likely been broken. I couldn't afford a foot injury. I had a roof to decorate. It was a heck of a time getting up the ladder with a wreath and Santa, his sleigh, and eight not so tiny reindeer with two good feet. I hated to envision the project with a broken foot.

"Sorry," she said, not appearing the least bit apologetic.

"It's not good to sneak up on people."

"Maybe that's what happened to Samuel. Snuck up on someone and she...I mean he or she...killed him in their frightened state."

That's how she was going to play this. Fine. She wasn't in her work uniform. "Or someone got in trouble for allowing her husband to see a patient he was forbidden to visit and was fired for it and now has time to accost people in a parking lot." Take that.

Tears filled her eyes. "My husband was found murdered Friday night. I was given leave."

I was a horrible person. It was my turn to apologize. "I'm sorry, Bonnie, that was uncalled for. It's been stressful lately. Probably more so for you. Samuel visited my mom on Thursday and upset her."

"Who let him?" Fire burned in her eyes. "It's in Gloria's chart that Samuel and strangers aren't permitted to speak with her one on one. I will talk to human resources and the patient care team and have it investigated for Gloria."

Either she was good actress, or I had it all wrong. The woman was livid on behalf of my mother. "Doctor Yielding is checking into what happened. You came over to talk with me because..." I trailed off.

"To ask for a copy of the divorce decree. The insurance agent is still stone-walling me. The date and signatures on the wedding license are blurred. I was going to make a fresh copy of our wedding license, but Samuel sent it to get framed, and the two places in town that do framing don't have it. If I can get a copy of the decree, the date on it could help settle everything."

"Knowing Samuel, he found a cheaper place online and sent it. Did you check his computer?"

"Can't. Detective Grayson took it as evidence."

My curiosity overtook good judgment. "What else did he take?"

"Lock box where we kept our documents. Financial records he kept at the house. Can I stop by your house to get a copy?"

I hated admitting the truth especially since Bonnie stood up for my mom. "I don't have one."

Rage sparked in her eyes. She grabbed my arm, her nails digging through my coat into my arm. Those things were a weapon. "Then get one."

"When I have time." I gripped her wrist. "Let me go."

Bonnie stared at her hand as if she didn't know how it got there. She shoved her hands into her coat pocket. "I'll keep asking you until you do."

"Call Milton." I threw my attorney to the she-devil. I had paid him a small fortune for the divorce since Samuel dragged it out.

"I have. He won't return my calls."

Couldn't say I blamed him if she left a message using the same tone of voice. It was Thanksgiving week. The beginning of hunting season. "He's out hunting. He usually comes back home Wednesday as his wife would kill..." The ugly word stopped me cold. How easy it was said. I was going to work on taking it out of my everyday vocabulary. "Would be very upset if he wasn't home for Thanksgiving."

Bonnie covered her face with her hands and released a heartbroken moan. "I just want to bury my husband."

"Helen, Samuel's mom. He tells her everything and stores

things at her house. I bet she has the divorce decree."

"Why would Samuel give his mother his divorce decree?"

"She's making a never-ending scrapbook for him." Or at least it had been never-ending. My heart broke for her. A mother should never have to complete the scrapbook of their child's life.

"She hates me. There's no way she'd help me."

"That's not true," I said, not quite knowing if I was telling the truth. Helen had not been happy with Samuel when we divorced. She assumed, rightly, that it was all his fault and told him in no uncertain terms he was an idiot. Samuel had been shocked. He was the quintessential momma's boy and it was the first time she chose another person over him.

"She didn't like me when we were married and hates me more now that Samuel is dead. She thinks I'm setting you up and is telling whoever she can."

"She told you that?"

"Not in those words."

"I'll stop by Helen's for you and see if she has a copy."

It was Monday. Errand day and Helen had no one to take her, unless Cassie stopped by to check on her grandmother, but I had a feeling the girl was deep in anger and grief and had no thoughts for anyone else. Since Helen was still thinking fondly of me, she might give a hint about Samuel's possible newly attained wealth.

Before I drove to Helen's house, I called Brett. I adjusted the heat in my SUV. The temperature was dropping. I hoped he had time to meet for lunch before he headed back to Virginia. I wanted to know what the judge said. Then again, it might be better not to be out in public when we discussed my case.

He answered on the third ring. "Be brief. I'm in Alexandria. Emergency hearing. Had to postpone the meeting in Season's Greetings to tomorrow."

When you had an in demand, hotshot attorney, you weren't at the top of the list. "The RV was trashed, local police have it under protective custody. Some guy named Gary Meadows posted on Samuel's Facebook that he told him trouble follows. And, I had a run-in with Detective Grayson. He was interviewing my mother."

"He was what? Hold on." Brett excused himself. A door opened and closed.

I shifted in the driver's seat, jotting down some ideas for some new Christmas gifts onto the notebook I kept on the passenger seat. My best ideas always seemed to come at the most inconvenient times. If I waited to write them down, they'd vanish, no matter how much I believed that I wouldn't forget them. I never remembered any of my great ideas at a later point in time, but the bad ones always reappeared over and over.

Brett returned to our phone conversation. "Detective Grayson questioned your mother? A woman diagnosed with dementia and living in a memory care unit."

Tears rushed into my eyes. I swiped them away. "Yes. He says questioning, but my mother said he was blaming her for Samuel's death."

"That's improbable."

"That's what the detective said. He insists my mother misunderstood. For some reason, he believes my mother was the last person to see Samuel alive."

"Why does he think that?"

"Samuel was at Season's Living on Thursday morning. Another guy confirmed he was there that day but said Samuel didn't come into my mom's room."

"Stay away from the detective."

"I'm not going to him. He's going to my mom. I won't let him harass her."

"I'll take care of it."

"What if he does it again before you can take care of it? You're busy."

"Merry, have I ever let you down?"

I bit my lip. When he was helping me wasn't the time to remind this ex-husband of all the times he hadn't.

"I withdraw that question. If the detective comes around, you tell him to call your attorney. Nothing else. No matter what he says or asks, the response is call my attorney. I'll be in Season's Greetings tomorrow. I'll call Season's Living and advise the staff to call me immediately if an officer comes to speak with your mother."

"You're my mother's attorney too?" Brett was picking up a lot of new clients: me, Grace, Abraham, my mom.

"If the detective makes it necessary, yes. I'll be sure to fill his superiors in on why Detective Grayson doesn't want to make that a necessity. On the other issues, I'll contact the local police and see if they have any theories on who vandalized your RV. I'll have members of my team investigate Gary Meadows. Stay off Samuel's Facebook page. A detective just might place something on the deceased's timeline to prove that an ex-wife is fibbing when she said she had nothing to do with the man."

"I know how I can prove that I wrote the correct day. My neighbor Cornelius Sullivan. He started a post on the Season's Greetings Facebook page complaining about the RV being in front of my house. If I had it there Thursday night, he'd have called the cops then. Just like he did last night when Grace and I were unloading it. He fussed about it Friday morning when Cassie drove it to me."

"There's some good news."

I kept friend requesting Gary Meadows to myself.

NINETEEN

I turned on the radio before heading to Helen's house, planning to get caught up on the goings on around our area. The news came on and the big story was a warning of an impending snow storm coming Wednesday evening as people were traveling to their holiday destinations.

"We advise travelers to leave early on Wednesday or wait until Friday. It's a doozy of a storm, and the less people on the roads the better. If you're one of the ones who think snow can't stop you, pack plenty of blankets, water, and non-perishable foods before you venture out. Expect worse bumper-to-bumper holiday traffic than usual on the interstate."

My heart sunk. I might be alone for Thanksgiving. Or if not alone, without Scotland. There was a chance Raleigh could get off work early but not her brother. He was scheduled from eight a.m. to four p.m., and if the weather was bad, he'd likely need to stay. I knew the day that all my children couldn't come home for a holiday would arrive, but I hadn't expected it to happen so soon.

"If you haven't stocked up on necessities for the storm, make sure to do it today before the worst hits or the shelves are bare," the newscaster advised.

I was nearing One Stop, the gas station slash convenience store where the winning lottery ticket was sold. There was a huge sign with "Winning Lottery Ticket Bought Here," written in a block font. Dollar signs were placed around the words. Samuel played every Tuesday and Friday, buying one Easy Pick and one ticket with his lucky numbers. Had Samuel won? Was that why the winner hadn't come forward? They were dead.

The message Gary Meadows left on Samuel's Facebook page flashed in my head, *Told you, man, trouble follows.* The theory had locusts swarming in my stomach. I fisted my hand and placed it on my stomach, hoping it stopped the brewing battle. Would an employee be able to tell me if Samuel bought the winning lottery ticket?

I parked in front of the store. I opened a browser on my cell phone and typed in lottery winner who—and the words "died tragically" popped up. With shaking fingers, I tapped on the link and read the stories. My hand shook even worse, so I tightened my hold on my phone, the case pressing into my palm and fingers, leaving a mark. Some of those tragic deaths were winners who had been murdered shortly after having won. I clicked over to my Facebook page and checked my friend request. Gary still hadn't accepted it. Was that what he warned Samuel about? Samuel had posted his first vague Facebook post after the winning numbers had been drawn. Had he been boasting about winning twelve million dollars?

Images flickered in my brain. The CDs in the driver door holder. Paper containers in the wrong order. Vinyl on the floor of the RV. The hole near the vent. The items in the wrong place in my garage. Someone was searching for the ticket.

A person who knew Samuel bought it. Was that what Samuel had eluded to and what he wanted to tell me? He won twelve million dollars. Why tell me? *To let you know what a catch you let get away.* My self-respect and my mother's well-being wasn't worth twelve million dollars, or any amount of money.

Coldness griped my scalp. I jerked my attention away from the phone and scanned the area. No one was lingering outside in the misting rain. There was one way to find out if Samuel bought his ticket here. Slipping out of my car, I yanked up the hood of my coat and ran into the store.

The store was empty. Since I was there, I grabbed a gallon of milk, a loaf of bread, and toilet paper before the local stores were cleared out. I placed the items on the counter, searching for any sign of any more information about the winning lottery ticket. There wouldn't be anything with Samuel's face on it, but it might state the day the ticket was bought.

"Customers have also been picking up a lighter and batteries in case the power goes out. Would you like to add some to your purchase?" The cashier asked.

I followed his suggestion and added them to my order. Beside me was a case filled with scratch-off tickets and a machine to print out the lottery tickets. Right above was a security camera. And if my guess on the motive for Samuel's murder was correct, the winning ticket brought him death instead of riches.

I handed over my debit card. "Did you sell the winning ticket?"

"Have no idea. I don't know who won." His gaze skittered around the store, almost like he was looking for someone else to help.

"Why does my question make you nervous?"

"We've had people asking us that ever since it was announced our store sold the ticket. My parents have been harassed by the police, scammers with fake tickets thinking my parents had the money to give them, and anyone else looking for a quick dollar. I keep telling my folks to take down the sign out front, but they said they had to have it up."

"Maybe the security footage shows who bought it."

He pivoted and stared at the camera that was pointed toward the machine and cash register. "If it does, I sure wouldn't share it with anyone. People deserve their privacy. With as many whackos as there are nowadays, they deserve to be safe. Is there anything else? I see someone needs help in the back." He placed my items into a bag, double bagged it, then handed it to me.

I was on to something here. The snow crunched under my feet as I walked to my car. I'd talk to Brett about it and see if he could request the tapes. Later. I doubt he'd be happy I was on my way to Helen's house. This was one of those times it was better to seek forgiveness from your attorney than get his permission first.

With my mission on my mind, I carefully navigated the snow-covered roads to Helen's house, praying the roads remained opened and relatively clear until we ran her errands and found a copy of my divorce decree.

Helen lived at the end of a paved road, her nearest neighbors half a mile away. She liked the peace and quiet, and now I was worried it was too peaceful and quiet. If someone came after Helen thinking she might have money, there was no one near to help her.

I parked in her driveway and carefully placed my foot on the walkway. It was slippery. There was a nice spot along the walkway to add some wooden hand rails that blended into the style of the house. I hated thinking of the widow falling on the ice when she went to get her mail. Helen didn't own a cell phone and could be stranded for hours, injured and in the cold. Whether she wanted one or not, I was getting Helen a cell phone. Even if I had to enlist her granddaughter's help. Helen had a hard time saying no to Cassie.

Helen opened the door before I knocked. "Come in." She shuffled out of my way. The gait different than her usual bouncing step. The light was gone from her eyes. She seemed frail. Old. The last few days had stripped her of her vibrancy—or rather the death of her son had.

"I'm so sorry, Helen."

She leaned into me. Sobs shook her body. "My boy. My boy is gone. Why would someone kill him?"

I wasn't sharing my theory with his mom. No reason was a good reason and knowing it was about money wouldn't relieve any of her grief. I led her to the couch and helped her sink onto the cushion. "Let's sit."

She grabbed a wad of tissues and mopped up the tears streaming down her cheeks. "I'm sorry. I can't stop myself from crying."

"Don't apologize." I kept an arm draped around her shoulders. "Would you like to talk about Samuel?"

The hardest part about death was no one wanted to talk about the deceased. When my father died, everyone acted as if uttering his name was a curse. People tripped over themselves with apologies if they uttered it. I wanted to tell them I loved hearing it. Needed to hear his name. I wanted a reminder that other people knew and loved him. Rather, a lot of friends behaved like he never existed, even going so far as to not utter the word "father" in front of me as if I'd break down into a wailing mess.

"What I want is to find out who killed my boy." She gripped my hand. The pressure turned my knuckles white.

I shifted uncomfortably. She knew I was a suspect. If it made her feel better to hurl verbal abuse at me, I'd accept it. I hated seeing Helen look old and like she was giving up on life. Her granddaughter needed her now more than ever.

She stroked my cheek. "No matter what the Morgantown detective hints at, I know in my heart you didn't kill Samuel."

"It means a lot to me that you don't believe that horrible accusation."

"Never about you, darling. Is there a reason you came by today? You have to know people will talk about it, and that detective could make a huge ado about you seeing me."

"I know Monday is your errand day and wanted to see if you needed someone to take you."

"I'd like that. I do need to get to the post office." She nodded toward a pile of Christmas cards. "Have you seen Cassie? I haven't seen my granddaughter since Friday. She stopped by briefly and no word from her since then. I was hoping she was staying with you."

"She's not at my house. Bonnie told me told that Cassie hasn't been there." Worry flooded through me. Where was she staying?

"I hope..." Helen trailed off, worrying her hands together.

"What?"

"It's probably nothing. Knowing my granddaughter, she wants extra attention, and this is her way of getting it. I wouldn't be surprised if the girl is probably sneaking in and out her window. I caught her doing it a few times and told Samuel. He said Cassie liked thinking she was a rebel, but he knew what she was up to. It was harmless. She was still showing up for her shifts at the book store, so he wasn't concerned about it."

Until she fell climbing out the window and broke something. "I guess it's good she has somewhere to go since she and Bonnie don't get along."

Helen looked away, brows drawn down and her lip trembled.

"What's wrong? Please don't tell me nothing."

"Rumors. One should never base facts on them."

"What are people saying?"

"Lynne, Cassie's mother, is in town."

I drew in a sharp breath. "Do you think Cassie is with her?" That was good. Right? Cassie needed someone to lean on. Except why now? After almost eighteen years, Cassie's mother reenters her life—right around the time Samuel won money. Had Samuel reached out to his ex? Maybe Samuel had chosen Bonnie over Cassie and to soften the blow, had found a way to bring Lynne back into his daughter's life. What better way to feel better about kicking your child out then handing her off to her mother?

"I think Cassie is trying to play everyone against each other." Helen let out a huge sigh. "Someone killed her father and she doesn't know who to trust. The police are pointing at you and I know Cassie is having a hard time believing that. Bonnie was at work, so it couldn't be her."

With Bonnie having a solid alibi, it meant the other possible suspect was Cassie. "According to Cassie's Facebook page, she believes I killed her father."

Helen clutched my hands. "She doesn't mean it. She's hurting and lashing out. Please don't take it to heart."

It was hard not to.

"Please tell me the real reason you came today. I'm certain your attorney wouldn't approve of you being here. If you're throwing aside advice, it's because you need something."

She had me. "A copy of the divorce decree."

"The divorce decree?" She looked puzzled.

"Mine and Samuel's. Bonnie has been pestering me about it."

"Of course, she has." Helen frowned. "The woman has left messages for me. I didn't feel like talking to her."

"She called Milton and he's out of town. I haven't received one in the mail yet, but Samuel had to have one to get remarried, and he wouldn't have thrown it away. Your house is the only other place I could think of that he'd store it."

"I don't recall seeing it." She tapped her lip. "Then again, my son knew I wasn't happy about it."

"Bonnie said it's not at her house. She's looked everywhere."

"I'll check in Samuel's scrapbook. Maybe he slipped it into the memory pocket. There are boxes in the attic of some of Samuel's mementos. You can look up there. He was rummaging around up there Thursday morning."

The day he died. "Sure."

I went into her garage and pulled down the steps leading to the attic. Cold air shot down. More insulation was needed up there. I climbed up, making a mental note to add it to my list of projects for Helen's house.

Boxes were scattered all around the attic. Some open, some closed. Samuel made a mess up here. Was he looking for, or hiding, something? The first box was filled with Christmas decorations. I pushed it toward the door, planning on hauling it down for Helen. There were a few more and I moved them over.

The back of the attic was more of a mess than the front. Old clothes, comics, and toys were strewn around. Samuel had been looking for something. But what? Set off to the side was a box filled with yearbooks and photographs. A magnetic photo album on top was open. There were pictures of a younger Samuel with various women and an empty spot where a picture had been, a few tendrils of the backing paper remained on the sticky sheet.

I flipped to the next page, again another missing photo. Throughout the book, there was a photo missing here and there. Who had Samuel removed from his photographed life? Lynne? Or had someone removed themselves from it?

I tucked the book under my arm and carried it down. The last thought refused to leave me. Had someone else tampered with the book? Did Samuel invite someone to his mom's home or had someone found a way into the grieving mother's home?

I tested the garage door. It was a sturdy metal door controlled by a standard door opener remote. Easy to hack. I knew that because Scotland warned me of the possibility if I switched over to one. He insisted I take him shopping with me when I replaced the door. I'd call Paul and ask him to check Helen's door for security issues.

Helen was sitting on the couch, staring at a scrapbook on her lap. Her thin fingers caressed the cheek of her son. "This is his last scrapbook. I never thought I'd make a last one."

I placed the one I found in the attic on the coffee table. "Would you like to look at it with me?"

Tears shone in her eyes. "Are you sure? I know your relationship with Samuel was painful at the end. I'm sorry he hurt you."

"He wasn't who I expected him to be," I treaded carefully, "and I'm sure I wasn't who he expected either. Some people make great friends but not so good spouses to each other."

"Was that how it was with your first husband?"

I nodded. "I'm great at making friends just not in finding true love."

"Or our expectations for true love are a little unrealistic. Even if a person loves you, they will disappoint you. Nothing is perfect. Even true love." She closed the book. "How about we look at this later? The snow is still falling. We should get going before the snow starts sticking more."

"Did you find the divorce decree?"

She shook her head. "Not in the attic either?"

"Nope. I found a photo album in the attic with some photos taken out of it." I opened it up.

Frowning, she flipped through the pages. "I've never seen this album. I fussed at him for not taking any pictures when he was in college. Said he didn't have any and here they are. Why did Samuel hide it up there?"

And lie about it. "Do you mind if I take it with me?"

"I don't know." She clutched it to her chest.

I pointed at the picture size blank spots. "There was someone who didn't want to be in his book anymore. It might be the person who killed him."

"Take care of it for me." She kissed the book then handed it to me.

"Do you still feel up to doing your errands?"

She planted her hands onto the couch cushion and pushed herself up. There was a fire in her eyes and her mouth was no longer trembling. Her strength had returned. "Yes. Let me get my mail."

TWENTY

"Do you mind parking by Harold's Hotdogs? I've been cooped up since last Monday. I'm having a good day today and would love to stretch my legs some."

"Are you sure? It's raining." I was surprised she was having a good day. Helen had arthritis in her hips and the dampness in the air usually set it off, coupled with a wet sidewalk, it would be harder for her to walk.

"I know the weather, and I know my body. I need to stretch out my muscles and joints or I'll never be able to use them." There was a tenseness in her voice I never heard from her.

She was an adult and could make health decisions for herself, plus I was sure she didn't want to be reminded about her precarious health situation. She had been diagnosed with breast cancer a year ago and had been in remission though the last mammogram had a hot spot. As Samuel and I divorced soon after her last appointment, I hadn't heard if it was nothing or if the cancer had returned. If she wanted me to know about her health, she'd tell me.

"I'm sorry." I pulled into a space right in front of Harold's. "I was out of line."

"Don't you fret. The last few days have been trying for both of us. I'll just head over to the bank then the post office. I'll meet you back here." She grinned at me. "After I stop at Harold's for a corn dog. I have a hankering for something fried even if it's not good for me. Want one?"

"Sure." I had meant to decline as Christmas cookie season was about to start, but the impish look in her pale blue eyes had me wanting to throw food caution to the side. "I'm going to head over to the bookstore. Rachel usually places an order for a Christmas sign depending upon her theme."

"While you're there, you can ask if Cassie is scheduled to work this week. If the girl doesn't come see me, Grandma will come to her." Helen centered a knowing look on me and exited the car, the bright red envelopes of her Christmas cards sticking out from her purse. She knew I hadn't planned just to go see about business. I was also checking on Cassie.

I headed toward One More Page, the bookstore owned by my friend Rachel Abbott. The store was in the middle of Main Avenue, making it the perfect location viewing of the annual Christmas Parade. It was why her window decoration sign was important to her. She knew a lot of people would see it and she wanted to draw them in. Rachel had a standing order for every Christmas, and I always made it right after the Morgantown Holiday Bazaar as she knew I was swamped making products for the show.

The doorbell buzzed as I entered the store.

"Welcome to One More Page," a voice echoed from the back.

For the most part, Rachel was a one-woman show. She made enough to stay afloat but not to hire more than one part-time worker, two times a week. Cassie's love of reading and frequent visiting of the bookstore got her the job.

"It's Merry. Stopping by for ideas for your window sign."

"Great! I'll be out in a few, placing an order for a new book that the internet is buzzing about. Want to get it in before the parade. I hope it makes it here in two weeks."

"Wishing you tons of customers." I walked over to the window and studied it. So far, it was a blank canvas, nothing to indicate the theme Rachel wanted. She usually had a few items on the large sill...books, stuffed animal, trinkets.

"Santa." Rachel's voice carried over to me. "It's all I got right now."

Not as elaborate as her usual themes. It was easier to work

with, which was good since my current life focus was figuring out a better murder suspect than me. I turned slowly, mapping out each area of the store in my head. Santa. North Pole was done at the craft show. We could narrow it down to one part of the North Pole.

"Santa's workshop," I said as Rachel entered the store area.

She grinned. "I was thinking more along the lines of Santa's office. For the front window, I'd like a naughty and nice list, the nice side I'd have names of residents, and the naughty will be well-known book villains."

Brilliant and easy. "I can have that done by the beginning of next week."

"Great. I'll send you the names." Rachel trailed off, her smile hinting there was something she wanted me to know but was above gossip.

I considered Rachel a good friend and enjoyed her company. The one aspect of her personality that annoyed me was her insistence she wasn't a gossip yet told everyone what she knew...once you inquired about it. She felt she wasn't gossiping if she didn't bring up the topic. I guessed she wanted to tell me something related to Samuel. It was currently the most gossip worthy topic in Season's Greetings. I'd venture into the subject by asking about Cassie.

"How has Cassie been? She's a little angry with me so I haven't wanted to call her since her father died."

Rachel heaved out a sigh. "I've been wanting to talk to you about Cassie."

What had Cassie been saying about me to Rachel? "Has she done something that worries you?"

"I haven't seen her since Samuel died. I left a message that I'd hold her job until she felt up to coming in."

"That's nice—"

Rachel held up a hand, silencing me. "On Thursday, a woman was talking to Cassie. It seemed like an intense conversation. Cassie seemed really upset. I walked over, and the woman left. I caught a bit of their conversation. The woman mentioned something about selling a vehicle."

Maybe I hadn't been the first one Cassie asked to buy the RV. "Who was she?"

"I hadn't seen her around town before. Cassie seems to know her. I saw them in front of Milton's office this morning."

My divorce attorney. Why?

After returning home from dropping off Helen, I called Milton. The message went straight to voicemail. The man was still hunting. Maybe the woman with Cassie needed an attorney, or Cassie was so distraught over something that the woman walked with her to Milton's office, doing a kindness for the girl. Milton and Samuel had been good friends for a while until they had a falling out awhile back, one Samuel refused to talk about. Cassie had talked about the fishing trips her and her dad had gone on with Milton when she was little. The teen was probably still fond of him, and it wasn't a surprise she'd want to see Milton after her dad died. It was likely Samuel had Milton draw up a will, or Cassie was checking to see if Milton knew about a will.

But who was the woman? And old friend of Samuel's? Could she be the person no longer in the photo album? Or Lynne?

I spread the photo albums on my workspace and booted up my computer. The pictures seemed to be from when Samuel was in college at WVU in Morgantown. It was a large school. I flipped through the album again, trying to find another familiar face among the pages. Since Season's Greetings was within two hours of WVU, a lot of graduating seniors attended the large university. Was the missing photo a picture of a local resident?

I couldn't remember Samuel mentioning who he hung out with at college. He had so many friends on Facebook, it would take a long time to narrow down which ones were from his college days, and the detective might be monitoring the page.

Cassie would know. Did I want to drag a teenager into this mess? If Samuel wasn't the one who ripped out the pictures, then it was tied to his murder. I couldn't bring her into this. I wanted her safe.

There was a number one in a blue circle on the corner of the icon for my messenger app. It was a message from Gary Meadows.

I don't usually friend strangers, but a pretty woman in Christmas attire catches my interest. Not to mention the seasonal name. Merry Winters. Decided you were worth a risk.

I wasn't quite sure he was, but I had no choice. Or so, I told myself. *I saw your message to Samuel Waters and was wondering how you knew him.*

How is that your concern?

He was my ex-husband.

I watched the messages. No response. My heart thudded. Was this a spy for Detective Grayson? Brett had warned me about the possibility. Would they come beating down my door any minute? Nothing I typed sounded sinister or like a confession. I read what I wrote. Nope. All sounded innocent.

You are that Merry Winters.

What did Samuel say about me?

You were a stickler for rules. He should've given you what you wanted when you asked for it. Wondered if it was too late.

Yes, I responded back quickly.

I guess he got what he deserved.

My fingers flew over the keys; *tap, tap, tap,* the clicks coming fast and furious. *That's a horrible thing to say about a person. He didn't deserve to be killed.*

I wasn't talking about that. Though the man shouldn't have been bragging. Not all one thinks or owns should be discussed in public.

He won the lottery. Didn't he?

There was another long pause before Gary responded back. *You didn't know.*

You did. You had warned Samuel about his social media vague bragging.

Yes, Gary wrote. *I told him he was setting himself up for a big fall.*

How do you know Samuel? He confided a lot to you. Was Gary the person in the photographs? Why did he pop back into Samuel's life now? Did he live around or in Season's Greetings?

I waited for an answer, heart racing. I drew in deep breaths to steady my nerves. The longer there was no response, the more I suspected Gary was a ruse—Detective Grayson in disguise. How did I know who Gary Meadows was? Or that he was who he really was? A person could be anyone on the internet.

After an hour of staring at my phone, I accepted the fact that Gary Meadows had nothing further to say.

I ventured onto his Facebook page and it was filled with movie quotes and lyrics. Shares of places to travel, investing, and fishing. Nothing personal at all on his page. Foreboding weighed me down. Gary Meadows was a pretender.

But why?

The troubling thought followed me as I turned off the light and headed to bed. My life was filled with a list of unanswered questions. All of them centered around Samuel's murder and being accused of it.

Maybe tomorrow, I'd find an answer. Tonight, I was too tired. And truth be told, I was losing hope.

TWENTY-ONE

The first hint of the sun rising streamed through the windows of my craft room, chasing away the darkness. A new day dawned, and I wasn't looking forward to it. I wanted to hide rather than venture out. Samuel's death shook the core of my world. I was looking at people I knew with suspicious eyes and questioning their intent, including a teenage girl. It wasn't me. It wasn't who I was. I didn't like my options: stay optimistic and risk my freedom or become hardened and save it in one way but lose it in another.

I couldn't sleep, so instead of tossing and turning, I caught up on orders. Trying to prove myself innocent of my ex-husband's murder had consumed a lot of time. Christmas orders were coming in fast and furious. I had heard two cha-chings while I was working on the current order: a set of his and her wine glasses with a Christmas wedding theme. A Christmas wedding, what could be more magical? Surprisingly, I had two weddings and neither took place around Christmas.

I hunched over one of Samuel's photo albums as my Cricut chugged away, cutting out the vinyl for an order. My task light was shining down on the magnetic album. Ebenezer whistled by the door and thumped against it.

"You can't come in here." I told him for the umpteenth time. "Customers don't like their gifts coming with fur."

I glanced at my phone. No calls from Brett. I had left him a message this morning to call me since I had figured out why Samuel was killed. Either Brett was driving, or he hadn't had enough coffee to deal with me. I knew he'd lecture me on not staying out of it, a fact he had to know I couldn't do. This was my life. How could I stay out of it?

Ebenezer banged again.

"I fed you breakfast." Even though I skipped it. "Quit it. I mean it."

He squealed. He reminded me of my daughter, having to say the last word.

The vinyl was cut. I grabbed a transfer sheet, trimming it to fit the phrase perfectly. The best way to layer vinyl was to cut transfer sheet pieces to the exact measurement as the foundation piece and line up the edges of the transfer sheet before placing it down. I had ruined some projects before I discovered the tip on YouTube. Now, I saved myself a lot of time and frustration by watching videos first rather than through the good old trial-and-error method.

"We're a Couple of Misfits" played on my phone. Brett.

I snagged my cell. "I know why someone killed Samuel. He won the lottery."

"How do you know this?" He sounded aggravated. Not a good mood to start the day or our conversation.

There was a thump in the hallway. Great. Now Ebenezer was hitting the wall near my bedroom. "Don't you dare gnaw on anymore walls," I corrected the rascal then answered Brett. "He always bought two tickets every Monday and Friday. Cassie keeps asking me about a ticket. It all fits together."

"Are the winning numbers the ones he always played?"

"I don't know. He bought one ticket with his special numbers and the other was an Easy Pick. Four of the numbers are his and his mom's birthday."

"There was no ticket found on Samuel." Horns honked in the background. "This traffic is horrendous."

"That's because the killer has it. All the police have to do is wait to see who turns it in."

"The winner usually has a time frame between six months and a year to collect their winnings."

I grew quiet. Brett sure knew that quickly, either he played the lottery quite a bit or he knew the motive. The man was keeping things from me. "You knew?"

"It's what you're paying me for. To find out those type of things."

"When were you planning on telling me?"

"I didn't have to, your message clued me in to the fact that you already knew."

I switched over from my Cricut program to a browser and plugged winning the lottery in West Virginia into Google. "Six months in West Virginia. Maybe they'll turn it in sooner." I didn't want to be a suspect for six months.

"If someone killed Samuel for the ticket, they're scouring the newspaper. They'll wait until things settled down before they claim the money. What proof do you have that Samuel bought a ticket that day and it was those numbers?"

"What proof does the detective have that I'm guilty? My theory is just as solid as his."

"Yes, which is why you're not in jail and still considered a person of interest."

"I have an official title." It was better than suspect, but person of interest was probably usually upgraded to alleged killer.

"That's one way to put it. Don't panic."

"I'm not panicking." Not yet. I was upset. I hated being a suspect. Who wanted to buy Christmas gifts and décor from an alleged murderer? And I'm sure your mother being a suspect in her ex-husband's murder wasn't a career boost for a police officer. Now Raleigh, she'd find a way to work it to her benefit.

"Traffic is bad. I'd rather not talk even using the headset. I'll call you as soon as I speak to the judge who presided over your divorce."

"I can meet you there."

"No. I want to get information about Samuel's behavior and he might be more forthcoming without you present."

Or in case he had a few words to say about me. "Maybe that's not the right angle. Why prove Samuel was horrible to me? He's dead. It does no good."

"You need a defense."

"I didn't do it."

"Sometimes that's not the best one."

"How about proving who the real killer is? I found a photo album that might have the truth hidden in it."

"What are you talking about?"

I told him about the album I found in Helen's attic and the missing photos. "The first picture that was gone was on a page with Samuel and other girls. I bet this picture is of him and a girl. I just have to find out who she is."

"No, that's not what you need to do." He cursed. "I hate this traffic. It's not going to give me time to swing by your house first."

"You don't need to come here first."

"I don't want that album in your possession. I'm coming to get it. Maybe I can push back the meeting with the judge."

"I can't give it to you. I promised Helen I'd take care of it."

"But—"

"I'm not going to argue with you, Brett. I won't give it to you. It's important to Helen. These are the only pictures she has of Samuel's time in college. She's never even seen them before."

"He hid them from his mom?"

"Yes. That's why I think the missing photos are important to this case."

"Merry, someone was murdered. If you really believe this book has a clue to the identity of the person responsible, it needs to be turned over."

"To the detective who believes I did it? He'll bury it."

"He can't if I turn it over to the local police. There will be a record of it. It's not safe for you to have evidence in a possible murder."

"Because it makes me look guilty?"

"Because a killer needs it to stay out of jail."

Brett's words dumped a whole lot of ugly reality onto me.

"I don't want to scare you, Merry. I want you to be cautious.

Please let me and the police handle this." He hung up.

I stared at the photos, putting my backlog of orders onto the do-later list. Who was missing? And who got rid of them? Samuel? The easiest way to narrow it down was finding out about his friends in college. Considering I married the man, one would think that I knew the answer. Samuel and I had lived in the now, the current years, our pasts were ours alone. It worked for us. For me, it was because I didn't find my past all that interesting to share, for Samuel it appeared he had something to hide.

There was a chance Cassie knew some of the people in the photo or heard stories about her dad's time at WVU. I called her cell. It rang a few times before the call disconnected. She was mad at me about the RV. There was one way to get her attention. Before I talked myself out of it, I typed: *I think I found the ticket. Wasn't it for an event though?*

Closing one eye, I hit sent. My conscience immediately scolding me for lying to the teen to get information I wanted. I had a feeling I'd regret it later. Like when Cassie came over to get her ticket. She wouldn't be so forthcoming with information when she discovered the truth.

Maybe I should text back and make up the type of ticket I found. Back out of the mess before it was created.

I'll be over. Cassie responded. Too late to back out now.

Ok.

It won't be until like two or three hours from now. Must stop at the funeral home. Dad needs a casket and I want to check the clothes Bonnie dropped off. I want Dad to be dressed like Dad. Not like how Bonnie wanted him to dress.

I felt even worse. I was a Grinch. Maybe I could find out what I needed on my own instead of forcing Cassie to come here on false pretenses. Though, I still had to think of a ticket I had meant. Was there a concert coming up that she'd liked and still had tickets available? I could buy one and play it off like her dad must've hidden it as a Christmas gift for her.

I opened Facebook and popped onto Samuel's page. On the

left-hand side of the page, it listed his studies: Communication Studies at WVU and Ceramics.

Ceramics? Why hadn't he mentioned that to me? We had crafting in common. I'd have loved it and might have considered some of his ideas for my business. The man was so analytical and money focused, I didn't think he understood the heart side to the crafting business. Our wares were bought as much on emotion as cost. The products I created weren't necessities to run a household, but filled emotional needs of the customers. Celebration. Remembrance. A piece of happiness to brighten their or someone else's day.

I poked around some more on his page, coming up with nothing but more frustration and anger toward Samuel. There were more instances of him vague bragging about his win, not only on his page, but on others. My heart hurt that his taunts might have very well caused his death. But who would benefit? Cassie? Bonnie?

Me?

There was only one way to pull myself out of the gloom and refocus on work. Christmas. I needed to have some Christmas cheer in my house, and a way to pass the time until Cassie came, and it wasn't late enough to visit my mother. Tuesday morning was her spa day: hair and mani-pedi. After yesterday, my mom needed some pampering and I didn't want to interfere. I had hoped on waiting until the weekend to decorate because my children would be down for Thanksgiving and I'd have help, but the weather wasn't planning on cooperating. The forecast predicted four inches of snow by the weekend. Lovely for holiday pictures, created a great ambiance, but not great for putting lights on the roof. Yesterday's snow hadn't accumulated much, so today was a good day to get it started.

If I wouldn't have too many neighbors complaining, I'd have decorated the outside right after Halloween. I wasn't much of a Thanksgiving decorator so it would've been easy to go from my tame, non-scary Halloween décor to overabundance, glittery Christmasland. While I was knee-deep in Christmas cheer, I'd figure out a good explanation of why I have now misplaced a ticket or was mistaken about finding one.

After donning my all-weather jacket, I tugged on my leather gloves and shoved my phone into my pocket, zipping it up so the cell didn't tumble to the ground. Even with an OtterBox case, I didn't think the phone could handle a two-story plummet.

I opened the garage and a strong wind rattled the door as I pushed it up. With the wind blowing, I opted to put up the icicle lights and wreath, leaving Santa and his team of reindeer for another day. There was no way I was lugging those up the ladder.

The closer I was to the metal shelving units holding the boxed lights, the more I felt like bugs were skittering along my skin, picking at my nerves like they were guitar strings. The icicle lights weren't on the second shelf. I always stored the lights in the order I placed them, leaving the top shelf for items I rarely used. I had to remind my son that lights didn't go on the top shelf.

I wrangled the ladder to the right-hand side of the house. It was the easiest spot to climb onto the roof and then work my way over to the center to hang the wreath. The hanging of the wreath was the most dangerous part of today's holiday decorating plan. The wreath went on the flat portion of the box gable roof. The walkway near that section of the roof was crumbling and the feet of the ladder weren't leveled. Another item on my to-do list.

I tested the ladder by bouncing on the first rung. I wasn't big on heights, but I adored Christmas lights and the only way to get them up was doing it myself. There wasn't much that would keep me from having the magical Christmas season I planned. I tied one end of a ten-foot rope around the wreath and the other around my waist, making sure the rope dangled behind me. Next, I looped the strands of icicle lights around my torso, crossbody purse fashion.

Since I wasn't putting everything up today, I hoped I heard less complaints from Cornelius. You'd think with such a Christmassy first name, he'd be on board with decorating for the holiday, but he loathed the Christmas season and he bombarded all of Season's Greetings with his reasons.

The main theme of his hatred of the season was people. He thrived on being a hermit and too many people were interested in his well-being during Christmas time. People brought over food, invited him to meals, sang carols from the sidewalk, delivered presents and all other sorts of goodwill, which he despised. No one expected anything from him and yet when the air started to chill, his normally congenial and dismissive disposition turned sour. Even more Grinch-like than the Grinch himself.

When I reached the roof, I scooted on my behind to the center and leaned over, using the grabber to lower the wreath the last few inches I needed. Singing "Jingle Bells" to calm my nerves, I lowered the grabber and the wreath. It took me a couple tries to place the wreath onto the hook.

The next mission to Christmasify the house: hanging the icicle lights, an easier task since Scotland had left the tabs in the gutter. I had the icicles on the right side of the house placed in record time. Keeping my arms out to stabilize my balance as I walked up the pitch of the roof, I headed for the other side. As I started the descent on the slope, my left foot shot out, skidding on a small icy patch.

Screaming, I fell stomach first onto the roof and grabbed the top edge, stopping my skidding and nearly wrenching my shoulder out of joint. I rested on the roof, choking back tears and waiting for my heart rate to slow. I pulled myself to my knees and sat on the roof, catching my breath. I didn't want to kill myself and thereby ruin my children's Christmas forever.

A gust of wind slammed into me. Once again, I grabbed hold of the roof, hanging on for dear life. The lights would have to wait until later. I righted myself, sitting firmly on the roof, and bracing my feet onto the slope. I should've brought the rope with me and latched myself to the structure.

How in the world would I get back to the other side? I rested my hand on my coat pocket. The fire department didn't need to waste their resources plucking a woman with a hare-brained idea for hanging up Christmas lights the day after a snowfall.

I could shimmy my way to the end of the roof and jump to the tree. I wasn't sure how good I was at jumping anymore. The last time I tried making a six-foot leap I was eighteen-years-old and trying to escape a dog—and soon some parents—chasing me. I was almost twenty-eight years older now, and my physical conditioning hadn't got any better. The dog had left some teeth marks in my ankle until I was rescued by the owner—Brett.

That was the first and last time I ever agreed to a dare. My mother hadn't been too happy when she received a call about my breaking and entering the house of a rather important family. I hadn't been trying to break into the house, but out of it, as Brett's parents returned home unexpectedly and I wasn't allowed to be there. I should've gone with my instinct of going out the front door and claiming to be a pizza delivery person. Maybe there was a good reason Brett's parents weren't overly fond of me.

The wind picked up and I was getting cold. The roof wasn't icy on the other side. I could crawl toward the ladder. It was the safest of all my plans. I pulled myself up and over then reached the ladder. Or at least where I had placed the ladder.

Open mouthed, I stared down at my ladder tipped onto the grass. Now what? Tears filled my eyes. Mother Nature had it in for her. I blinked away the tears, the small amount already staining my glasses and dotting a few points of my vision. If I cried, I'd still be stuck, and my face would freeze. How in the world would I get down now?

Jump? Nope. I needed all limbs working to craft and finish decorating my house. I sat down on the roof, the cold seeped through my jeans. Cupping my chin in my hands, I braced my arms on my raised knees, and heaved out a sigh. I had no choice. I had to call for help.

I tugged out my phone. A muffled bang floated to me. I paused with my finger on the home button. I remained still and quiet. What was that noise? *Bang.* It sounded like it was coming from inside my house. Ebenezer was running loose but he wasn't big enough to knock over anything that loud.

My eyes widened. Someone was in my house! The ladder hadn't fallen over. It was placed on the ground. "Get out of my house! I know you're in there. I hear you. I'm calling the police."

The back door opened and closed.

I scrambled on my hands and knees to the other side of the roof. A figure wearing a down jacket jumped up and grabbed the top of the fence. An orange cap was pulled low on their head. There was a flash of bare ankle as their sweat pants pulled up. I fumbled with my phone, trying to activate the camera and take a picture. The phone slipped from my hand, cartwheeled down the roof and smacked onto the ground.

I didn't have a picture of the culprit.

Or a way down.

TWENTY-TWO

Now what? I gingerly sat on the roof and contemplated my situation. Was there a way I could get Cornelius's attention? The surefire way was to turn the Christmas lights on as he was a stickler for rules, but the plug was near the ground and if I could reach the plug, I wouldn't be in this predicament.

Next plan? I squished myself into a tight ball, trying to stay warm. No other bright, or even not so bright ideas sprung into my mind. I shivered. The wind was cutting through my jacket. A strong gust blew. I braced my hands on the roof, and hunched over, praying a crosswind didn't catch me. This was getting worse.

Brett would be calling me back. I could rely on that and the fact that if he didn't reach me, he'd come to see what I was up to. Cassie should be coming by soon and she'd put the ladder back. Unless, she was the one who knocked it over and snuck into my house to find the ticket herself. There went finding out who Samuel was eliminating from his college years. Samuel was raised here. Lived here his whole life. Everyone knew him, heck even my attorney—that was it. Milton. Milton had been friends with Samuel from toddlerhood until their junior year of college. He'd know who was missing from the photos.

"Are you all right?"

I scooted to the edge of the roof. Paul was looking at me.

"Yes. The ladder blew over. I was trying to figure out a way down."

"I heard over the scanner that some crazy woman was crawling across a roof." Paul placed the ladder close to me and held it steady.

Could always count on Cornelius's dislike of Christmas. "In this instance, I'll let being called a crazy woman slide." I started down the ladder.

"When I heard the address, I figured you were putting up the Christmas lights. I called the dispatcher and said I'd stop and check it out since I was in the vicinity. The weather this weekend will be terrible, and I knew you wouldn't want to put it off until the following weekend when it cleared. Why didn't you call for help? Scotland told me you were the independent type though this seems to be taking it too far."

A rock formed in my stomach. I wasn't sure how I felt about my son talking about me to his friends. Had my boy disliked Samuel so much he was trying to find me a better suitor?

"I dropped my phone." I stepped off the last rung and bumped into Paul.

He placed a hand under my elbow, steadying me. "Careful, I'd hate to see you get hurt."

His voice was low, intimate. My face heated. I moved away from him, deciding it was best not to acknowledge the comment as I was confused by his tone. "Thanks for your help. I need to locate my phone." And peek in my attic. The bare ankles of the intruder had an idea rooting into my brain: Cassie was living in my attic. How many people walked around with no socks in winter?

"I'll help you."

"That's all right. I'm sure you have more important things to do." I wanted to check out my suspicions on my own. If it didn't appear Cassie had taken up residence in the attic, I'd call the police.

"I know Scotland would appreciate it if I stuck around to make sure you found the phone and it worked. With everything that has happened the last few days, he'd be upset that I left you without a means to call for help."

Paul was right. No need to act stupid because I wanted to protect Cassie. From what? Who would care that she was staying in my attic? *Because you're afraid she knows something about her father's death.* The truth was like a punch in the stomach. Deep inside, I still suspected Cassie and I tried ignoring it. I didn't want to believe it was true.

It was better I had someone with me. "Okay. But first I need to check the attic. I've been hearing noise up there and I saw someone jumping over my fence."

Paul's eyes widened. "Merry, we have to call the police."

I shook my head. "I think I know who."

Understanding flashed in his eyes. "Does Cassie have a key to your house?"

"I never gave her one, but it would've been easy for her to lift it at some point and make a copy."

"Do you want to check the attic first or look for your phone?" Paul patted his coat pocket. "I have my phone if that makes a difference."

Warmth rushed through my heart and head. I wasn't sure why I was so pleased that Paul was asking me what I wanted to do. It was a small thing, yet it made me extraordinarily happy. "The attic first. If I'm wrong, I don't want the person to have enough time to come back and either hide evidence or..." I trailed off, not wanting to voice aloud any alternatives. None of them were pretty. I opened the front door and Paul followed me inside.

Ebenezer greeted us with whistles of excitement and tried to run out the door.

I shut it before he escaped. "I'm going to build him a habitat downstairs once I have some time."

"I can help you or build it for you." Paul leaned down and scratched Ebenezer's head. The guinea pig remained still, enjoying the attention way too much. "Whichever you'd like."

I started to say neither then stopped. Paul was trying to be a friend, and I could use a few more. It wouldn't hurt to have some help especially since I had no idea how to build a guinea pig habitat. "I'd appreciate it."

"Just let me know the times that are good for you and I'll check my schedule."

We went upstairs. The pull down for the attic was near the

guest room. I was surprised Grace hadn't heard someone walking around in the attic. Well, she had gone down to the kitchen, and I was sure Cassie stayed as still as possible.

Or I was wrong about who was up there. I hesitated.

"Want me to go up first?" Paul asked, reaching for the string that lowered the ladder.

"I'll go first. I'm ready." I motioned for Paul to tug down the ladder.

With one smooth yank, the ladder unfolded. Carefully, I made my way up, hoping with everything inside of me that it was Cassie and there was nothing incriminating against her. Even though it meant that I was still the number one suspect on Grayson's list.

I flicked on the attic light. In a corner, there was a scrunched up My Little Pony comforter and a pillow. Stepping closer, I saw a backpack with a t-shirt peeking out. I knew that shirt. I had bought it for Cassie when we went to Hershey park.

"It was Cassie." I was relieved—for a moment. Now, if only I could find evidence that she had nothing to do with her father ending up in the dinette bench seat of the RV.

There was a banging on my front door.

Paul headed down the ladder. "I'll get that for you."

The pounding continued as Paul made his way down, jumping down before he reached the last rung. The sound intensified. I hurried after Paul, wanting to offer whatever kind of protection was possible. Whoever was at my door was angry.

Paul yanked open the door.

Cornelius stepped back for a moment, confused. He huffed and puffed. "I saw what you did. Don't think I won't call the home owner's association about this."

Paul leaned toward me. "What is he talking about?"

"The Christmas decorations I put up." I gave Cornelius my best Christmas smile. "I'm not going to turn them on tonight."

"You can't win me over with your sweetness." He shook his finger at me like I was a naughty child tramping through his yard. "You've been trying to turn those lights on sooner and keep them on longer since you moved in."

He was right. Every year, I attended the Christmas planning meeting and asked about moving up the date. Every year, it was vetoed. I couldn't help it. I loved Christmas lights. The brightness during the darkest part of the year made the world seem so much more hopeful and bright.

"I promise I won't turn the lights on sooner, Cornelius."

He crossed his arms and evil-eyed me. "Don't believe you."

"If I do, just call the cops."

"Don't think I won't. And you better not think of permanently parking that traveling circus vehicle in front of your house. It's not supposed to be here. I called the HOA and Milton about it. Told him as your attorney, he should do a better of job of making sure you abide by the law."

"He's my divorce attorney," I said. "He doesn't care where I park my RV."

"He should along with every other person in this neighborhood." He huffed and stomped across the street, muttering under his breath about the crazy, Christmas lady.

Our HOA consisted of twelve houses and rules were minimal: no goats, no horses, no Christmas lights on until Black Friday, and no obstructing the road. That one came about because the kids in the neighborhood liked to play football in the street. The problem wasn't so much the kids in the road as they ran to the yards whenever a car drove down the road, but the huge makeshift goal posts they created. One day, a goal post tipped over onto Cornelius's car as the kids tried to haul it out of the way.

A sound came from my backyard. What was it? I strained to hear. The faint hints of "We're a Couple of Misfits" reached me. Brett. The fall didn't break my phone. I needed to leave a five-star review for the OtterBox case.

"My phone. It's my lawyer. My other one." I raced through my house to the back door. By the time I stepped out into the backyard, the phone quit ringing. It was somewhere back here. I secured the door to make sure Ebenezer stayed in the house. I didn't want to have to chase him around the neighborhood.

I searched through the bushes under the windows of the kitchen. "Where are you?"

The phone rang again. Brett was determined to reach me and knew my habit of leaving my phone in a different room.

"What did you find out?" I asked out of breath.

"Do you have a copy of your divorce decree?" Brett's voice was strange, a cross between gargling and choking.

"What's wrong?"

"Do you?"

"No. I haven't received one in the mail. Since you're at the courthouse get a copy. Get two. Bonnie needs one also." Saved me some time.

"There might be a problem with that," Brett said in the new strange tone I never heard come from him.

"You're my attorney. They'll give you one."

"They can't give me a document that doesn't exist."

"What?" I screeched.

"Everything okay?" Paul stood behind me, his breath drifted across my cheek. His hands settled a little too comfortably on my shoulders. *He like likes you, Mom.*

I jerked away. Paul's touch slipped off, and I increased the distance between us. As I hustled into my house to take the private call, I called out to Paul, "Thanks for your help."

"Sure thing." He sounded disappointment.

"Brett, what are you talking about?" I watched the dejected man walk away. Should I have offered more of an explanation? I didn't know how to navigate or what to call the relationship between me and Paul. He had been my son's friend. My son said Paul was interested in me in a romantic way. Paul's actions hinted at that. The truth was, I wasn't ready to confirm or deny if my son's intuition was correct.

"There's no copy of the divorce decree at the courthouse. My appointment with the judge was bumped, and since I was here, decided to get a copy for my case file."

"It's not there?"

"I've had them check every file cabinet and in-box. It's not here."

"I'll see what my attorney has to say." I ended the call.

At least I knew why Grayson didn't believe a word I said, he thought I was lying about being divorced. Knowing my voice betrayed me, I texted Milton. *Found a photo album of Samuel's and am wondering who a few people are. Can you help me when you're back in town?*

Almost immediately, he responded. *Sure can. I can see you at my office in twenty minutes.*

While I was there, I had one more question for Milton: Why wasn't my divorce decree at the court house?

TWENTY-THREE

Strangling the steering wheel, I headed to my attorney's office. This was what it felt like to want to harm someone. It wasn't a pleasant feeling. My nerves felt on fire, every organ tight, and my brain pinged from one thought to the next, most of them on ways to harm Milton. Best divorce lawyer in town. Ha. It was like ordering a lovely rum cake from a baker and receiving a fruitcake. No one in the world wanted fruitcake.

Did Cassie know there wasn't a divorce decree on file? Did that mean I was still technically married to Samuel? My heart squeezed for a moment, rendering me breathless and frozen in place. I rubbed at the spot. If so, I was still Cassie's stepmother. Responsible for her. I groaned. This situation was getting more complicated.

"Thanks a lot Samuel. And Milton."

Rage built. Why hadn't Milton, or the judge for that matter, filed the decree? How hard could it have been when the document was signed in the courthouse? It was a long hallway, six steps, through a metal detector, and two doors away. Heck, they'd have to walk past the office to leave the building.

Milton's office was a mere block away from the courthouse. He had no excuse for not filing it. He was in the courthouse at least three times a week, or so he had told me when I scheduled appointments and complained about his lack of availability. I whipped around the corner and slowed down as the police station was at the end of the block. My income already took a hit this week, no sense adding an unnecessary bill.

All the street parking was taken. I continued down the one-way street and turned, inching past the police station to the overflow parking lot for the business and the courthouse. I chose the spot farthest from the buildings as I didn't want anyone seeing my car near the police department and creating some interesting gossip.

The cold hit me the moment I stepped out of the car. The ducks who refused to go South for winter and lived year-round in the reservoir area across the street quacked at me. The critters were a source of contention between the residents of Season's Greetings as some found them a nuisance and likely contaminating the water, while others marveled at the ducks' antics. Personally, I was fond of them, though they took away from the Christmas ambiance this time of year. It wasn't like we could round them up and put them in Christmas sweaters.

I cradled the albums to my chest, wishing I opted for my winter jacket. I hadn't remembered it being this cold when I was on the roof, though I hadn't just stepped out of a car where the heat was blasting. The sudden temperature change was what got me.

The wire light wreaths were hung on the streetlamps, and red ribbons were tied around the parking meters. The town was preparing for Christmas. By next Monday morning, the street would be alive with the Christmas spirit: holiday vignettes displayed in windows and others frosted with "snow," wreaths on doors, holiday music piped from the police station. Some people saw the old buildings and thought run-down and faded, I saw a history lived, open to exploring.

Why was my life in a tailspin? I maintained a happy and cheerful disposition. I was kind to people. Kept Christmas well and lived with the Christmas spirit all year long. Why did that make people think I didn't know my own mind? I was a pushover. I had no backbone. Samuel found out I had one. Or then again maybe not. He figured a few dollars, or rather twelve million of them, would persuade me to stay married to him. I stomped away from my car.

"Merry Christmas, Merry." Someone called out.

I hmphed a response. Not very Christmas like. Not Merry Winters like. *Don't let anyone change your spirit.* My dad's voice drifted into my head. I hadn't had an easy life. Abandoned as a baby. Bullied as a child because of that. Married a man I loved only to discover he didn't love me enough to stand up to his family. Struggled financially for many years. Yet through it all, I remained hopeful. Happy. Filled with love and forgiveness. I was forty-five years old. Why lose it—correction—give it away because of Samuel and Milton?

Life wasn't perfect. It was good. I had amazing children who loved me. Friends. A hobby I loved that turned into a job and now might be my career. The good outweighed the bad. And, it was almost Christmas.

I smiled. My spirits were picking up. My gait changed from a march into a leisurely stroll. Take time to see the good in the world. I was focusing so much on the evil and bad, I forgot to refill my spirit. There was a couple walking hand-in-hand, heads bowed toward each other, conversing in quiet, excited whispers. She lifted her hand and giggled. An engagement ring gleamed. He held tightly to a velvet box. Eloping. The courthouse was nearby.

Love. It was a beautiful emotion. A lone duck waddled down the sidewalk. There were always a few ducks who remained behind and took up residence in the water reservoir across the street from the parking lot near the courthouse. They usually remained there unless someone disturbed them, or the temperature dipped too low and DNR rounded them up to move them indoors. Usually kids throwing rocks into the water or cars speeding by. The noise sent the ducks into a frenzy.

I leaned over and shooed at her or him, trying to direct the duck back to its home. "You don't want to go that way. Nothing but lawyer offices and two eateries. One's a hot dog place so they won't be interested in you, but Charlie's Hometown Grub might add you to the menu. If you're a mommy, your little ones are the other way."

The duck quacked and continued in the direction I advised

against.

"You're definitely a male. You're not listening to me." I side-stepped to get in front of the duck and waved at him. "Come on, dude, go in the safe direction."

He quacked at me, a series of loud duck curses. At least that was what it sounded like to my ears. He arched his neck forward, snapping at me.

"Fine. Have it your way." I sighed and stepped aside. The duck waddled down the sidewalk as if he knew exactly where he was going to. "You'll find out you should've accepted the directions I gave."

Why hadn't the judge given the clerk the decree to walk it to the proper office? Didn't matter. I'd find the decree and file it myself. Today. If Milton was running late, I'd call his wife and ask her to open the office. I was a little scared of that option as Barbara wasn't the type of person you asked favors from. It wasn't that she expected any back, it was just that she didn't like them period and let you know about it. From the picture Milton had of her on the wall, she had been a very happy young lady in her youth. She beamed at the world, a delighted glint in her eyes. The woman nowadays wore a permanent frown and acted like life was getting in her way.

I always wondered what happened from the time she graduated from college and married Milton to now. The story went that they meet their junior year of college, she had been trying to win his affections since the day she saw him walking into the first class they attended together. At first, Milton only had eyes for another, later noticing Barbara and knowing she was his soul mate.

The blinds were closed, no light seeping through the slats, though I heard banging coming from the office. What was going on? I paused at the window and peeked inside, cupping my hands over my eyes. There was faint movement coming from the back of the building. I twisted the knob and the door opened. I walked into Milton's law office.

Bland and empty were the words to describe it today. Two

closed boxes were on the floor near the table where the microwave and Keurig were kept. The coffee pods were gone along with the coffee cups Milton stored beside the brewer. Good to know that my drawn-out divorce financed an office redo. The place needed a sprucing up as the décor style was Ikea mixed with camouflage.

The framed degrees that had hung on the wall were in an open box on the faded couch where I had waited for my appointment. Milton didn't have a secretary and used a wooden sign on a platform, "Meeting in Progress," to let clients know to stay in the waiting area. It was in the middle of the small hallway that led to the private office and the bathroom.

The pictures of his rock-wall climbing hobby, chili cook-off wins, and fishing trips with his friends, including the one of a teenage Milton, Samuel, and a girl who I presumed was Milton's wife, were also gone. It had seemed a conflict of interest to hire an attorney who had been Samuel's friend at one time, but everyone I asked said Milton was the best attorney in town and I should snag him before Samuel hired him. They had been friends since they were young children, the relationship cooling between them when they returned from college.

The girl in the picture. What if it wasn't Barbara, but someone Samuel had dated? The mysterious Lynne? The girl had been standing between the two men, and it would explain the total one-eighty facial personality change. The reason Barbara didn't have the same bubbly personality was because it wasn't Barbara in the photograph.

The photographs were in the box with framed degrees. It wouldn't take long to pull the picture out and snap of photo of the one with the girl. The young girl was smiling, leaning more toward Milton than Samuel. Her hair cascaded around her shoulders, long bangs obscuring her eyes. There was something familiar about the shape of her face. The smile. *Her name might be written on the back.* The thought plucked out at my desire for knowledge and battled against my conscience. It was one thing to take a picture of the photograph and quite another to take it out of the frame to see whose name was written on the back.

Before I talked myself out of it, I placed the albums on a chair then opened the box. My hand shook as I took out the photo. I moved the metal hinges on the back of the frame and slid the backing from the groves in the wooden frame. Written in pencil was Samuel, Grace, and Milton. College. Freshman year.

A door in the back of the office closed. Cold air came from the direction of Milton's private office. "Milton?"

It was quiet. Too quiet. Where was he? I wandered back to the office. Nobody was in there. I placed the photo albums on the desk, my gaze being drawn to the open laptop placed on the edge of the screen. The screen was on the start-up screen of Chrome. One of the easy click boxes was for Facebook, and the small image of the Facebook page held my attention. Was that my picture?

I checked the office for Milton. He must've stepped out for lunch, not hearing me come in. I nudged the mouse over to the box and clicked it. Milton was signed on to Facebook—or rather Gary Meadows' page was up. Milton was Gary Meadows. I clicked on the messaging icon. Milton had been interacting with Samuel, Evelyn Graham, and me. There was a message from Evelyn, sent yesterday: *Why are you ignoring me? I did what you wanted.*

Milton convinced the nurse to let Grayson speak to my mom. My attorney was setting me up for Samuel's murder. With shaking hands, I snapped pictures of the Facebook page. Nearby, I heard a door creak open. It was time to leave. I grabbed the photo albums and headed for the front door. I hurried into the main office, snagging the photo of Milton, Samuel, and the unknown woman as I passed the stacked boxes.

"What are you doing?" Milton's angry voice bounced off the walls.

The albums slipped from my hands, scattering by my feet. Quickly, I leaned over and gathered them to my chest, pivoting toward the door. I left the framed photograph on the ground. A crack spread from one end of the photo to the other.

Milton squared back his shoulders and stalked over, his hefty weight shifting in a menacing way. At first glance, Milton seemed like a shorter and balder version of Santa and he was usually as jolly as Santa checking off the nice list. When he morphed into his lawyer persona, there was an instant switch. His gaze turned steely. His gait was more of a stalk than a stroll. The weight he carried in his middle seemed more like a rock than a bowl full of jelly. He picked up the damaged photo frame. "Why were you taking this?"

"I remembered you had a photograph of a younger Samuel on your wall and I wanted a better look at it. He hadn't changed much."

"No, he hadn't." Milton breathed in deeply, his broad shoulders and rounded gut straining the buttons on his camouflage hunting jacket. "That doesn't explain why it was in your possession."

"I thought Helen would like a copy. Renovating your office?"

"So, you were just going to take it with you?" Milton said. "What's going on, Merry? You're acting really skittish."

I hadn't realized it, but I'd been backing up the whole time I was talking. "Just have a lot to do today."

"You're leaving before you talked to me. I thought you had something important to show me."

"I wanted a copy of my divorce decree. But if you're busy, I can come back later." With the police.

Milton grimaced. The lawyer was gone and now I was witnessing a child on the naughty list having to fess up. "Merry, you're not divorced. Samuel never signed the decree."

"Wh—" Sounds locked in my throat.

Milton walked back to his office and returned quickly with a document in his hands. My heart thudded. Had I closed the Facebook page?

He held out the bottom page of the decree. Only my signature was on the bottom. Merry Noel Winters.

"Why didn't you tell me?" I was still married to Samuel. I lied to a homicide detective. Inadvertently. I had a feeling the detective wouldn't believe it. Matter-of-fact, I now had a motive for murdering my ex-husband—he wasn't my ex-husband.

"Samuel never showed up in court to sign it." Milton walked passed me and stood near the front door.

"Why didn't you tell me?"

"Because I thought I could convince him to change his mind. I was wrong. He asked me to stop by with the decree on Thursday because he was ready to sign it. I knew he was up to something, and I was right. He wanted to keep money from you." Milton paused, a glint in his eye. "A lot of it."

He saw Samuel on Thursday. Before he died. For all I knew, the meeting took place in the RV. "I don't want his money. I'm going home."

"After everything he put you through, dragging out the divorce and making you incur more legal fees, you deserve some of the money."

I tried to walk passed him. He held out an arm blocking me. I stepped back. "I don't care anymore. I'd just like to go."

He locked the front door and moved his bulk to block the exit. "Show me the albums."

Alarm bells went off in my head. I clasped them to my body like a shield. "I want to leave."

"Not until I get those albums."

That was the last thing I wanted to do. I backed up, nearly tripping over a rolling chair. Milton charged toward me. I kicked the chair in his direction. It slammed into him. I ran down the hallway toward the private office. Milton cursed.

I reached Milton's office and slammed the door shut. The door knob twisted. I threw my body against the door, pressing it close, and locked it.

Milton pounded on the door. "Merry, I need those albums."

"And you would've had them if you hadn't started acting like a creep." I scanned the room for something to protect me. The double-line landline phone. It was hefty. I unhooked the phone from the cord.

Where to hide the albums? Frantically, I searched for a place.

Closet? Too easy. Desk. It was locked. Under the rug? Stop. Milton would know where to find the albums in his office. What I needed was a cavalry and proof of the album. Milton was the one who tore out the pictures. I was sure of it.

"I won't hurt you," Milton said in a pleasant voice.

Right, like I'd fall for that. Bet he said that to Samuel before he shoved him into the bench. I fumbled my cell phone out of my coat pocket. I hit Brett's number.

"Merry—"

"I'm at Milton's office. Get here now."

Milton pounded on the door. I let out a little yelp.

"What's going on?"

"I think he killed Samuel." I hung up the phone. I didn't have time to talk. I snapped pictures of the photo album, sending them to Brett one after the other. It was quiet. Oh my God! There was another way into the office. The back door. My gaze fell on the door that I had assumed was a closet. Milton was coming for me.

I had to escape. I unlocked the door and leaned out, listening for Milton. Nothing. There was a scratching sound at the closet door. I scurried out of the room, the books tight in my grasp. The front door was clear. Freedom.

A fist shot out from a gaping blackhole in the hallway striking me in the collar bone and knocking me backwards into the wall. I screamed. The bathroom. I forgot about the bathroom. My head clunked on the dry wall. My body slid to a sitting position. The books tumbled from my hands. I tried to reach for the closest one. My hand laid by my side, refusing to budge.

Frantically, he flipped through it. "I didn't want to do that."

Liar. I kept the reprimand to myself and tried pushing myself up. The throbbing in my head was making it hard to move my feet. My muscles weren't obeying.

"Where did you get these albums?"

I inched over, hoping once my senses returned I'd have a clear shot to the front door.

Milton fixed his attention on me and frowned. "Answer the

question."

I pressed my lips together. No way was I telling him.

"Samuel gave them to you. What did he tell you?"

Since it didn't sound like he was asking a question, I didn't confirm or deny where he thought I got the albums. Better he thought Samuel handed them to me rather than Helen.

Milton held his hand out to me. "Let me help you."

So, he could knock me down again. I didn't think so. I hid my hands behind my back, craning my neck to the side. The blinds were closed, and I couldn't see through the small window at the top of the door. It was hard to tell if Brett had arrived.

"I won't hurt you."

Tears welled in my eyes. I blinked them away. Showing fear wouldn't help me. Men like Milton drew strength from it. I was horrible at choosing men, whether to marry or call a friend. "You knew I didn't want to be married to Samuel anymore. He was a threat to my mother's well-being. You should've told me that he didn't sign the decree."

"I thought I could change his mind." The way his gaze darted around told me that wasn't the complete truth. There was something else. Now wasn't the time to push the man for it. "I was wrong. I'm sorry about that."

The consequence of Milton's withholding the information smacked me as hard as his fist had. "That's why the detective thinks I murdered Samuel. I lied about the divorce."

"I'll tell him you didn't know."

"Why would he believe that? He's positive I killed Samuel. You saying I didn't know is hardly likely to change his mind. It doesn't make any sense that you wouldn't have told me. He'll think you're trying to protect me."

"Not if I tell him everything..." Milton trailed off. His shoulders rounded forward, and his stomach pouched out. The intimidating figure left and in its wake was a defeated and shamed man. Leaning against the wall, Milton slid to a sitting position. "I'm so sorry, Merry. I don't know how all of this happened. Yes, I do. I just never thought it would lead to all of this. I didn't kill Samuel. But, I might have helped orchestrate it. I told a woman from his past about the lottery ticket. I figured it served him right to have to deal with her, since I'd likely have to deal with someone from my past."

Shadows crossed in front of the window. One. Two. Three. Four. Five. Season's Greetings didn't have that many officers on duty during a shift. I figured Brett would come even if ordered not to, but the extra body?

I didn't have to contemplate for long as Detective Grayson peered through the window. Our eyes gazes locked. His brows rose. I gave him a shaky smile.

"Now is your chance to right your wrongs," I said. "We have company."

Milton sat in one of the gray leather chairs reserved for clients. He was slumped down, reminding of me a child getting a well-deserved scolding. Two of the three local officers left. The one remaining behind was stationed near the door, making sure no one came in and was searching for evidence in the boxes Milton had packed up. Detective Grayson wasn't any more willing to accept "I didn't kill Samuel" as proof of innocence from Milton than he had from me. That made me feel a little better.

Brett had pulled the second leather chair far away from Milton and stood between me and my divorce attorney. My head was leaned against the seat rest, holding a bag of frozen mangos to the back of my head and causing me to peer through the bottom half of my glasses to observe everything. It was hurting my neck and giving me a headache.

Grayson closed one of the photo albums and pushed it away. He brought the second one in front of him and opened it. "I'm having a hard time figuring out how these albums caused a battle. There's nothing out of the ordinary in them. What led you to believe Mr. Dellwood killed Samuel?"

Okay, so I wasn't quite off the hook with the detective. "That's the issue," I said. "There's nothing in some of the spots. The photos were removed. Milton was angry I wouldn't hand him the books. Why get so angry if you weren't hiding something? Huge." Like murder.

"Ms. Winters has made a good point. Care to explain, Counselor?" Grayson fixed a hard stare on Milton.

"As I said, I believed Samuel had given them to her and shared a personal detail about my life I'd rather not get out." Milton shifted uncomfortably.

"What would that be?" Grayson tilted his head toward me and Brett. "I can request them to leave."

"No, Merry has a right to know. This has affected her life more than anyone." Milton drew in a deep breath then released it. "It has to do with the picture Merry was looking at."

"The one of you and Samuel with that girl. I thought that was Barbara."

Milton let out a sad chuckle. "No, that wasn't Barbara. It was my girlfriend in college. As a joke, and because we wanted an easy class, Samuel and I took ceramics. It was a lot harder than we realized. Samuel was pretty good at it, I was only interested in impressing a pretty girl I fell hard for."

"Why did you hang up the photo?" I asked.

"To remind myself to be careful of my choices. I fell in lust, we had sex many times and one of them resulted in a pregnancy. When the kid was born I was ecstatic. I had a son. When he got a little older, I realized her son wasn't quite right. No way was he mine."

"Your son," I corrected. Milton was a horrible human being. I was willing to forgive him for striking me, but not for dismissing a child—his child—in such a cruel way.

"She said he was, I denied it. Our relationship faltered."

"You left her because your child wasn't perfect." The disgust was clear in Detective Grayson's voice. At least that man had a redeeming quality.

"Whether he was truly mine or not doesn't matter," Milton

said. "What matters is that Samuel knew about that transgression and was blackmailing me for it. He brought me pictures of me and the girl and said if I agreed to let him back date the decree, he'd give them to me. If not, he'd post them on social media and let everyone know the man who was planning on running for city council dumped his kid because of a disability. So, I happened to let it slip a few times that Samuel won twelve million dollars."

"That's why so many people posted links to GoFundMe campaigns on his Facebook page," I said, regretting it immediately as Grayson's attention zinged over to me. "Why did you post on his page as Gary Meadows? And how does Evelyn Graham fit into this? You were logged into Facebook as him and—"

The detective's ire shifted to me. "I have this, Ms. Winters."

"This is when I'll invoke my right to an attorney before I say anything else," Milton said.

TWENTY-FOUR

"I don't think he killed him," I said as Brett walked me back to my vehicle. "Why say so much if you knew it would make you a suspect in a man's death?"

"Because he said exactly what he wanted to say. I don't trust the guy." Brett's steps were heavy, anger echoing through with each one.

"I don't trust him either. Yet, I still don't think he killed Samuel."

"Why not?"

"Because he had a chance to really hurt me and didn't."

Brett froze and gaped at me. "Are you serious? That's it. That's your reasoning? He didn't kill you, so he didn't kill Samuel."

I narrowed my eyes. "Don't talk to me like I'm stupid."

Brett flushed. "Merry—"

I held up my hand, silencing him. "You are. If Milton was trying to get away with murder, why have me around to tell people what he did? Why reveal what he did to the police? He felt heartsick when he told me that he thought he orchestrated Samuel's death by telling people about the money. Samuel wouldn't be the first lottery winner murdered right after, or before, he received his winnings. I bet Samuel hadn't signed the ticket yet. He'd want to make sure that we were divorced first, or I might have been entitled to some of the money."

Brett nodded. "That's what I figured. It's the only reason your ex-husband would want to back date the divorce. Where's the ticket?"

I shrugged. "That's the twelve-million-dollar question."

We continued to my car and as it came into view, it was my turn to abruptly stop. The passenger door of my SUV was wide open. Papers fluttered by me. I stomped on one then picked it up. My insurance card. I bet my registration was also loose. I moved toward my car.

Brett snagged my arm. "Hold up."

He was right. Proceed with caution. There was a missing lottery ticket, and this was the second vehicle I owned that was vandalized. I was regretting not telling the police about the intruder leaving my house this morning. What if I was wrong and it wasn't Cassie camping out in my attic? Or even if it was, had I made the correct choice in protecting her? The intruder in my house, the vandalism of the RV, could have helped proved my innocence. Brett's earlier words flickered in my head: You tend to allow your emotions to rule over common sense and self-preservation. He was right.

Brett pulled out his cell and called the police. The police department was within eye sight and no one there had noticed someone tossing everything out of my vehicle. Of course, the police had been busy with saving me from Milton.

I drew in a sharp breath. Milton had slipped out of the office to trash my car or his confession was a way to tie up the police. The guy was nothing but a conniving liar and likely a murderer. "He did this."

He pocketed his phone. "The police are on the way."

"This is the reason for Milton's confession. He stalled us long enough for someone to search my car for the ticket. With Samuel dead and almost buried, the other most likely candidate to have the ticket was the person the police zeroed in on as the murderer. Me." I pointed toward the police station. "He knows where the police station is located. They'd notice someone searching my car. Best way to get away with it was to have the officers somewhere else. Like his office."

Brett frowned. "You're in danger. Whoever is looking for the ticket doesn't know you don't that have it. Eventually, they'll lose their patience and demand it. What will stop them from harming you?"

"I have to agree with your attorney." Detective Grayson joined us, snapping on a pair of gloves. "The murderer believes you have the ticket."

"At least you don't think I'm the murderer anymore."

"You made a good suspect." Grayson picked up an item from the ground and deposited it into a bag.

I ignored the comment. "Whoever it is has to know I don't have it now. They ransacked the RV, my vehicle, and I think my garage." I ticked off on my fingers all the times I noticed things were out of place. "I might be forgetting one."

Both men stared at me.

"Has anyone approached you about the ticket?" Grayson asked.

"Cassie. She said she left an event ticket in the RV. I think she meant the lottery ticket. Samuel would've told his daughter he won. I also hinted to her that I found a ticket."

"Why?" Brett practically screamed at me.

"Because I wanted her to look at the photo albums and tell me who was missing. She was ignoring my calls. The only thing she was interested in was the ticket. I used it."

"When were you meeting her?" Grayson asked.

I glanced at the phone. "An hour ago. She was going to come over. I stood her up." Yet, there were no messages from her. "She must've looked herself. I bet she was the person who jumped over my fence."

"Do you think she kill—"

My eyes widened. "No. She wouldn't have killed her father. She loved him. He was her only parent."

"Birth mom is not in the picture?" Grayson asked.

"She hasn't seen Cassie since she was a baby. Samuel never talked much about her. Just that she had wanted a baby but realized after a few months she didn't want to be a mother and left.

He married again a few years later and divorced. Married again. Let's just say that happened a couple of times. I think Samuel was looking for a mother for his daughter rather than a wife for himself, so the marriages never lasted long."

"Is there anyone else you can think of that has talked to you about the ticket? The lottery? Anything suspicious at all?" Grayson asked.

"No." I stopped talking as memories weaved in and out of my mind. Oh my God! No. It couldn't be. With shaking hands, I pulled my cell phone from my pocket and brought up my designing app. Think of it like a decal. Add each piece in the main component and check if it layers together. The name on the picture floated into my head.

"Merry, what are—"

I held up my hand. I needed silence, no extra words in my head. I wrote lottery in a large box and start piling in all the instances of vandalism. Comments I remembered. Long time to get RV. Checking the underneath storage compartment. Told me to check Samuel's Facebook. Tears cascaded down my cheeks. No. Not my friend. Not my Grace. My heart shattered.

Samuel had talked to Grace, but not about wanting to rent a booth. It was about Milton. The man who left her because their son understood the world differently than others.

"Merry, what's wrong?"

"I know who's been looking for the ticket. Grace Turner."

Brett sucked in a breath. "Abraham's mom. My other client."

Grayson sent a sharp look in Brett's direction before settling a sympathetic one on me. "The woman's son was with you when you discovered Samuel's body."

I nodded, tears clogging my breath.

"Her son was the one I talked with Saturday. He mentioned you wanted him to help you move stuff out of the RV," Grayson said.

"Yes, the trees."

The trees. Abraham had to have the tree with the bit of red on the top. Abraham was frantic for that tree. Had Grace asked her son to get it for her? Was she afraid it could implicate her in Samuel's murder? What if she came to Season's Greetings to have it out with Milton and he told her about the lottery ticket. That amount of money would ensure her that Abraham would have the proper care he needed when she died. Her son, the light of her life, would be taken care of. It was her one worry about life, or rather death.

"Do you think she might have killed Samuel Waters?" Grayson's gentle voice broke me.

"I don't know." I covered my face with my hands and wept.

TWENTY-FIVE

Brett followed me home. Why wouldn't he listen to me and go back to Virginia? It was a three and half hour drive home for him. I knew he thought I needed him. What I needed was to be left alone to sort out my emotional turmoil. Or as alone as one could be with a police officer and a detective keeping tabs on you. I had told the detective about Grace coming tomorrow and he said he'd be ready for her.

I was certain I lost Brett when I stopped at the drug store and spent an inordinate amount of time in the feminine product section. In case that hadn't worked, I ordered a pizza from the local pizzeria while I was parked in their lot and designed Christmas t-shirts while I waited for my early dinner. My plans for the remainder of the dwindling day was eat, craft, and try to keep my mind from Grace. None of those activities required Brett. I figured he had better things to do with his time. I was wrong.

Thumping the back of my head on the seat rest, I moaned. Even though we had a cordial relationship, it didn't mean he needed to protect me by staying the night in my house. There was a fine line between professional issues and personal. Samuel was personal. Brett and I had to keep our relationship professional. Attorney-client.

Brett got out of his car. I shoved open my door. "Go home. I mean it."

"I've never known you to be so stubborn and refusing to see possibilities. Why can't you see that you are in danger? You've always had quite the imagination." The scorn in his voice was hard to discount.

I knew his mind slipped to our divorce. We had a whirlwind courtship, met in May and married in September, and neglected to discuss important issues we'd face in our marriage and in raising children. Young love was always in a rush. After Raleigh was born, I was excited to start the Santa tradition. Brett wanted it nixed, saying it was lying and created a false sense of expectations and self-esteem issues for children whose parents couldn't afford their wishes. It was another way for those children not to measure up and feel like Santa disliked them and contributed to the notion that poor equaled naughty as Santa only delivered to good.

I had been crushed my husband wanted to deny our child an experience that showed wonder, magic, and belief in others. Belief beyond yourself was my true driving force. It was my life. My parents had taken in a child that wasn't theirs and loved her. Saved me. My mother lived every day as a wonderful, magical moment with endless possibilities no matter what happened the day before or what you currently possessed.

"To me, Christmas wasn't about imagination. It was about tradition and hope." I slammed the door shut, careful not to drop my pizza, and hit the lock button. It beeped. "I can't do this. Go home."

"I loved your Christmas spirit. I just had concerns. I loved your hope. Your belief. I needed someone who had an abundance of it because I knew it was what I lacked. My mission wasn't to be a Grinch in your life."

Brett believed I picked a holiday over him. He couldn't understand it was about our different approaches to life. I believed I could do anything because my mom spoke of hope. I wanted that for our children. Brett disagreed. Hope without reason or a plan was setting people up for failure and was an unrealistic expectation that destroyed their spirit, not helped grow it.

"There's no reason for us to rehash this out in the cold. We're divorced. You're married."

"Is that why you don't want to discuss what happened to us?" Brett whispered. "Because I'm married."

"Because we're divorced, Brett. You know Raleigh still has visions of us rekindling our marriage in our golden years. I don't want to give our children a false hope."

"I thought you were all about hope."

Twinges of anger were building. Why was Brett doing this? Balancing the pizza on one hand, I pointed at myself then at him. "Not about this. As I said, I embrace magic and reality. Santa will come but he might not bring what you asked for. Santa can't bring you a live alligator no matter how good you are."

"You're comparing me to an alligator."

"I'm comparing you to something that's impossible to have."

"I'm not. I'm separated."

An emotion fluttered in my chest, a tangled mess of longing, fear, confusion, and anger. Why tell me now? Why not earlier? Why at all. Unless...no, we couldn't—I couldn't—redo the past. I turned my back on him and walked to my front door. "This isn't going to work. You're my attorney. It's becoming personal and it shouldn't. Why we aren't married anymore doesn't matter. It has nothing to do with my being a suspect in Samuel's case. We have to have a professional distance between us."

"If that's what you want, I agree to those terms." His tone didn't match the words. "We'll maintain a professional decorum. You are my client. Not my ex-wife. Not the mother of my children."

"Now that we have that settled, you can go home."

"I have some appointments in Morgantown. I'll stay in Season's Greetings tonight and head over in the morning."

"Why not now? You can stay with the kids."

He held up his hand and shook his head. "Remember, professional. No talk of children."

The man was exasperating. "Fine. If you prefer a bed-and-breakfast, there's a lovely one in the heart of town. It has a wonderful view of the town Christmas tree and since it's not lit it won't disturb your rest. Or there's a motel at the end of town. They have a business center and a gym. That might be more to your liking."

"To best serve my client's needs, I'm staying here." Brett motioned for me to step away from the front door.

I took a gamble and stepped closer. "That's not in her best interests. Her ex-husband was found murdered and she's a suspect."

"Was a suspect. Grayson has seemed to move on to another. And the deceased is your husband."

"You're a cruel man, Mr. Calloway."

"You have to face it. You're still married to the man."

"Even more of a reason you shouldn't be bunking down in my house."

A smile played at his lips. "Technically, you're a widow. You're not breaking any vows or doing something immoral by having a man in your house."

"This isn't funny."

He heaved out a sigh. "You're right."

The front door opened with a push. In my haste to leave, I hadn't tugged it close or locked it. This wasn't good. Someone was looking for a lottery ticket and I basically handed them a written invitation to enter my house. "Brett."

"Merry, what's wrong?" He dropped the phone back into his pocket and wrapped an arm around my shoulder, moving in front of me. This time, I didn't block his attempt to offer protection.

"My door wasn't shut all the way." I wandered into the living room and placed the pizza on the coffee table. Nothing seemed out of place. The living room was in the same order as I had left it. The couch cushions were in place. The mantel still had family photos line up.

"Do you remember closing it?"

"I can't say for certain."

"Let's check before we call the police." Brett's attention was on the photographs, all of them snapshots of daily life. Scotland and Raleigh opening Christmas presents, playing horseshoes in the backyard, Raleigh and I baking, Scotland teaching me how to play a video game.

The wistfulness in his gaze spoke to my heart. I squeezed his hand. "I can print you out a copy of those."

He clasped my hand. "Let's check the other rooms. Stay behind me."

Hand-in-hand, we crept in. Mine shook while his grip was firm and reassuring. The heat from his hand warmed mine. My temperature seemed to have dropped fifteen degrees. He looked at me, eyebrows raised.

"You okay?"

I nodded. The feeling of being all right evaporated when we moved from the dining room into the kitchen. The kitchen was a disaster zone. The refrigerator was open. The drawers tugged out. Food, plastic ware, and utensils had been dumped on the vinyl floor. The newspaper was shredded into pieces. If it wasn't for the grip I had on Brett's hand, I'd have tumbled to the floor.

"I'm taking it you are not responsible for this mess."

"No."

We stood quiet in the kitchen, listening for footsteps overhead. Nothing. It was eerily quiet. Not even any scratching of tiny toenails on the hardwood floors or the muffled thump of a furry critter jumping downstairs.

"Ebenezer." I cried and ran out of the kitchen for the stairs. I took them two at a time, my short gait almost causing me to fall up the stairs. "Ebenezer." My voice shook.

Brett ran up behind me, with his longer stride, he overtook me and blocked the landing. "The burglar might still be here."

"Ebenezer's missing. I have to know he's safe." My bedroom door was open. Dread filled me, crushing my spirit. Tears slid down my cheeks. I left Ebenezer alone all day. Defenseless. I should've come home sooner instead of waiting Brett out. I was a strong woman. I wasn't a coward. I should've told him firmly he was not coming home with me and there would not be a personal relationship between us. Our lives were tied together because of our love for our children, but not combined.

"Who's Ebenezer?"

"He's my companion. He's my pet. My traveling buddy."

"We'll find him. I promise."

I pushed past him. We were wasting time. I ran into my room. It was trashed. My clothes dumped on the floor. The drawers tossed to the side. The wall had a hole where one of the drawers had hit it. I dropped to my knees and lifted the edge of the comforter. It was too dark. I wriggled underneath. Ebenezer wasn't under the bed. I scooted back out, my fast pace tugging up my shirt and leaving a slight rug burn on my stomach.

"Merry, we have to leave." Brett held his hand out to me.

I pivoted and crawled toward the dresser. Ebenezer wasn't hiding there either. Where was he? I sat back on my heels. Panic was building again along with the tears. I stood and scanned the room. On the floor were small pieces of dry clay. I didn't make pottery, but I knew someone who did. Grace. She was already in town.

My tears dried. "There's a sledgehammer in my garage. Get it and meet me at your car."

"Merry?" Brett's voice was filled with trepidation.

I didn't blame him. My temperament usually stayed at one place for a long period of time. Mood swings weren't my thing—until it came to someone hurting my children. Then it morphed in a nanosecond and stayed in Mama Bear mode until I destroyed the threat. It was time to do just that.

"We're going to give Grace what she wants."

TWENTY-SIX

Even though it was only six thirty, the sky was dark and clear, almost like it was cleaning the slate for the impending storm to arrive tomorrow. I wished it had come tonight then Ebenezer would've been safe at home and I wouldn't be on my way with Brett to destroy what had, briefly, been a dream come true.

"This is a bad idea." Brett said, giving me the side-eye.

I cradled the sledgehammer in my arms. "You can drop me off at the fire station and leave. Paul will help me."

"Who's Paul?" A muscle in his jaw twitched.

"A friend who's willing to help me."

Brett clenched his teeth. Okay, that wasn't nice. I needed all the help possible to destroy the dinette and get the ticket. It had to be in the bench, likely fallen through a crack. It was the only place that hadn't been searched thoroughly. I knew of no other place Samuel would've hidden the ticket.

"Bonnie might have the ticket. It might be why she's so determined to have the divorce decree," Brett said.

"Which there isn't one and I'm sure that truth is all over town by now with Milton arrested. If she has the ticket, she'd tear it up. No way would she let me have the money. Too many people know Samuel bought the ticket."

"How can you be sure she knows you're still married to Samuel?"

"I don't want rational arguments right now. I want to get Ebenezer back." I heaved out a sigh and clutched the sledgehammer tighter. "I feel this all-consuming need to bash something."

"Dinette is the best option." Brett pulled into the parking lot of the fire station.

Paul was already there, sitting on the hood of his sports car. He hopped off when we pulled up beside him.

I got out, being careful not to hit Brett's car with the sledgehammer. "Thanks for meeting us here."

"Chief says feel free to use any of the crow bars." He handed me a pair of safety googles. "No one has asked about the RV or done anything to it. An officer has been driving by a few times at night to make sure everything was quiet. I called the police to let them know we were doing some minor renovations tonight. I didn't want them getting suspicious with all the cars in the lot."

Or other people might if there was more than one car here. "Brett, can you pull your car behind the building?"

"Why?"

"This way someone driving by won't see two cars. It might make them not want to stop."

Brett narrowed his eyes. "I don't think that's a good idea."

"I think it's a great idea," Paul said, opening the bay door. "I'll move my car. If the kidnapper is a local, they'll recognize it and know I'm here and won't stop. An out of towner wouldn't know and they'll stop."

"Do we want a potential murderer stopping while we're here?" Brett's feelings on the plan came through clear in his voice. He thought we were out of our minds.

"It'll make it easier for the police to arrest them," I said. "The officers know what we're doing. I'll ask Paul to contact the dispatcher and have them know only one car should be out here, if another is in the lot it's trouble."

"You're taking a big risk, Merry," Brett said.

"I just want this over with and Ebenezer back home."

"You're risking your life for just a—"

I spun. My hand wrapped firmly around the neck of the sledgehammer. "Don't you dare say Ebenezer is just a guinea pig.

He's innocent. And defenseless. Only a cruel, soulless person would harm an innocent being."

Paul opened the bay doors and motioned us inside. About time. Less talk. More action. I opened the door to the RV and stepped inside. No happiness wrapped itself around me. No feelings of joy. All of it had been sucked out of the place that had for a brief moment been a dream come true.

"Good riddance." I donned the safety glasses and took aim. *Crack.* The dinette shuddered and shifted slightly. I smashed it again. And again.

The table crashed to the floor. Brett moved it out of the way.

Paul handed Brett a crow bar and held out another one to me. "It might be better to pry off the wood. Don't want to damage the ticket."

He was right.

I placed the sledgehammer down. The three of us pried away the pieces to the bench, tossing them to the side. Some of the pieces were stained and I tried not to think of why and blocked Samuel's image from my mind.

I sat back on my heels. Disappointment cascaded through me. Every piece of the bench was removed. No ticket. There was a sound near the bay door. A scratching.

"I left the door open a crack," he whispered. "Someone is trying to get in."

"Merry, hide somewhere," Brett said.

Before I disagreed with Brett, I heard a familiar voice calling my name. Abraham. He was distraught. "Stay here. Both of you."

"Merry Christmas, you here?" There were tears in his voice.

I walked down the steps. "I'm here, Abraham."

He beamed at me. Ebenezer was cradled in his arms. The little bundle of fur was safe and content, half-asleep, head drooping over Abraham's arms. "You're safe. Nothing bad happened to you."

"No, Abraham. I'm fine. I thought you were coming tomorrow," I spoke a little louder, hoping the guys knew I was safe and not to charge out. Abraham wasn't a threat to anyone. "Why did you think I wasn't safe?"

"Your house was so messy. Mama said it was like that when she walked in. She told me to take Ebenezer to keep him safe. I did."

"You did a good job. You didn't walk inside with your mom?"

He shook his head. "She asked me to wait in the car until she was sure you were home. Since we came early."

"How long did you wait?"

Abraham tilted his head to the side, brows and nose scrunching up. "How long did Mama ask me to wait? She didn't give me a time. I just stayed in the car until she came out."

"How long was she in my house?"

"Merry, did we do something wrong?" He was hurt. Confused by all my questions.

"No, you just came earlier than I expected. I feel bad you were at my house and I wasn't home."

"The weather man said snow was coming. It would stop me from seeing Ebenezer. I asked Mama if we could come today instead. She said okay but I had to listen to everything she said and do as told. No arguing today or disobeying. I did a good job. Mama said so." He beamed at me.

"I'm sure you were the best. How did you know to find me here?" I already knew. Grace was there when the police suggested I have the RV moved to the fire station for safekeeping.

"You're mad." Abraham stepped back, still holding Ebenezer, gaze skittering around.

"Let me have Ebenezer."

Abraham held him tighter. Ebenezer squealed and struggled to get free. "Why are you mad? I'm your helper."

"I know, Abraham. I'm not mad at you. I'm tired. It's been a long day. Please let me have Ebenezer." My request only had Abraham wrapping Ebenezer even more firmly in his arms.

Abraham's eyes widened, and he stumbled backwards. "The dead man is back. Behind you."

I threw a glare over my shoulder. Brett. Should've guessed. He looked nothing like Samuel, but Abraham had only seen a dead man in my RV and he was assuming the man walking out was one and the same. "Go back."

"Give Merry her pet, Son." Brett spoke in a quiet and firm manner. His dad voice.

"You're the mean man."

"No, he's not," I said. "That's Brett. Raleigh's dad."

Abraham smiled. "I like Raleigh."

"How about you put the hamster..."

"Guinea pig," Abraham and I corrected.

"Abraham." Grace's voice bounced off the open bay area like a shot. Abraham winced and loosened his hold. Ebenezer wiggled from his grasp and tumbled to the floor, making a beeline for underneath a fire truck.

Tears built in his eyes. "I can't stay the night at Merry's anymore."

"No, you can't." Her expression softened. She walked over to Abraham and hugged her son tightly. "I love you. You're a good boy. A good man."

"But I didn't listen. I didn't stay in the car when you went to get Merry's purse for her from her car like she asked. You couldn't find it. I thought Merry took it with her and forgot. I was going to have Merry call you."

Grace winced and shook her head. "I did some things I shouldn't. Merry knows."

Red lights filled the bay. The police were here. Paul hovered in the doorway. Brett stood beside me, angled to jump in front of me. It wasn't necessary. No one was in danger.

Abraham fixed a pleading look on me. "You'll forgive her, Merry Christmas? Mama won't stay on the naughty list with you."

The bay door was lifted. Orville and another officer walked inside, approaching us cautiously, hands near the butt of their weapons.

"Milton Delwood..." I said the name and trailed off, flicking a questioning gaze at Abraham.

Grace nodded. She rose on her toes to cradle her beloved son's face in her hands. "I broke things that didn't belong to me. Merry's things. And I lied to her. I tricked her, so I could take something of hers."

"Mama, lying is bad." His voice trembled. "Merry is our friend. You don't hurt friends."

"I know, honey." She looked at me. Pain and sorrow clear in her eyes. "I did what I thought I needed to do for..." She trailed off.

I knew the ending of the sentence. For him. She didn't want those words to install themselves in Abraham's head and have him blame himself. I didn't want that either.

"Ma'am, we need you to come with us." Orville took hold of her elbow.

Abraham took a step forward to follow. Orville shook his head. "Not you, Son. Just your mom."

"Mama, where do I go?" Panic laced his words. He swayed back and forth, the tempo increasing. "Where do I sleep? How do I get home?"

"What about his father?" Brett asked.

"He left me and Mama." Abraham rocked back and forth, panic growing. "He'll leave me alone again."

Torrents of tears ran down Grace's face. "No! He doesn't deserve a chance to know Abraham."

Ebenezer ran out from under the truck and sat on Abraham's feet whistling and shrieking until the young man picked him up.

"Abraham can stay with me," I said.

"It might be a long time," Orville said. "Are you sure?"

"Yes." I hooked my arm through Abraham's. "Let's take Ebenezer home."

Leaning my forehead on the guestroom door, I fought back tears. It was midnight and Abraham finally settled down and fell asleep. The young man alternated between weeping and raging. He had gotten hold of his mom's boyfriend, and the guy promised to be in

Season's Greetings on Friday. The man told me he was trying for tomorrow but feared if the snow made it impossible to travel, Abraham would grow more upset. I agreed. It was better for Abraham's well-being to give him a date that was entirely possible.

What was I going to do? Ebenezer helped soothe Abraham. What would happen tomorrow or Thursday and Grace wasn't here? Or even months later. How could this be explained to Abraham?

I went back to my bedroom, pacing around the small space. How did all of this happen? I wanted to rail at Samuel. It wasn't his fault. Nobody forced Grace to make the decision she had. Decision. I had a hard time thinking murder. It didn't fit Grace's personality. I couldn't picture her murdering someone. But she had. She pretty much admitted it tonight. She was careful with what she said as everything was confusing enough to Abraham.

My heart and brain were having a hard time accepting it. A man dead. Two mothers, a daughter, and a son brokenhearted. All for a stupid ticket that gave a person twelve million dollars. Did Grace still think it was worth it?

I picked up my phone and did something I had never done before. Called Bright.

"Merry?" Her voice was sweet with a musical lilt to it. "Is that really you? I thought you hated chatting on the phone. Is everything okay?"

I burst into tears.

"Did the Grinch steal your Christmas?" Her tone was hard, protective. "If he did, I'll come after him. I can Halloween it up. I have a broom around somewhere and can portray a witch really good."

"No," I hiccupped. Once my breathing was under control I told her everything. Samuel. Cassie. Milton. Grace. Brett.

"Guard your heart right now, honey."

"I don't want it to harden." I used the comforter to swipe away my tears. Rudolph's nose was now sopping wet.

"You can guard a heart without it becoming hard. Years ago, you told me about a teenager who had a big holiday gift wish. This girl knew it was unlikely that she'd get a car but clung to the tiniest hope that the possibility existed. That gift didn't come. It didn't turn her bitter or hardened her heart toward the holiday or make her doubt her parents. She still loved Christmas and the joys that came with it. She didn't stop believing that dreams could come true, she knew how to let her dreams fly yet keep them grounded. Handle this situation the same as you did your Christmas wishes, see all the good possibilities and accept the reality without it changing you."

And that was what I didn't know how to do this time—not let people's behaviors alter who I was.

TWENTY-SEVEN

This was the worst start to the holiday season I ever had, and that included being left on the church steps on Christmas Eve. At least I had a stocking to protect me from the elements and it was done before the start of the Christmas Eve service. I had a fighting chance for survival. Samuel's murderer—Grace—killed more than just him and stole so much from so many people, the fallout wasn't even over yet.

I was starting to understand how Christmas could be ruined for people. The holiday would never be the same for Abraham. He now had a negative memory to the beginning of it and I wasn't sure it was something he had the ability to get past without his mom. Grace's boyfriend wasn't a substitute for her. And neither was I. I tried. I tried hard, but Abraham was depressed, and hints of anger appeared and disappeared.

Right now, he was barricaded in the guest room after I explained to him for what seemed like the thousandth time that his mother wasn't coming to take him home. He wanted Grace—needed Grace—and she was going to be denied to him for a long, long time. Brett had come over to explain the situation to him but only made things worse. To Abraham, Brett was the man who appeared out of the RV where he had seen a dead man. He had connected the two together and wasn't able to separate them. I believed part of his confusion was because his mother had never been away from him for so long.

The only source of comfort for Abraham was Ebenezer. As much as I loved and would miss Ebenezer, I was considering allowing Abraham to take my companion home with him.

"I gave her names of some other attorneys," Brett had told me. "It's a conflict for me to advise her because..."

"Of me." I had begged Brett to take her case instead. To help her and Abraham.

He couldn't. He was heading home before the snow started. I told him he could stay as Raleigh was planning on arriving this afternoon instead of waiting until tomorrow, Thanksgiving. He said it was time he went home and there were other cases demanding his attention.

I knew the truth. The disappointment on my face, and Abraham's wailing, had broken Brett. This was a situation where justice couldn't be served without hurting someone who didn't deserve it. Abraham was losing his mother. His soft place to fall. His protector. It was killing Brett. I saw it in the dejected way he ambled out the door, head down, shoulders slumped. For the first time, Brett looked old and as if life had worn him down.

This afternoon, I felt the same. Old. Tired. Defeated. I stared at the boxes of Christmas paraphernalia filling my living room. Even those items weren't bringing any joy to me. Sighing, I dropped onto the couch. I still couldn't believe that Grace killed Samuel. She hadn't confessed. All she said was that she was looking for the ticket. It wasn't much to me, but enough, along with the vandalism of my RV, home, and car, for Grayson to hold her.

Half-heartedly, I opened the box for the Christmas tree and lugged it to the corner of the fireplace near the window. I set up the stand then put the bottom part of the six-half-foot pre-lit tree into it.

"Mama gets a living tree. They smell better." Abraham's voice came from the top of the stairs.

I tempered my joy, not wanting to scare him off or give the impression that I had great news for him. "I like living trees too. Since I leave trees up for a long time, it's safer to have the artificial one."

"Maybe you could get a small living one. Put it up later. They smell good." He clumped down the stairs. The scratching of nails on the hardwood floors followed him. Ebenezer was keeping close tabs on Abraham.

"That's a good idea." I hefted out the second part of the tree.

"I'll do that for you Merry."

The shortening of my name brought a rush of tears to my eyes. The trust between me and Abraham had a crack in it. I was no longer Merry Christmas, just Merry. I had helped take his mom from him. "Raleigh will be here tonight."

Abraham shrugged and finished assembling the tree. There was no joy or excitement in his face. He was going through the motions.

Why, Grace, why?

There was a knock on the front door.

I dabbed the tears away and took in some deep breaths, doing my best to control the despair squeezing at my heart. "I'll be back."

Abraham jerked toward the door, hope glittering in his eyes. "We have company? Is it…" He trailed off. The expression on his face let me know he was too scared to voice the hope aloud—his mom was coming for him.

I didn't venture a guess and hurried to the door before Abraham built his dream up too much. I hated to do anything else that crushed him. I tugged the door open. A cold gust of wind blew in along with my former stepdaughter. Correction, my stepdaughter Cassie. I was still married to her father. The girl was shivering, chilled to the bone. She wore a light sweater, t-shirt, leggings and flip-flops. What was the child thinking?

I snagged the afghan from the back of the couch and wrapped her in it. "What are you doing out in this weather dressed like that? I know you own socks."

"How would you know?" Her chattering teeth added a strange accompaniment to her words.

"Because I used to do your laundry. Your dad kept you well-supplied with socks."

Cassie loved socks. It was her thing. I had never seen the child wearing a matching pair as she liked to mix them in complementary pairs. Fox and owl. One pink-striped sock. One gray-striped sock. Cow and a horse. Polar bear and penguin. She loved animals and crazy stripped socks. Samuel loved finding designs his daughter didn't have. He was so excited one day when he found her a unicorn and dragon pair.

"Want me to start a fire, Merry?"

"Who's he?" Cassie's eyes widened, and she huddled into one corner of the couch. She licked her lips. Ebenezer raced around the room, picking up on Cassie's nervous energy.

"He's a friend of mine," I said. "He's staying with me until a friend of his can pick him up."

"My mom had to go away." Tears welled in his eyes. "No one will tell me when she'll be back."

Compassion filled Cassie's eyes. "My dad went away too. He won't ever be back."

Abraham sat beside her and took her hands in his. "I'm sorry. My dad went away when I was real little, and he never came back either." He pointed at her ankle. "You're bleeding. Merry, she's hurt."

I squatted down and reached for her ankle.

Cassie placed her other foot on top of it. "I'm fine. It's not bleeding."

"Let me see." I pushed at the foot blocking my view.

"You're not my mother," she snapped at me.

"Yes, I am." I snapped back. "Your dad never signed the divorce papers."

Abraham jumped up from the couch and paced in front of the fire place. Our anger was upsetting him.

"What?" Cassie popped up. Her ankle now in full view as I was still sitting on the floor.

She wasn't bleeding. She had a tattoo. A mother-daughter tattoo and what Abraham saw was the red from the swirly heart. In the middle were the initials EG and CW. The skin was red and puckered. It was a fresh tattoo.

"When and where did you get this?" I was livid. It looked infected. Why did she get a tattoo for her mom? The woman abandoned her and never looked back. Her dad raised her. Spoiled her. And just died. Why not one for him?

I knew. The rumor about Lynne being back was the truth. The woman had wormed her way into her daughter's heart. A girl who'd inherit twelve million dollars.

"None of your business," she sounded panicked.

"Yes, it is. It looks infected. You didn't let a friend do this to you."

"Why are you mad, Merry? You think tattoos are bad?" Abraham asked.

"Not if they're done properly and by experienced tattoo artists," I said. "And if it's something the individual wants and wasn't talked into it."

"It was." She rubbed her thumb and ring finger together.

No, it wasn't. Deep down, Cassie was worried about the reconnection with her mother.

"Where have you been staying?"

"With a friend." She rubbed her fingers together faster.

"Don't you mean in my attic or with your mom?"

Cassie paled. "I should've asked you. I didn't want to go back to my house. I don't trust Bonnie."

"Bonnie had nothing to do with your father's death."

Cassie shrugged and stared at the ground.

"The snow is coming down hard." Abraham said.

I looked out the window. It was hard. Thick snow falling at a steady pace. I hoped Raleigh changed her plans and would stay home until tomorrow. I didn't want her traveling in this weather.

"I'm cold," Cassie said. "Can I borrow some socks?"

I nodded, it gave me time to figure out what to do with this new information. "You can also change into one of my shirts and leggings. Yours are soaked."

She wrapped the afghan around herself and headed up the stairs, pausing halfway up. "I came to get my ticket you found. Is it in your room?"

I had totally forgot about that fib and added a new one onto it. "No. I'm sure what I found wasn't what you were looking for."

"Oh." Cassie clomped up the stairs.

"Can we finish decorating?" Abraham asked, a slight smile on his face.

"Sure." I was glad Abraham's worry about his mother eased a bit. Maybe Cassie's presence made Abraham see his time here as more of the sleepover his mother had promised. I'd invite her to stay over as well. The girl had arrived barely dressed, and I had a feeling her mother, Lynne, wasn't interested in Cassie's welfare.

Abraham and I finished decorating the tree and the mantle before Cassie came back downstairs.

"Sorry, Merry, I fell asleep on your bed." She looked at the ground.

"That's okay." I smiled and tucked a lock of her blonde hair behind her ear. She leaned her cheek into my palm. Tears trickled onto my hand. I tipped her head up. "Honey, what's wrong?"

"I'm sorry. I really am."

"Don't apologize to her." A woman's angry voice boomed down on us.

My head jerked toward the sound. Evelyn Graham—Lynne—EG—was glaring down at me. She moved down the steps, one step at a time, hand hovered near her hip like she was readying to pull something out. A gun.

The woman wasn't worried about Cassie because her daughter let her in. It would've been easy for her to retrieve the ladder from in front of the house where I left it yesterday and go to the back and climb in through my bedroom window. That was why she was sorry.

"Where's my dad's ticket? I searched everywhere." Cassie stepped away from me. "If you'd just have given it to me, I wouldn't have called my mom for help."

"I don't know where it is."

Abraham shifted to the right. I followed suited, wanting to

keep him behind me and calm. His nervousness could be mistaken for anger and a woman with a gun was likely to shoot and kill a man she deemed a threat.

"You said you have the ticket and then said it was the wrong one. You want my dad's ticket." Anger shook her voice. "You think it's yours."

"No, I don't. I'd give it to you. I made up that story because I wanted you to come over and look at a photo album."

Evelyn laughed. "You think the girl is that stupid? A photo album. Did you want to sit with her and reminisce about her dad who you divorced?"

"No, I wanted her to tell me who was missing from an album. I was trying to find out who killed Samuel. Because it wasn't me."

"I know you went to the RV last night," Evelyn said. "You went to get it."

"It wasn't there."

"I told you we should've kept the RV." Cassie shifted her weight from foot to foot and twisted her hands into the hem of her t-shirt.

"We needed the money." Evelyn glared at her.

Not to mention getting rid of Samuel's body.

Cassie dipped her head. I had a feeling the girl gave her mother the money from selling the RV and hadn't seen a penny of the money since.

My cell phone was on an end table near the Christmas tree. Was there a way I could get over there and send a text for help?

"Samuel told me he gave the ticket to you." Evelyn approached me. "You demanded it."

I snorted. I couldn't help it. "The only thing I wanted from Samuel was a divorce. Which I never got."

"And that's why you can't stay alive," Evelyn said. "You'll get the money."

Cassie stared at her mother, tears trailed down her pale cheeks. "When did you talk to my dad? You said you came because a friend told you he had died. You came for me. You lied."

Evelyn's eyes widened for a second. She pulled the gun out.

I raised my arm, using it as a barricade to keep Cassie behind me. "Samuel hid that ticket so well no one will ever find it. Just leave before you make things worse." Even to my ears, the order and potential consequences sounded lame.

"You're lying. You have it. That's why he came up with the plan of hiding in the bench. He'd surprise you and you'd give it to him to make him leave. When he got in to test it out, I realized I didn't need him to get the ticket. Traveling all day exhausted me so I had to take a seat for a while."

She sat on the bench, hoping her weight stopped him from getting out. It worked. I fisted my hands. Samuel broke my heart. Hurt my mom. But, he didn't deserve to be murdered.

"Merry Christmas, she has a gun. Guns are bad." Abraham walked toward her.

"Stay there." Cold sweat broke out all over me. My breath felt thick in my lungs and my limbs heavy. This was total all-encompassing fear.

"Mama says men protect women." Abraham hulked toward her.

Evelyn moved the aim of the gun onto him.

"No." I jumped in front of Abraham, colliding into him and nearly bringing us both to the ground. Abraham steadied me. I stood in front of him, it did little good to protect him as the young man was nearly a foot taller than me. "He doesn't understand. Just leave him alone."

Cassie was crying, muttering over and over she was sorry.

My anger grew. Evelyn killed Samuel and used his daughter. Her daughter. She preyed on the grieving girl's emotions, acting like she loved the girl to get her hands on the lottery ticket.

A movement near the window caught my eye. Evelyn sensed it too. Her gaze traveled in the same direction. The snow was piling up. The clouds were eliminating what little light there was. I prayed harder that my daughter stayed home. My children knew they didn't have to knock before they entered their home.

Don't think about that. Stay in the now. Enough trouble here without imagining more. The advice did little to bring me total calm, but it kicked in my designing mode. Look at everything around me, put all the pieces of the situation together and find a way to get us out of the mess.

"Raleigh isn't coming home today is she?" Abraham asked. "Too much snow."

"Who's that?" Evelyn asked, an evil spark in her eye.

"Merry's daughter," Cassie said.

A grin stretched Evelyn's thin mouth, like the Grinch when he thought of his most diabolical plan. But all he wanted to do was steal Christmas, not suck out the last breath and rip out the heart of a mother by killing her child. I couldn't escape knowing Raleigh might walk into this. I could get Cassie and Abraham out. All I had to do was stay alive long enough to save the kids.

The lights. "I'm going to ask Abraham to turn on the Christmas lights and then I'll get the ticket."

She pointed the gun at Abraham. "Don't you move. I thought you said you didn't have it."

"I lied," I said.

Cassie's expression said I betrayed her. I was willing to give up the ticket for Raleigh, my real daughter, but not her who I had sworn I loved as much as one of my own.

"The problem for you is Samuel signed it," I said. "The only one who's entitled to the money is his wife."

"I can fix—stop that." Evelyn glared at Abraham.

He was swaying back and forth.

"He's upset because he can't turn the lights on," I said. "I promised him."

"He isn't right in the head is he?" There was a flicker of empathy in her eyes and I played on it.

"Routines are important to him. He knows the Christmas lights go on now. I'm Merry Christmas."

Evelyn raised a foot and itched at her ankle. There was gauze wrapped around it. Matching mother-daughter tattoos. Grace wasn't the only one who wanted that tree, so did a certain heavily made-up customer. Had she searched my garage for the ticket and feared her fingerprints, or blood, was on the tree?

"You were at the event." I said it more as a statement than a question.

"I shouldn't have fussed over that stupid tree. You just wanted to keep it so much, I figured it was a clue to the ticket."

"Nope, I just don't like bossy customers."

"Merry Christmas..." Abraham pointed at the light switch near the front door.

"Can he?" I asked. "I promise you, I'll get you the ticket."

"So, he can run out the door for help? I don't think so."

My heart plummeted for a second, bouncing back up when Evelyn walked over and turned on the switch.

"There we go, problem solved. Everyone follow Merry to the ticket."

Where to go? The kitchen had been trashed. Upstairs? The attic? My gaze flickered toward it. Cassie moved her head slightly left to right and tapped her chest. No. The noise I heard in the attic was Cassie searching it.

Where? Think. The laundry. Samuel's dirty laundry. "It's in my car."

"Your car?" A hard look was fixed on Cassie.

The teenager whimpered. Evelyn had sent Cassie to search my vehicle. I wrapped my arm around her shoulders, drawing her to me. "It's in a dirty laundry bag I picked up from my mother. Samuel had dropped off laundry for her to do."

"Send the guy to get it." She nodded at Abraham.

Darn. I hoped she'd leave the kids in the house and follow me out.

Abraham sent me a questioning look. I smiled at him. "It's okay. You're fine."

He reached for his coat.

"No coat." Evelyn waved the gun toward the door like it was a wand. "Go on."

Mumbling under his breath, Abraham took the keys from me and went to the car. As he approached the door with the bag, I snagged it from him, slammed the door shut and locked it.

Evelyn screeched. The side of the gun struck me in the head. I fell to my knees.

"You stupid woman."

Cassie started crying.

I fought through the pain wanting me to curl into a ball. "You'd never forgive yourself if you hurt him. He isn't going to know what to do. He can't process situations like this. Cassie and I will find the ticket. It's in one of the pockets."

Evelyn grabbed the bag and dumped the contents over me and Cassie. Cassie drew her knees to her chin, dropped her head onto them and cried. This was too much for her. Her dad's clothes. Her mother wanting money, not her. The scent of stale, dirty laundry enveloped me. Slivers of anger wormed their way into my heart. Samuel had actually brought my mother his dirty laundry.

I grabbed a shirt then a pair of pants, searching frantically through the pockets and any spot where I thought the seam could be split, like at the collar, and a ticket hidden inside. Nothing.

Evelyn crouched down, nearly sitting on her heels. "You're lying to me."

A bundle of fur launched through the air toward Evelyn's face. Instinctively, her hands rose, and she screamed. The gun landed in the laundry. Ebenezer! He was trying to help. He landed smack in the middle of the laundry and scurried around in utter glee. No, of course he wasn't trying to save us. He was a guinea pig, not a guard dog. Ebenezer just wanted to play in the pile of dirty clothes. Maybe I should think about getting a dog. A large one.

Or just not let murderers into my house.

But Ebenezer's glee of dirty clothes had been a distraction and caused Evelyn to drop the gun. Something I needed to take advantage of. I flattened myself on the laundry and wiggled around until the gun pressed into my stomach.

"Run, Cassie." Evelyn needed the gun—and the ticket—more

than she needed her daughter to stay here.

Evelyn snatched a handful of my hair and yanked. I scooped up a bundle of dirty, stinky laundry and hugged it tight. Tears blurred my vision. My glasses slid down, almost falling into the laundry, I tipped my head back, resettling my glasses and relieving some of the pressure. As long as Evelyn had hold of my hair, she couldn't get the gun. Where were the police? Cornelius should've called them by now. A work shirt was under my nose. I turned my head to get away from the smell.

Ebenezer lifted his head from a section of the pile, wiggled his nose, and dove back in. Why hadn't I adopted a dog? There had been a nice, sturdy German shepherd at the adoption event.

The pain in my head lessened. Evelyn must've realized her error. No free hand meant no chance getting the gun. I jerked my head backwards, slamming the back of my skull into Evelyn's face. She howled. A part of my head felt wet. I was free. For now.

A pounding rattled the door.

"Go, Cassie."

The girl was immobile.

"I'll kill you too!" Evelyn held her hands to her face. Blood seeped through her fingers.

Evelyn's scream scared Ebenezer and he ran out of the pile of clothes.

Not without the gun. I scooped up the laundry and ran with the bundle. Had to get it away from Evelyn. Away from Cassie. I lied again. "I have the gun and ticket. Run, Cassie!" I lied again about the ticket, praying Evelyn believed me and followed me into the kitchen. Not the smartest place as there were knives in there but it was the quickest room to get to. I just need the woman away from Cassie.

There was a movement by the back door. I unlocked and opened the door, tossing the clothes and gun into the snow, not caring what caused the shadow lurking in my yard and ran back into the living room. I froze. A body collided into me from behind, grabbed my shoulders and steadied me.

Evelyn screamed. "Stop it."

Cassie's sobs grew. She was on Evelyn. Hitting. Scratching. Biting. Doing anything she could to inflict bodily harm on the woman who killed her father.

A voice I had assigned to a Grinch said, "I got this, darling." From behind me, Grayson emerged and gently pried the girl from her father's murderer and directed her into my arms.

Orville and another local officer ran in from the kitchen. Someone still pounded on the front door.

"Did the whole force come?" I wanted the knocking stopped. It increased the headache caused by the violent hair pulling.

Detective Grayson cuffed Evelyn.

The door creaked open. "Mom..." Raleigh. "Cornelius is about to break your door down."

He stomped into my house. "The Christmas lights are on." He slapped the light switch down.

"She did it." Cassie pointed a shaking finger at Evelyn who was surrounded by one of Morgantown and some of Season Greetings finest. "It was her."

Cornelius puffed out his chest, pleased with himself. "About time the law in Season's Greetings took things seriously."

After what seemed like days, but was only hours, Detective Grayson left, promising Abraham he was returning with his mother in about an hour. I had told the detective I didn't want to press any vandalizing charges against Grace. I didn't want Cassie charged either. The girl was grieving for her father and the mother who abandoned her twice. I think this time was more painful for Cassie because it destroyed all her hopes and dreams of what it would be like if she reunited with her mother.

Raleigh sat beside me on the couch. "Are you okay?"

I nodded, not sure if I was okay. But, I had to be okay. I wasn't going to let what happened ruin the day for me. My daughter was home. My son would arrive soon. I was determined to have a lovely

Thanksgiving.

"Mom, you've been ignoring your mail." Raleigh handed me a stack of mail in colorful envelopes. "Christmas mail. You're favorite kind. Open this one first." Raleigh shoved a gold envelope decorated with seasonal stickers into my hand.

There was a bright red envelope hidden behind her back. Like the ones Helen had mailed out. "Let me guess, that one is not from your brother."

My children loved giving me the first Christmas card of the season and Raleigh was trying to stack the deck in her favor. I wasn't playing favorites. "I'll open the red one first."

It was from Helen. The card was shaped like a present. Paperclipped to the card was the lottery ticket and a note: *You're the only one who didn't ask me about it.*

Raleigh drew in a sharp breath. "You're a millionaire, Mom."

For a moment, I thought of everything I could buy with that money. The freedom it brought, then I remembered Samuel's fate. A daughter with no father. No mother. A mother terrified of the bleakness of her son's future when she died. The money could provide a comfortable and safe life for Abraham. Help Cassie get on her feet.

I had invited Cassie to stay with me while everything was sorted out. She declined preferring to stay in her childhood home where memories of her father were strong. While Cassie didn't want to live with Bonnie, she didn't want to throw her out either. She knew the woman loved Samuel and was also grieving. I was proud of Cassie. I wanted to be proud of me. I couldn't keep it. "It's not mine. I can't keep it."

"Aren't you still married to Samuel? His widow." Raleigh asked gently. "Because that means his ticket is your ticket. It rightfully belongs to you."

She was right, but I didn't want to profit from Samuel's death. The man who I believed was my ex-husband. "I don't know. Samuel did sign the decree that was on Milton's desk, but Milton had told me that it was backdated. I don't know if that makes it invalid. Your dad said Milton is no longer cooperating with the police. It's all one big mess."

Placing the card and ticket back into the envelope, I stood. "I have an errand to run. I'll be back before your dad and Scotland arrive."

"You should ask Helen to join us for dinner. We always have plenty of food."

I kissed the top of my daughter's head. She knew how to read me and push my buttons. "I will."

The radio stations weren't playing Christmas music yet, so I left the radio off, preferring the quiet to any upbeat tempo or sad songs. Why hadn't Helen kept the ticket for her and Cassie? They needed the money more than I did. *You're the only one who didn't ask.* I was thankful Evelyn believed I had the ticket rather than going after the ailing, older woman.

Because Samuel told her I had it. Had he said that because he suspected Evelyn would hurt someone for the ticket? Had he feared for Cassie and his mom? It didn't sit well with me he was willing to put me in the path of a deranged woman, but I'd also rather it be me than them. I'd never know Samuel's reasonings for lying to the woman. It was also likely he went along with her plan, believing at some point he could overpower her, saving himself, his daughter, and his money.

Did it really matter now? The question filled my head as I pulled into Helen's driveway. The answer was easy. No.

The moment I stepped foot on Helen's porch, the door opened.

She was pale. Dark smudges were under her eyes. There was a weariness in her eyes and in her body. Her shoulders were rounded forward as if it was too much effort to stand straight. Her legs quaked.

"You're sick." I gently took hold of her elbow. "Let's get you into bed. I'll make some soup for you and—"

"I'm dying, Merry. That's why I sent you the ticket."

No. It wasn't true. She felt like she was. She wasn't *actually* dying right now. She was sick. Very sick. She'd get better. I'd take care of her and make sure of it. I led her to the recliner and helped settle her comfortably. "I'll go make you some soup."

She took hold of my hand, forcing me to remain still. "I need you to listen to me. I'm dying. The cancer is back and has spread."

I shook my head, tears slid down my face. "Cassie needs you."

"Honey, I don't get a vote on the matter. The doctor said it could be a year or months. We just don't know. I did know I wanted my granddaughter protected and taken care of. I know you'll spend the money wisely."

"It was Samuel's money. It should rightly go to Cassie."

"No, Merry it was mine. Now, it's yours." Helen fluttered her hand toward the stairs. "In a shoe box in my closet are lottery tickets I've bought over the years. You'll see the Easy Pick numbers are always the same. My birthdate, my husband's birthdate, and the day we got married. I never thought I'd ever experience that much pain again in my life as the day Edward died. I was wrong."

She had experienced a greater grief, her son dying. "I'm so sorry, Helen. Evelyn, Lynne, will pay for what she did."

"Nothing will bring him back. Not even all that money. I don't want Cassie to have it. People will use her. It will destroy her. Cassie acts tough, but she is fragile. Without her father, she'll be desperate for love, and someone will love her to get the money. I want her to have real love. True love." She squeezed my hand.

"I'll set up a trust for her. My ex-husband Brett is an attorney. He'll help us do it or know who can."

"Once I'm gone, you can. Right now, it hurts too much. My son died because of that money. I should've never told him I'd give him the ticket. He told me it would be better if he claimed the money rather than I do and he inherited it. The government would take more of the money. If he even got it. I should've known he'd brag about it and that it would ruin him. I don't want that for my granddaughter."

"Money doesn't destroy everyone."

"I know." She locked gazes with me. "Eighteen is too young for all of that. I'm too old and tired to deal with it. I trust you, Merry. I know you'll do the right thing for Cassie, you, and others. Please accept it."

The money could help a lot of people. "I'll set up a trust. Keep it private so no one knows."

Helen smiled. "In your name. It's better that way."

"Fine, in my name. Cassie will get a scholarship to go to college."

"If you can convince her of that, you'd have earned the money. The girl is stubborn. Says she wants to be an artist. She told me, 'Artists art. They don't school.'"

I snorted. "I'll find some good art schools for her to check into."

"Good. While you're doing that, find yourself a new RV."

"I'm not spending it on myself. It's for your granddaughter."

"My son owes you an RV. It was a promise to you he never should've broken." She rapped her knuckles on the armrest. "The day he told me his brilliant plan for your mom, I wanted to throttle my boy. Money just shone too brightly for him. This lets him, in a way, make it right with you. Cassie would like to know that her dad did that. Made amends with you."

"Okay. One used RV for me."

"I know the perfect one." Her eyes twinkled. "Been doing some poking around on the internet. Found you a beauty."

"You've been doing a lot of planning."

The humor faded in her eyes. "That's what you do for the people you love."

Tears blurred my vision. I hugged Helen. "Want to spend Thanksgiving with the kids? Raleigh is home and Scotland is on the way. We'll pick up Cassie on the way."

"If Bonnie's invited, too. That's another woman Samuel needs to make right with."

"I know she wanted to go on a cruise."

Helen cupped my cheek. "Let's look into that. I'd like to know some of my son's mistakes were corrected before..." She trailed off.

She didn't need to say the end of her sentence—before she

died. "I love you, Helen. Samuel was misguided at times. Had hare-brained ideas. One thing that couldn't be said was that he didn't treat his daughter well. He loved his daughter. You taught him how to love his child. It was incredible to see."

Tears shone in her eyes. "Thank you. That's all a mother wants to know. She done good with her children."

I drew her into my arms and told her what her aching mother's heart needed desperately to hear. "You done good."

CHRISTINA FREEBURN

Christina Freeburn has always loved books. There was nothing better than picking up a story and being transported to another place. The love of reading evolved into the love of writing and she's been writing since her teenage years. Her first novel was a 2003 Library of Virginia Literary Award nominee. Her two mystery series, Faith Hunter Scrap This and Merry & Bright Handcrafted Mysteries, are a mix of crafty and crime and feature heroines whose crafting time is interrupted by crime solving. Christina served in the US Army and has also worked as a paralegal, librarian, and church secretary. She lives in West Virginia with her husband, dog, and a rarely seen cat except by those who are afraid of or allergic to felines.

Mysteries by Christina Freeburn

The Merry & Bright Handcrafted Mystery Series

NOT A CREATURE WAS STIRRING (#1)

The Faith Hunter Scrap This Series

CROPPED TO DEATH (#1)
DESIGNED TO DEATH (#2)
EMBELLISHED TO DEATH (#3)
FRAMED TO DEATH (#4)
MASKED TO DEATH (#5)
ALTERED TO DEATH (#6)

Henery Press Mystery Books

And finally, before you go...
Here are a few other mysteries
you might enjoy:

CROPPED TO DEATH

Christina Freeburn

A Faith Hunter Scrap This Mystery (#1)

Former US Army JAG specialist, Faith Hunter, returns to her West Virginia home to work in her grandmothers' scrapbooking store determined to lead an unassuming life after her adventure abroad turned disaster. But her quiet life unravels when her friend is charged with murder – and Faith inadvertently supplied the evidence. So Faith decides to cut through the scrap and piece together what really happened.

With a sexy prosecutor, a determined homicide detective, a handful of sticky suspects and a crop contest gone bad, Faith quickly realizes if she's not careful, she'll be the next one cropped.

Available at booksellers nationwide and online

Visit www.henerypress.com for details

THE SEMESTER OF OUR DISCONTENT

Cynthia Kuhn

A Lila Maclean Academic Mystery (#1)

English professor Lila Maclean is thrilled about her new job at prestigious Stonedale University, until she finds one of her colleagues dead. She soon learns that everyone, from the chancellor to the detective working the case, believes Lila—or someone she is protecting—may be responsible for the horrific event, so she assigns herself the task of identifying the killer.

Putting her scholarly skills to the test, Lila gathers evidence, but her search is complicated by an unexpected nemesis, a suspicious investigator, and an ominous secret society. Rather than earning an "A" for effort, she receives a threat featuring the mysterious emblem and must act quickly to avoid failing her assignment...and becoming the next victim.

Available at booksellers nationwide and online

Visit www.henerypress.com for details

ARTIFACT

Gigi Pandian

A Jaya Jones Treasure Hunt Mystery (#1)

Historian Jaya Jones discovers the secrets of a lost Indian treasure may be hidden in a Scottish legend from the days of the British Raj. But she's not the only one on the trail...

From San Francisco to London to the Highlands of Scotland, Jaya must evade a shadowy stalker as she follows hints from the hastily scrawled note of her dead lover to a remote archaeological dig. Helping her decipher the cryptic clues are her magician best friend, a devastatingly handsome art historian with something to hide, and a charming archaeologist running for his life.

Available at booksellers nationwide and online

Visit www.henerypress.com for details

MURDER ON A SILVER PLATTER

Shawn Reilly Simmons

A Red Carpet Catering Mystery (#1)

Penelope Sutherland and her Red Carpet Catering company just got their big break as the on-set caterer for an upcoming blockbuster. But when she discovers a dead body outside her house, Penelope finds herself in hot water. Things start to boil over when serious accidents threaten the lives of the cast and crew. And when the film's star, who happens to be Penelope's best friend, is poisoned, the entire production is nearly shut down.

Threats and accusations send Penelope out of the frying pan and into the fire as she struggles to keep her company afloat. Before Penelope can dish up dessert, she must find the killer or she'll be the one served up on a silver platter.

Available at booksellers nationwide and online

Visit www.henerypress.com for details